THE SCOUT'S ACCOUNT

In the Shadow of the *Mayflower*

Also by Paul Brodeur

Fiction
The Sick Fox
The Stunt Man
Downstream

Nonfiction
Asbestos and Enzymes
Expendable Americans
The Zapping of America
The Asbestos Hazard
Restitution: The Land Claims of the New England Indians
Outrageous Misconduct: The Asbestos Industry on Trial
Currents of Death
The Great Power-Line Cover-Up

Memoir
Secrets: A Writer in the Cold War

THE SCOUT'S ACCOUNT

In the Shadow of the *Mayflower*

by

Paul Brodeur

To order additional copies of this title, contact your
favorite local bookstore or visit www.amazon.com

Cover and book design by Marianne Swan
Image on front cover, courtesy of Plimoth Plantation, Kristen Oney
Photo on the back by Bill Ravanesi

Printed in the United States of America
ISBN: 978-1-939739-86-5

For Stephen
whose idea this was

And with special thanks to Jon Swan
for his encouragement and advice

Foreword

The Native People who lived in Northeastern America when the English Pilgrims arrived in 1620 spoke dialects of the Algonquian tongue but did not possess a written language, and were thus unable to leave their own record of what happened afterward. For this reason, the best way to understand how they felt and why they acted toward the newcomers as they did is to tell their story from the perspective of a Native American who witnessed the landing of the *Mayflower* at the tip of Cape Cod and lived through the tumultuous period that followed, including the massacre of the Pequot, the uprising known as King Philip's War, and the resulting decimation and dispersion of the Native inhabitants. This novel attempts to accomplish that purpose and to describe the colonization and conquest of the Native People by the Pilgrim and Puritan invaders.

The land as it was when

the Mayflower arrived in 1620

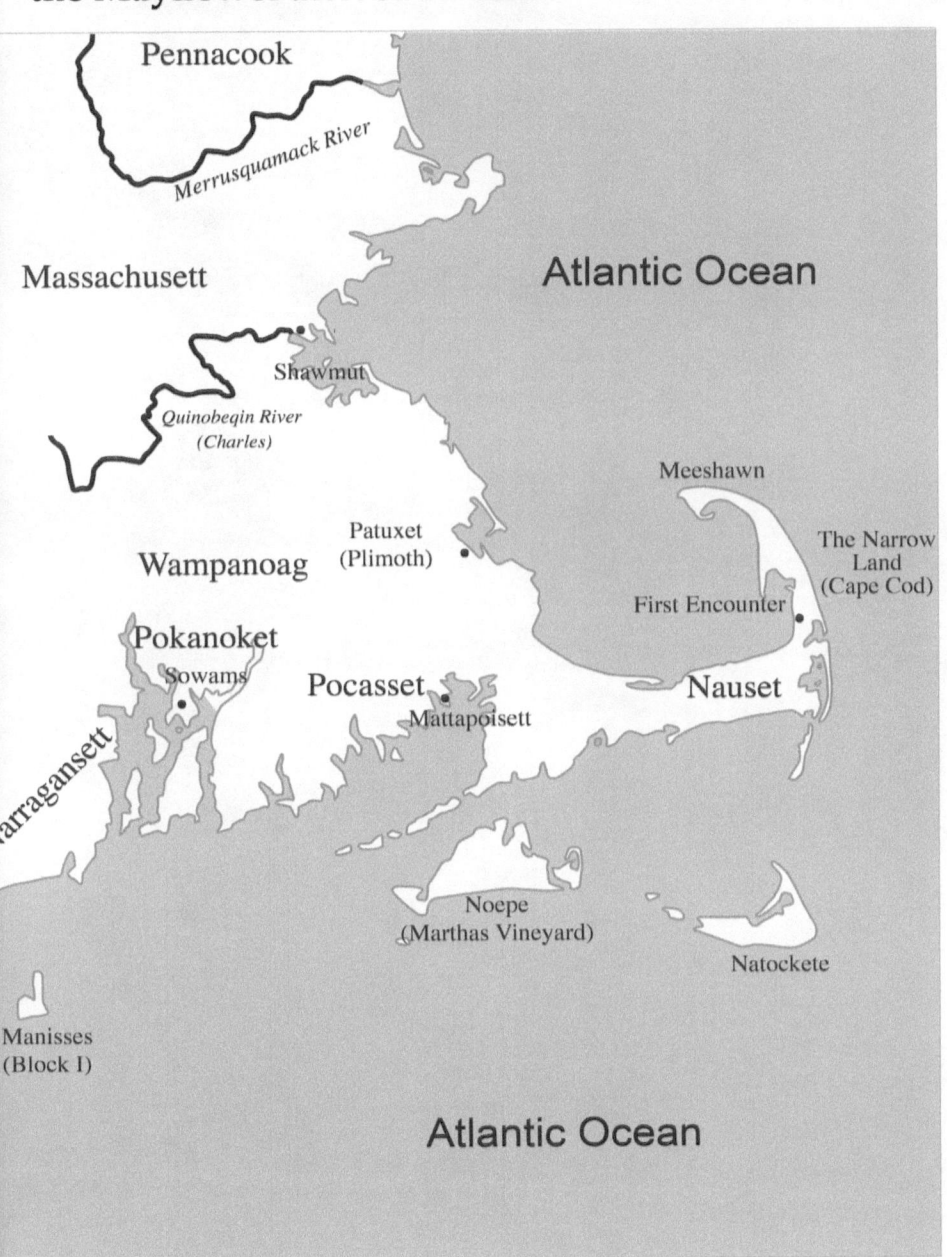

Pennacook

Merrusquamack River

Massachusett

Atlantic Ocean

Shawmut

Quinobeqin River
(Charles)

Meeshawn

Patuxet
(Plimoth)

The Narrow
Land
(Cape Cod)

Wampanoag

First Encounter

Pokanoket

Sowams

Pocasset

Nauset

Mattapoisett

Narragansett

Noepe
(Marthas Vineyard)

Natockete

Manisses
(Block I)

Atlantic Ocean

Part One

ADVENT

Chapter One

When the messenger arrived with a summons from the sachem, the young man named Squeteague stopped slicing strips of blubber from a pilot whale that had become stranded in a tidal marsh and set off at full speed. He was a tall and sinewy youth with the slender legs of a long-distance runner for which he was already known among the Nauset, who had adopted him after his father had been kidnapped by English seamen to be sold into slavery, and his mother had succumbed to the pestilence that other European sailors had inflicted upon the inhabitants of the region. Harvest moons had risen into the sky sixteen times since he had been born, which allowed him to grow his glossy black hair below shoulder length and tie into a braid. Now, after a run through dense forest, he arrived at the ocean side of the peninsula his people called the Narrow Land, and the English called Cape Cod. There, he found the sachem Aspinet—a lean, hawk-nosed man—standing at the edge of a sand cliff above the sea whose breakers were crashing upon the berm below.

"Strangers from across the sea," Aspinet declared, and pointed toward the horizon at what Squeteague, who had never seen sails, imagined was a cluster of clouds. "Perhaps the Englishmen who took your father have returned. Yesterday, they were making their way toward the Monomoyick. Today, they're heading in the opposite direction toward our brothers, the Payomet. You, Squeteague, will be my scout. You will run along the beach to keep them in sight. You will watch them if they come ashore. You will observe everything they do. And, most important, you will warn the Payomet so they are not taken unaware."

At this point, the sachem gave a slight push that sent Squeteague sliding down the cliff to the beach below and his hope of being reunited with his father soaring to the sky above. In spite of the morning chill that accompanied the month of first snow, he pulled off his deerskin shirt and moccasins, and, clad only in a pair of leggings began to lope along firm sand at the water's edge, keeping the cloud-like sails abreast of him. All that morning and afternoon he ran, stopping neither to drink nor eat, until, late in the day, when the land beneath his feet curved west in the direction of the setting sun and the sails he had been following turned toward the shore. At that point, he saw a large and oddly shaped vessel beneath them—higher at one end than the other—upon which he could make out the figures of men.

Could his father be among them? Might the English have brought him back to his homeland as it was rumored they sometimes did with other Native People they had taken captive?

At dusk, some of the figures climbed into the sky upon what appeared to be webs of sinew, the sails fell as if from trees, and a large hook-like object dropped into the water with a splash. In the darkness that followed, the ship became silhouetted by the moon and lit with small fires that bobbed up and down with the swells of the sea. Full of anticipation that his father might have returned, Squeteague kept the vigil the sachem had commanded. Then, tired from his long run, he covered himself with beach grass and fell asleep.

During the night, he dreamed that his father had swum ashore and enfolded him in a joyful embrace, but at first light he awoke to find everything as it had been before. Perhaps the foreigners were keeping his father hidden.

As soon as the sun rose above the horizon, men climbed once again into the trees, the sails billowed into the sky like clouds, and the large hook emerged from the sea. Within a few minutes, the ship got underway, hindered for a time by a current that would have made Squeteague's pursuit easier had he not found it necessary to run in soft sand in order to keep out of sight.

Several hours later, he lay behind a dune as the ship rounded the last point of land—called Meeshawn (end of the path)—and entered a habor with deep water. Once again, men climbed into the trees, the sails dropped away, and the hook fell into the water. The gravity of his mission began to weigh upon Squeteague, who found himself alone on the outermost tip of the Narrow Land, where the vessel carrying the foreigners had come to anchor. Englishmen, the sachem had called them—the same people who had clubbed his father to the ground and dragged him away as Squeteague, then ten years old, had run zigzagging among them across a marsh and into the forest. Men he had not been old or strong enough to fight—a failing that had haunted him ever since, even though his fellow Nauset, admiring the dexterity of his escape, had named him after the sea trout that slipped easily through their weirs and from their fish-bone hooks. At this point, the ship swung about to reveal a stern into which had been carved the design of a flower. Mindful of Aspinet's instruction to observe everything, Squeteague transcribed it with a forefinger in the wet sand beside him.

By morning, the tracing was erased by an incoming tide. Soon, however, he would learn that the flower was the same as the fragrant blossoms that filled the woods in springtime, as well as the name of the vessel he had followed. The wind had shifted toward Squeteague's hiding place and with it came the smell of unwashed bodies. A small boat carrying half as many men as the years of his age was launched from the ship and rowed ashore, where its passengers climbed out, fell on their knees, and shouted toward the sky. Squeteague found himself wondering if they were angry or pleased with their gods, but then they started marching in single file in his direction. To his great disappointment, his father was not among them.

For the rest of the day, he shadowed the Englishmen, who were led by a short stocky man with a red beard, careful not to find himself downwind of them. That was easy because the Englishmen, who carried strange-looking sticks and wore metal on their chests, stumbled as they trudged over hills of soft sand. Indeed, so slow was their progress that Squeteague had time to find water at a spring—the first he had drunk since the day before—and to gather groundnuts to eat. As darkness fell, the Englishmen returned to their ship with wood they had collected, and built fires to warm themselves. Not so Squeteague, who hunkered behind a dune to spend a second night of vigil, during which hope of seeing his father again gave way to foreboding.

The next day came and went with no activity or sound on the part of the Englishmen, except for a constant murmuring of voices and some solemn singing. On the third day, large sections of wood were ferried ashore, and several of the Englishmen began fitting them together. Some women and children also came ashore carrying baskets piled high with garments, and were accompanied by men carrying their long sticks to a nearby pond, where they commenced to wash the clothes, the children, and themselves. On the way back, they stopped to gather mussels from rocks along the shore, which Squeteague could have warned them against because of a tide that had made them unfit to eat. All night long, he heard the sound of retching coming from the vessel.

Only a handful of Englishmen rowed ashore on the following day—the rest recovering, Squeteague guessed, from sickness brought on by the poisoned shellfish they had consumed the night before. That afternoon, he was visited by a Payomet whom Aspinet had instructed to bring him some dried beans and find out what he had observed. Squeteague told the Payomet everything that he had seen and done since setting out on his mission, except for the design he had traced in the sand, which had been washed away by the tide. He did not mention his bitter disappointment at not seeing any sign of his father.

A day later, eight men led by the same red-bearded chief rowed ashore and began marching single file along the beach, while Squeteague kept them in sight from a vantage point in the forest. To his surprise, he suddenly saw a small group of Payomet walking along the shore, and alerted them to the presence of the Englishmen by giving the cry of a hawk hovering above its prey. As the Payomet ran into the woods, the Englishmen set off in pursuit, but soon fell far behind as they followed footprints the Payomet had left in the sand. When darkness fell, they lit a fire and camped for the night.

In the morning, the Englishmen resumed their exploration until they came on a spring and fell upon their knees to slake their thirst. The next day, shadowed by Squeteague, they found stubbled fields that the Payomet had planted with corn and mounds of sand covering Payomet graves. On a high hill above the shore near the mouth of a tidal creek, they came to an area where the sand had been flattened, and, digging down, found a large woven basket filled with dried corn. Squeteague watched them take as much of it as they could carry, before starting back in the direction from which they had come. Their thievery infuriated him, for he knew that the Payomet had buried the corn in anticipation of planting it the following spring, and that its loss might cause them hardship. It also reawakened the ache in his heart left by the loss of his father. What right had these foreigners to land on his people's territory, march about as if they owned it, and steal whatever they came upon?

That night, it rained and the Englishmen became lost and soaked to the bone. The next day, still lost, they entered a clearing in which a birch sapling had been bent in an arc to the ground and a pile of acorns lay surrounded by a circle of sinew. Too late, one of them stumbled upon the noose, and, snagged as the sapling jerked upward, was left dangling by the leg in a Payomet deer snare. As the man cried out in dismay, his companions looked fearfully into the forest around them and raised their long sticks as if ready to fend off an unseen enemy.

Hiding nearby, Squeteague looked on with grim satisfaction and wished he had brought his bow and arrow.

To the sound of knocking and rasping, the Englishmen finished putting together the sections of wood they had brought ashore to make a small open boat equipped with mast and sail. Meanwhile, Aspinet relieved Squeteague with a pair of Payomet scouts and gathered his warriors to attack the foreigners if they should land at a place of convenient ambush. Soon afterward, a Payomet runner reported that a boat carrying the foreigners and their long sticks had arrived in falling snow at the tidal creek, where they looted several graves and took more corn, as well as a canoe with which they explored the upper reaches of the creek. Before returning to their ship, the English removed clay pots and reed baskets from several wetu—shelters made of saplings bent into the ground at both ends to form arcs that were covered with mats woven from grass and sea straw. Aspinet made sure his warriors knew about the desecration of the graves and thefts from the wetu in order to strengthen their resolve.

He had no need to strengthen the resolve of Squeteague, who was ready to repel the invaders at any cost.

A few days later, sixteen Englishmen set out in their shallop and sailed to the tidal marsh in which the pilot whale Squeteague had been butchering had stranded itself. Only now there were several stranded whales being worked on by more than half a dozen Nauset, who fled when they saw the boat approach. The English soldiers, who were led by the same red-bearded man, disembarked at the mouth of a creek and, dividing their forces, sent some men with the boat to explore the coast, while others tramped through the surrounding woods, unaware that their every move was being observed by the Nauset. That night, some of them

8

stayed in the shallop, while others crowded into a makeshift camp fashioned from tree trunks, and fell into a sleep interrupted by the howling of wolves in the forest.

In the dim light of daybreak, the English soldiers sat down to a breakfast of gruel, but no sooner had they begun to eat than a great cry arose from the forest in which Aspinet's warriors had gathered and the sky was filled with the arching flight of dozens of arrows that rained down upon them, turning the sandy beach around the camp into a field of bristles. However, none of the arrows found its mark, and the Englishmen proceeded to take cover and point their long sticks toward the forest to the accompaniment of deafening noise and clouds of gray smoke.

In his first combat, Squeteague shot arrows into the sky with a powerful bow made of ash—sometimes keeping as many as three in the air at once—until his quiver was almost empty. Then, catching sight of the red-bearded captain, he notched an arrow in his bowstring and ran forward, trusting that his fellow Nauset would follow. When he got within a few yards of the English soldiers, who had formed a semicircle, he dropped to one knee, drew the bowstring back to his ear, and loosed the arrow at their leader, but before he could see whether it had hit its target, musket shot whistled so close that he was forced to flatten himself face down in the beach grass. When he raised his head, he realized that his Nauset comrades had fled into the forest behind him and that he was alone. Taking to his heels, he also ran into the forest, dodging this way and that as missiles sent by the Englishmen blasted the bark off the trunks of trees around him.

Squeteague focused his frustration upon Aspinet. "We outnumbered the red-bearded chief and his men!" he cried. "We could have driven them into shallow water and slaughtered them with our tomahawks!"

Surprised at the ferocity of Squeteague's outburst, Aspinet placed a hand upon the young man's shoulder and told him of a time some years before when a foreigner named Champlain had sailed along the coast and landed among the Monomoyick, who lived a short distance to the south. "A quarrel broke out between the Monomoyick and a landing party of the foreigners, who called themselves Frenchmen. As a result, the Monomoyick attacked them, killing several and sending others fleeing to their vessel with arrows sticking from their bodies like quills from a porcupine. But the Frenchmen returned and killed many Monomoyick with the devices that emitted the terrible sounds you heard today. So you must understand, my son, that the weapons of the foreigners are powerful and it may be best to fight them another day when conditions are more to our advantage."

Squeteague could not see the wisdom of Aspinet's position. For the rest of his life, he would remember the skirmish with the red-bearded captain and his soldiers, which occurred at a place called First Encounter Beach, as a lost opportunity to drive away the invaders, who would boast that they had prevailed against the inhabitants of the New World in their initial confrontation.

From the Manomet who lived in the direction of the sunset, Squeteague and his fellow Nauset learned that after the encounter by the shoreline the English had sailed their shallop across the bay to the abandoned village of the Patuxet, whose inhabitants had been wiped out several years earlier by plague brought to the land by European fishermen. There, the newcomers, who called themselves Pilgrims, found fields scattered with skulls and bones before returning to the ship that had carried them across the ocean. Several days later, they sailed the *Mayflower* across the bay and anchored off Patuxet, which they named Plimoth Plantation, and proceeded to build a settlement of log dwellings on a hill. During the winter, Native People in the vicinity kept close watch on the newcomers without attempting to make contact. However, at the beginning of spring, Massasoit, sachem of the Pokanoket and revered leader of the Wampanoag—"People of the First Light" who lived by the sea—visited the settlement and signed a treaty with the Pilgrims that bound each side to the aid of the other in case of war.

Squeteague, whose suspicion of the newcomers remained deep,

learned that Massasoit had made the alliance to protect the Po-kanoket from his bitter enemy Canonicus, sachem of the nearby Narragansett. The Pilgrims had their own reason to fear Canonicus. He had sent them a bundle of arrows wrapped in the skin of a rattlesnake, and been sent back a snakeskin filled with musket shot and gunpowder by their governor, William Bradford, who ordered an eight-foot palisade to be built around the settlement. Then news arrived from Virginia that the Powhatan had killed three hundred and forty-seven English settlers at Jamestown, and the Pilgrims at Plimoth Plantation had all the more reason to worry they might be assaulted and overwhelmed.

Squeteague also learned that a Patuxet named Tisquantum, who was Massasoit's interpreter, had been kidnapped at the same time as his father by an English sea captain named Thomas Hunt, but had escaped being sold into slavery and returned to his homeland, where he was showing the newcomers at Plimoth Plantation how to plant corn and where to catch fish, lobsters, and eels. Squeteague was eager to meet Tisquantum, who was called Squanto by the English, because he wanted to know what had happened to his father. So when he heard that the interpreter and Governor Bradford had come to nearby Monomoy (Chatham) in search of provisions, he set out for the village. By the time he arrived, however, he found Tisquantum lying on a mat of woven reeds, bleeding heavily from the nose, and pleading in a feverish mixture of Algonquian and English that Bradford pray for him to join the Englishmen's God in heaven.

Kneeling beside the interpreter, Squeteague introduced himself. "I am Squeteague, the son of Pocassonnet, who was kidnapped along with you by the Englishman Captain Hunt. I'm hoping you can tell me what became of him."

For a moment, the dying man looked at his young visitor as if he were a spirit from the dark place he was about to enter; then he raised himself on an elbow and took Squeteague by the arm. "You have the look of your father, a brave but unfortunate warrior. On board the ship that was carrying us into slavery, he struck a sailor who had abused him and cursed Captain Hunt, who had abducted us. Whereupon, the captain drew his cutlass and dealt your father a death blow and ordered him thrown into the sea for the fish to eat."

It had been almost two years to the day since Squeteague had followed the ship called *Mayflower* along the shore. He was now a man of eighteen harvest moons and determined to avenge his father's murder.

Chapter Two

During the winter of 1623, Massasoit fell ill with typhus brought by Dutch traders to the village of Sowams, his chief residence, which was situated at the head of Narragansett Bay. The disease would almost certainly have killed him if he had not been nursed back to health by a man named Edward Winslow, whom Governor Bradford sent from Plimoth to attend him. Upon his recovery, a grateful Massasoit swore undying allegiance to his English allies and, seeking to consolidate his influence with them, warned that Obtakiest, leader of a Massachusett band living next to Wessagussett, a small English settlement to the north of Plimoth Plantation, had made common cause with other sachems, including those of people living on the Narrow Land, to mount an attack upon the settlers.

Other than Massasoit's word, there was no evidence of an impending assault. However, the red-bearded captain, whose name was Miles Standish, was eager to settle the score for insults that he believed had been directed at him by a pair of Massachusett warriors named Wituwamat and Pecksuot, whom he had encountered earlier at Manomet. Accordingly, he assembled a force of

seven men and sailed in the shallop to Wessagussett. There, pre-
tending to have come for trade, he invited Pecksuot, Wituwamat,
Wituwamat's teenage brother, and a friend into a cabin for a meal
of corn and pork. When his guests had begun to eat, Standish
snatched the knife hanging around Pecksuot's neck and stabbed
him in the heart while his companions murdered Wituwamat, as
well as his young brother and the brother's friend. After slaugh-
tering several more Natives, Standish and his companions fought
a brief encounter with Obtakiest before forcing him to flee. Then,
soaked in the blood of their victims, they returned in triumph to
Plimoth, carrying the severed head of Wituwamat, which they im-
paled upon one of the palisades that surrounded the fort.

The killing spree initiated by the pugnacious Standish had a terrifying effect upon the Massachusett, as well as upon the Nauset
and other people living on the Narrow Land, who deserted their
villages and fled into swamps and forests to escape what they
feared would be wholesale massacre at the hands of the Englishmen and their dreaded muskets. There, unable to plant the corn,
beans, and squash that sustained them, they died of starvation
and a new outbreak of plague that not only killed them in droves,
but also struck down their leaders—among them Aspinet of the
Nauset, Canacum of the Manomet, and Iyanough, the young sachem of the Cummaquid.

Squeteague, esteemed because of the bravery he had exhibited during the skirmish with Captain Standish at First Encounter
Beach, tried to rally his fellow Nauset, who had sought refuge
on islands in Monomoy Bay. "We outnumber the foreigners!" he
cried, echoing the protest he had made to Aspinet. "Let's join with
our brothers and drive them away!"

But the dispirited Nauset remained too fearful of the English
and their muskets to heed his counsel. As a result, he decided that
it was time for him to leave the Narrow Land—a difficult decision
because he loved the sandy peninsula on which he had been born,
with its abundance of fish, shellfish, and water fowl. Half a day's
walk to the west, he came to the land of the Cummaquid, where

he found Iyanough lying on his deathbed and dreading what was going to happen to his people. "The God of the English is said to be all powerful," the young sachem warned in a voice that was barely audible. "He is offended with us and will destroy us in his anger."

Squeteague had heard such talk before but gave it little credence. The abduction and murder of his father and the plague brought by the foreigners that had killed his mother had persuaded him that the English and the deity they worshipped were not to be feared so much as despised for having inflicted torment upon innocent people. However, not wishing to cause Iyanough distress in his last hours, he remained silent and continued on his way. The next day, he visited the Manomet, whose sachem Canacum had died a week earlier. A brother of the dead leader told him that it had been Standish who had insulted Wituwamat and Pecksuot for not showing him sufficient respect.

Squeteague had no way of knowing how much or little of this might be true. At twilight, however, he came upon gruesome evidence of the red-bearded captain's wrath, for as he passed the fort the Englishmen had built to defend their settlement he could not fail to make out the head of Wituwamat which had been affixed to a palisade.

During the days that followed, Squeteague wandered through the land southwest of Plimoth, taking care to stay clear of Standish and his soldiers, who were now known far and wide as *Wotowequenega*—cutthroats. On the shore of what the Wampanoag called the "bay with many coves" (later known as Buzzards Bay), he encountered a large band of Pocasset, who had come there with their sachem, Corbitant, to gather quahogs and oysters and to spear eels in the Mattapoisett River. Upon learning that Corbitant opposed the treaty Massasoit had made with the English, Squeteague gained an audience by introducing himself as someone who had tried to kill Captain Standish in the only battle Native People had fought with him.

"A pity your arrow didn't find its mark," Corbitant said. "The

English Captain and his soldiers have succeeded in making our people afraid of their muskets."

"But if we gather together, can't drive them into the sea?"

"To fight against such powerful weapons with bows and arrows wouldn't be wise," Corbitant counseled. "However, the greed of the foreigners for furs has already persuaded some of them to furnish us with muskets of our own. This could be their undoing, for if we bide our time we can one day be as well armed as they."

"And what of Massasoit, who loves the English for restoring him to health?"

"Massasoit is a great sachem but he's made an evil bargain. He has made peace with the English in order to protect himself from his enemy—Canonicus and the Narragansett. To consolidate his power, he has brought the English invaders to his heart and dishonor upon himself by betraying the Massachusett, as well as the Nauset, Pocasset, and other Wampanoag People who live by the sea."

When Squeteague told Corbitant about the murder of his father at the hands of Captain Hunt, the Pocasset sachem recounted the trials of Epenow, a Wampanoag chief who lived on the nearby island of Noepe, which the English explorer Bartholomew Gosnold had named Martha's Vineyard. "Even before your father, Epenow was taken prisoner and transported across the sea by an English captain named Harlowe. There, in a great village called London, he was exhibited as a curiosity and delivered in servitude to a nobleman named Gorges, who wished to establish trading colonies in our land. After learning the language of the English, Epenow came to realize that they valued above everything a yellow substance called gold, and persuaded Gorges that there was much of it to be found in the sand cliffs of his native island. Whereupon Gorges sent Epenow back from England with a captain named Hobson so that he might reveal where this gold could be found, but as soon as Epenow came in sight of his homeland he leapt over the side of the ship and swam to shore, while his brothers who had come out in their canoes to greet the ship unleashed a hail of arrows to protect him."

Squeteague was fascinated to hear such a tale. "And you say all of this happened before the English landed at Patuxet, which they now call Plimoth?"

"All of it and more. Others of our fathers and grandfathers were captured and taken to the land of the English never to return."

"I'd like to meet this sachem called Epenow."

"I'll send you to Noepe with a message asking him to receive you," Corbitant replied.

The trip to the island took two days of paddling a large sea-going canoe against strong tidal currents, and when Squeteague and the pair of Pocasset who accompanied him arrived they were weary. After resting for several hours, he accepted Epenow's invitation to join him in his wetu for a meal of deer haunch and acorn squash, which was preceded by the customary offer of a pipe and tobacco. While passing the pipe back and forth, Epenow scrutinized his young guest and asked who he was and where he had come from.

"I'm of the Nauset who live on the Narrow Land," Squeteague replied. "When I was a boy, my father was abducted before my eyes by an English sea captain who later killed him. When the ship carrying the English settlers now at Plimoth came to our shores, our sachem, Aspinet, told me to follow it and learn where it might land. Afterward, I took part in the fight between my people and the soldiers led by Captain Standish who came ashore near our village. If we had possessed enough courage, we could have driven them into the sea, but we had never heard or seen the strange noise and smoke of their weapons, so we ran away. It's a shame I shall carry with me forever."

"You have no cause for shame," Epenow said, "but Corbitant is right—the muskets of the English invaders are too powerful for us to oppose with bows and arrows. Only by acquiring such weapons for ourselves can we hope to drive them from our land. As for Massasoit, he's being harassed by his enemy Canonicus, chief of the Narragansett, so he believes he has no choice but to remain a friend of the English who, for the moment, pretend to have good intentions toward him. But what will happen when Massasoit is no more?"

Squeteague was beginning to understand the complex web of uncertainty and fear that the arrival of the Englishmen and Massasoit's friendship with them had begun to build among the Wampanoag People. He was about to ask Epenow what could be done to avoid the trouble he foresaw, but the sachem had anticipated his question.

"One day we'll have to make peace among ourselves and rise up against the English. Otherwise they'll take our lands and leave our forests empty."

When Squeteague returned to the mainland, he headed north along the Mattapoisett River, taking care to avoid villages of the Pokanoket for fear that his sojourns with Corbitant and Epenow, widely regarded as critics of the treaty Massasoit had made with the English, might provoke reprisal. Unaware, however, that Massasoit had a fishing camp at the southern end of Assawompsett Pond, he stumbled upon it before the sun had set, and was detained by a pair of warriors who were standing guard.

Disarmed of his tomahawk and bow and arrow, Squeteague was taken to a tall man of powerful physique, whose only suggestion of status other than his grave and distinguished demeanor was a chain of white bone beads he wore around his neck. After the guards described how they had come to seize the trespasser, Massasoit told them to leave, motioned Squeteague to sit on a bearskin hide, and inquired who he was.

"My name is Squeteague and I'm a Nauset," Squeteague declared, proudly.

"Then you know that your sachem, Aspinet, as well as other sachems of people living on the Narrow Land, have conspired with Obtakiest to attack my English allies."

"Aspinet is dead of the foreign sickness," Squeteague replied, "as are Iyanough of the Cummaquid and Canacum of the Manomet."

Massasoit nodded to indicate that was aware of this. "It is painful to me that my tributary people by the sea have betrayed my wishes by going against the English."

"Aspinet had good reason to go against them," Squeteague declared. "The English captain named Standish and his men stole corn from the Payomet and looted the graves of their dead. Afterward, he and his soldiers came to our village."

"And you thought to drive them away with bows and arrows?"

"It takes the English much time to reload their weapons. If we had run upon them, we could have driven them into the sea and made short work of them with our tomahawks."

Massasoit smiled. "You're very sure of yourself for someone so young. What makes you wish to make short work of the English?"

"They kidnapped my father when I was a boy. A captain named Hunt took him across the sea in order to sell him as a slave in a place called Spain, but in the middle of the ocean he killed my father and had him thrown overboard for the sharks to eat."

"How do you know such a thing?"

"I was told so by the interpreter named Tisquantum."

"And where might you have met him?"

"In Monomoyick before he died. I'd heard that he had also been kidnapped by Captain Hunt and I wanted to find out if he knew what had happened to my father."

"Not all the English are like Hunt," Massasoit said. "He was an evil man."

"Others were also evil. Men such as Harlowe, who abducted the sachem Epenow.

Massasoit regarded his young visitor with new interest. "So you have met Epenow?"

"As well as Corbitant."

"You're a rash young fellow to admit this to me. Both of these sachems oppose the treaty I've made with the English. I consider them to be my enemies."

"Just as the English are mine," Squeteague replied. "My father's death at their hands is something I will avenge."

"And how do you propose to do that?"

"By cutting off as many of them as I can find."

"Hear me!" Massasoit commanded. "As the leader of the Wampanoag I can't dwell on every evil that's been done in the past but must consider what's best for the future. I could have had the English slaughtered during their first winter here. Instead, I fed them and helped them to survive. Did I do so out of pity in my heart? No, I acted for a greater purpose. When I became sachem of the Wampanoag People, we numbered many thousands, but because of the pestilence brought upon us by the Europeans we soon became less than half of what we had been. Some of our neighbors escaped the sickness and remained strong—the Narragansett, for example, who under their sachem, Canonicus, would like to make slaves of us to the last man, woman, and child. The Narragansett now exceed us by threefold. Should I stand by and allow them to conquer us? Or should I make peace with the English, as I have done, so that if the Narragansett attack us the English will be obliged to come to our defense with their guns?"

Squeteague fell silent as the opposing arguments of Massasoit, Corbitant, and Epenow jostled with one another in his brain. In the end, there seemed to be no easy answer. According to Massasoit, survival of the Wampanoag depended on keeping peace with the English, but what of the conviction of Corbitant and Epenow that peace with the English would inevitably lead to the dispossession and destruction of the Wampanoag?

Massasoit was watching him intently. "You're a young man of admirable spirit. However, I can't allow you to go about killing my English allies. Swear to me that you'll put aside your need for revenge."

"I cannot do that."

"Then, with reluctance, I shall have you put to death."

Squeteague now realized that his impetuous declaration of hatred for the English had placed him in danger of losing his life. Never again, he decided, would he allow passion to rule his speech in such a manner. Meanwhile, he found himself at the mercy of a man who commanded respect that bordered upon reverence from the Wampanoag and was demanding that he relinquish his duty to his murdered father.

"Shall I have your promise or not?" Massasoit demanded.

For a moment, Squeteague contemplated making a run for it and taking his chances with the guards outside. Then, realizing that he would stand little chance against armed men, he nodded in assent. "With reluctance," he replied. And only for the time being, he told himself.

Massasoit smiled at the bold answer of his young visitor. "In return for sparing your life, I shall require that you travel to the territory of the Massachusett and track down Obtakiest, who has plotted against my English friends. When you find him, you will kill him and send word that you have carried out my command. Afterward, you will keep me informed about the intentions of others who may be plotting against me."

Squeteague winced at the order that he kill one of the few people who had exhibited the courage to oppose Standish and his murderous companions. Under the circumstances, however, he had no choice except to agree, and did so with another nod of his head.

Massasoit raised a hand to signify that the interview was over. "Go," he said, "and do not fail to reflect on the necessity of keeping peace with the English. Perhaps one day you'll come to understand it."

Chapter Three

When Squeteague left Massasoit's fishing camp, he traveled northeast through deep forest to the region surrounding the abandoned settlement at Wessegusset, where he learned that Obtakiest had taken flight and disappeared. Close by was the main territory of the Massachusett, who were members of the loosely allied Wampanoag Confederation, and led by a squaw sachem named Wianna. She had inherited her title when her husband, Nanepashemet, had been killed by raiders a year before the colonists arrived at Plimoth. Since then she had consolidated her power by bringing several neighboring bands under her control, with the result that the Massachusett had come to occupy much of the land around the meandering Quinobequin (Charles) River, which the English king had named after himself.

Following Nanepashemet's death, Wianna had been left with two sons—both too young to inherit their father's title—and in whose place she had been designated by tradition to rule. Also by tradition, she would one day be required to marry Webcowit, her dead husband's powwaw, or medicine man. In the meantime, she was an attractive and lusty widow in her early thirties, and when the young and handsome Squeteague ventured to come among her people, she wasted no time inviting him into her wetu and seducing him by lying back on her bed of otter pelts and lifting the flap of her breechclout to reveal a pair of shapely thighs. For a few seconds, Squeteague stood spellbound before her. Then he tore off the leggings he was wearing and lay down beside her. Like most Nauset boys, he had been free to experiment with girls and had lost his virginity early on, but he had never engaged in sex with a woman who was so thoroughly knowledgeable in the art of giving and receiving carnal pleasure. For a time, he made love to her in a frenzy that elicited one orgasmic spasm after another— each of them accompanied by hoarse cries of gratification—until, satiated, she rolled out from beneath him and reciprocated in a manner he had not experienced before.

From then on, Squeteague was a nocturnal resident in Wianna's wetu and an accomplice in the many ways of lovemaking she found desirable. He also began to accompany her on official journeys, during which he came to know the Nipmuck, who lived to the west near Mount Wachusett; the Pocumtuck, who lived farther west beyond the Quinnehtukqut (Connecticut) River; the Pennacook who lived to the north by the Merruasquamack (Merrimack) River; and Pilgrim traders who were spreading into the interior from Plimoth and whose language he learned so that he might do business with them by swapping beaver pelts for muskets, metal tools, and cooking utensils. Thus did he not only become Wianna's lover, but also her chief agent for barter and trading.

When Massasoit learned that Squeteague was living with the Massachusett, he summoned him to Sowams to learn what Wianna's intentions toward the Pokanoket and their English allies might be.

"She wishes to maintain peaceful relations with both the Pokanoket and the English," Squeteague told him. "Her people, like yours, have been too weakened by the plague for it to be otherwise."

"I'm glad to hear this," Massasoit said. "Canonicus and his Narragansett are giving me enough to worry about without hostility from the Massachusett."

"The English have shown a great desire to acquire beaver pelts and the squaw sachem has chosen me to assist in bringing it about."

Massasoit smiled in a way that implied he suspected there was more than trade to account for Squeteague's living with the Massachusett. "You have pursued a wise course by making friends with the English," he said.

"Rest assured I haven't forgotten it was they who murdered my father," Squeteague replied.

"Just so long as you remember to do nothing to jeopardize the treaty I made with them. The peace must be kept so they will honor their agreement should the Narragansett attack."

A peace that will be temporary, Squeteague told himself, as he recalled Corbitant predicting how the Native People might one day be armed with muskets, and Epenow questioning what would happen when Massasoit was no more.

By this time, Wianna's eldest sons were about to assume their rightful titles as sachems of a pair of Massachusett coastal bands. The day was also approaching when she would be obliged to marry the powwaw Webcowit. Even though the marriage would be one of convenience, appearances required that she no longer keep a young consort in her otter-pelt bed. When the time came to explain this to Squeteague, she gave him a beaded deerskin shirt, a beautifully wrought copper bracelet, and a belt of the finest wampum—highly prized beads made from the shells of quahogs and used as currency.

"Slippery one," she told him, "you have swum in me to the delight of my nights. Perhaps you should now look for a wife who will give you sons."

But Wianna had simply wanted to see the dismay that came over her young lover's face, because she had no intention of relinquishing him. Indeed, for several more seasons, they continued to enjoy what the righteous settlers at Plimoth would have condemned as adultery—a crime punishable among them by death—whenever Webcowit went off on one of his healing missions. During this time, Squeteague continued to act as business agent for Wianna with English traders from Plimoth, and with the suppliers of beaver pelts, from the Nipmuck, Pocumtuck, and Pennacook. He also witnessed the profound change that occurred in the region in 1630, when nearly a thousand Puritan settlers led by a man named John Winthrop arrived from England with a royal charter to establish the Massachusetts Bay Colony.

The seal of the new colony showed a Native warrior calling upon the English to "Come over and help us."

The Bay colonists settled at first on a peninsula called Shawmut (land near water) that would become known as Boston. However, they soon began to spread into the surrounding area, purchasing territory the Massachusett and Nipmuck had used in common for centuries for a few beads and trinkets. Like their predecessors at Plimoth, the newcomers were separatists who believed in reforming the Church of England that had persecuted them over the years for their dissenting beliefs. From the start, however, they engaged in persecuting anyone among them who disagreed with the dogma proclaimed by their ministers, who asserted that religious authority should always prevail over civil government. This, in turn, allowed them to justify a claim to the lands in what they called "The New World" by God-given right of discovery, also known as the theory of *vacuum domicilium*, under which unsettled or unimproved territory, such as the forests the Native People roamed, could be theirs for the taking.

Squeteague knew little about the religious quarrels that had propelled the Puritans to journey to the New World, but he was a keen observer of how quickly they were settling on land along the coast and making incursions as far into the interior as the valley of the Quinnehtukqut River. He was also a witness to the zeal with which they preached a harsh and unforgiving religion. In the town of Naumkeag (Salem), he listened to a stern-faced minister

wearing a black-frock coat describe a wave of smallpox current-
ly decimating the Massachusett as "the righteousness of God's
judgment against the wicked savages." Making double use of the
Native population, the preacher then warned his congregation
that, "God will make a rod of the barbarous heathen to punish you
for your sins." Other ministers advised potential converts among
the Massachusett that a disapproving Jehovah would smite them
with additional plague if they did not accept the wisdom of the
Gospel. John Winthrop, who had become governor of the Massachusetts Bay Colony, had a more practical approach. He welcomed the decimating effect of smallpox upon the Native People
as the Lord's way of "clearing title to what we possess."

The arrogance of the English colonists at Plimoth and Boston toward those who dissented from their views, as well as their thirst
for land and beaver pelts, was not lost upon Squeteague, who became more and more skeptical of Massasoit's policy of keeping
peace with them at any cost. "These are a strange people who have
come among us," he told his mistress queen as, drenched in per-
spiration, they lay side by side after a bout of lovemaking. "They
believe they must save each other from evil or their God will condemn them to burn forever. They punish each other harshly for
trivial offenses such as dancing and letting their hair grow long.
They whip people they consider lazy or stubborn. They imprison
one another for drinking. They will flog a man for kissing his wife
in the street. They'll hang a man and a woman for the pleasure we
have just taken with one another. It's a wonder they dare to make
children, for they suffer no one to enjoy himself."

Two years after the Puritans arrived at Shawmut, Canonicus decided to attack the Massasoit and the Pokanoket in
strength. However, Pokanoket scouts observed the approach of
the Narragansett warriors in time for Massasoit to send messengers to Plimoth to invoke the treaty he had concluded with the
settlers a decade earlier. As a result, Standish and a group of soldiers marched to a small trading post the English had established

near Sowams in time to rescue Massasoit, who had sought refuge there, and to confront Canonicus and his Narragansett warriors, who quickly backed away in the face of their muskets.

As it happened, Squeteague had been visiting the trading post to exchange furs with the English and when the Narragansett war party surrounded it, he had volunteered to fight in behalf of its defenders. Once the threat had dissipated, Massasoit summoned him to his wetu to thank him for his loyalty. "You have demonstrated your allegiance to me in the manner of a true warrior," he said. "Perhaps you now understand the wisdom of my having made an alliance with the English."

Squeteague acknowledged that the arrival of Standish and his men had turned the tide of battle. At the same time, he reminded Massasoit that honor required him to seek vengeance for his father's murder.

The sachem placed both hands on his shoulders. "Try to put aside your need for revenge. And be assured that only with greatest reluctance would I have put to death someone whom I admired at first sight, and whom I have come admire more than ever. Indeed, from this day forward I shall consider you as a son, and wish that one day my own sons may grow to be the kind of man you have become."

Squeteague was moved to the brink of tears. The great chief of the Wampanoag had offered to become the father he had lost so many years before. Although he continued to entertain doubts about the wisdom of his surrogate father in having made peace with the English, he decided that for the moment he would put aside his hatred for them and not take any action to carry out his vow of vengeance.

Soon after his return to Shawmut, plague struck the Massachusett once again. As if the God of the Puritans possessed the vengeful powers ascribed to Him, one of Wianna's sons succumbed to smallpox, the other survived with a hideously deformed nose, and nearly a hundred of her people died of the disease. Devastated by the calamity, Wianna began selling choice pieces of land to the settlers in the hope of appeasing the vindictive deity they worshipped. She also ended her affair with Squeteague, fearing that some of her newly Christianized subjects would reveal it to the Puritan authorities. However, in light of their past liaison, she allowed him to continue acting as agent for the lucrative beaver trade being conducted between her people and merchants of Plimoth Plantation and the Massachusetts Bay Colony.

As for Squeteague, who longed for the sea that washed the shores of the Narrow Land, he salvaged a Dutch-built trading sloop that had been driven ashore in a gale and abandoned on one of the islands in Boston Harbor. After repairing the vessel, which he named the *Nauset*, he hired several Saugus as crewmembers and began to trade for furs with Native People who lived to the north along the sea coast, and the Narragansett who lived to the south by the bay of that name, as well as the Pequot who occupied land between Narragansett Bay and the Quinnehtukqut River. He soon found out that the Pequot and their tributary, the Western Niantic, had been doing business with Dutch traders from Manhattan, who had recently established a trading post called the "House of Good Hope," situated fifty miles up the Quinnehtukqut from the sea. He also learned that the Dutch and Pequot had negotiated a treaty under which all Native People, no matter what their affiliation, would be granted access to the trading post.

On his first trip to the Quinnehtukqut in the spring of 1634, a river sachem told him that the agreement had recently been broken by the Pequot, who had ambushed and killed several Narragansett trying to trade at Good Hope. The Dutch retaliated by capturing the Pequot sachem, Tatobem, and demanding that his people pay a ransom to have him back, but when the Pequot sent them payment in wampum, the Dutch who had wanted beaver pelts instead of wampum, killed Tatobem and returned only his body. For this reason, Tatobem's son, Sassacus, had vowed revenge.

In fact, Sassacus had already taken what he presumed to be revenge, as Squeteague found out when he sailed downriver on his way back to Boston, and came upon the hulk of a pinnace that had been burned to the water line. Some Western Niantic, close allies of the Pequot, explained that a few days earlier the vessel's Dutch captain had kidnapped two Niantic men and forced them to guide him upriver. However, other Niantic warriors had followed along the riverbank and waited until the ship had anchored for the night before coming onboard under the pretense of wanting to trade. By that time, the Dutch captain had become drunk, which made it easy for one of the Niantic to split his head with a tomahawk and for others to kill the rest of the crew and rescue the captives before setting the ship on fire.

Unfortunately for Sassacus, the captain of the pinnace was not a Dutchman but an Englishman named John Stone.

Squeteague found himself of two minds about the killing of Stone. On the one hand, he felt admiration for Sassacus, who believed (even if mistakenly) that he had taken blood vengeance for the kidnapping and murder of his father, just as he longed to take revenge for the kidnapping and murder of his own father by Captain Hunt. On the other hand, he knew that the Puritans would not tolerate the killing of an Englishman, and wondered if they would seize upon it as an excuse to avail themselves of the rich beaver resources in the interior. His concern was heightened when he discovered that Puritan authorities were demanding that the Pequot hand over the heads of those responsible for Captain Stone's "foul murder," as well as a large amount of wampum and many pelts. The fulminations of the Puritans intrigued Squeteague, who knew that they considered Stone to be a drunkard, lecher, braggart, bully, and blasphemer, and had banished him from the colony for life after bringing him to trial on the charge of adultery, for which crime he would have been hanged if, in addition to the reckless lady's aggrieved husband, there had been the second witness required by English law.

Could the Puritans be looking for an excuse to go to war?

Hoping to avoid undue notice, Squeteague was keeping the

Nauset at Jeffrey's Creek, a small cove north of Salem, but, after several more voyages to the Quinnehtukqut, his activities came to the attention of Governor Winthrop, who summoned Squeteague to appear before him at his headquarters in Boston. The governor was an elegant man, with piercing eyes, a carefully trimmed beard, and an imposing manner. For his part, Squeteague, who had dressed himself in his best deerskin leggings and the beaded shirt Wianna had given him, remained alert as Winthrop looked him over.

"My commissioners tell me you have a ship and are trading in furs without permission to do so," the governor said.

"I've been trading with the people of Your Excellency's colony in behalf of the Squaw Sachem of the Massachusett," Squeteague replied.

"The Squaw Sachem has been generous in sharing her lands. However, that doesn't give you the right to conduct commerce with the Pequot and their allies."

"So far I've merely explored the river where the Pequot and Niantic do business with the Dutch."

"The Dutch, Pequot, and Niantic are in league against us," Winthrop declared. "They pretend to want peaceful relations, but what they really want is to control the fur trade in the Connecticut River Valley."

"Any furs I acquire will be brought to the Bay Colony," Squeteague assured him.

"And who stands to profit from such trade?"

"Everyone, Your Excellency. The Native hunters who supply the pelts, I who bring them back to Your Excellency's colony, and the Commissioners who send them to His Majestie's kingdom across the sea."

Winthrop smiled to acknowledge Squeteague's business acumen before resuming his interrogation. "Can you explain why the colony should need you to act as a go-between in the fur trade?"

"Because I speak the Algonqian tongue, as well as many of its dialects, and can bargain to best advantage with the Native hunters and trappers who supply the beaver pelts."

The governor sat back in his chair and scrutinized Squeteague with appreciation. "Suppose the Colony were to grant you permission to trade in the Connecticut Valley? Might you be willing to undertake some additional service?"

Squeteague replied that he would welcome the chance.

Winthrop leaned forward, placed his elbows on the desk before him, and made a steeple of his fingers. "We face an uncertain situation on the frontier. We have an ally in Massasoit of the Pokanoket and in Uncas of the Mohegan, but we have little knowledge about the intentions of Canonicus and Miantonomo, sachems of the Narragansett, or Ninigret of the Niantic, and even less about Sassacus of the Pequot. Some of these tribes are hostile to one another and all would seem to want the fur trade for themselves. What we need is someone like you—someone of their blood—who can move freely among them and whose eyes and ears we may depend on to furnish us with information about their plans and strategems. Then, once our merciful God has finished loosing his fearsome pox upon them, we'll be able to drive out the Dutch and take over the fur trade for ourselves."

Squeteague could scarcely believe his ears. Here was the Governor of the Massachusetts Bay Colony not only revealing Puritan strategy, but also offering him opportunities that, while keeping the vow he had given Massasoit, would enable him to help his people in ways that might far exceed any blood vengeance he had ever dreamed of taking for his father's murder. What form these opportunities might present he could not immediately fathom, but of the fact that they would exist he was certain, and he was hopeful that they might establish him as a successful fur trader.

Beyond that lay the realization of how quickly he had risen in the world around him to become at the age of thirty the lover and accomplice of the Queen of the Massachusett, the adopted son of the great sachem Massasoit, and now an agent and scout for the Governor of the Bay Colony. Holding his breath, he tried to control the pounding in his chest.

"I will be honored to provide Your Excellency with such service," he replied.

Part Two

AMBUSH
AND
MASSACRE

Chapter Four

During the next two years, Governor Winthrop and authorities of the Massachusetts Bay Colony continued to demand that the Pequot furnish them with a large supply of wampum in compensation for Stone's murder, as well as the heads of his killers. For their part, Pequot emissaries claimed that the killers had either succumbed to smallpox or could not be found, but sent partial payment of the wampum tribute the Puritans had demanded and agreed to sign a peace treaty. Meanwhile, Squeteague had begun providing muskets to Native hunters in the Quinnehtukqut Valley in return for furs he delivered to trading posts English settlers were establishing on the river that would become the towns of Hartford, Windsor, and Wethersfield.

The first visitor to the site of Wethersfield was a man named John Oldham, who had led a pioneering trek through the wilderness from Massachusetts to the Quinnehtukqut River in 1633, and was blamed by the local Natives for a devastating outbreak of smallpox that occurred soon after his departure. Oldham had come to Plimoth Plantation a decade earlier, but had been banished from the colony for opposing its strict religion. Known as "Mad Jack" for his moody temperament, he had once pulled a knife on Miles Standish, who later drummed him out of the colony by forcing him to run a gauntlet of soldiers who thumped his backside with the butt ends of their muskets. Oldham then moved to the Massachusetts Bay Colony, where he became an advisor to Governor Winthrop, who furnished him with a pinnace to develop trade along the Connecticut coast and in the Connecticut River. On a voyage to the region in July of 1636, he came upon the *Nauset*, which Squeteague had anchored at the river mouth.

Pulling alongside, Oldham hailed the *Nauset*, asked to speak to her master, and found himself face to face with Squeteague.

"I believe I asked to speak to your captain," he said.

"I am the captain," Squeteague told him.

"You say you're such, yet you have the look of an Indian."

"I am both the captain of this ship and a member of the Nauset People who live on a territory we call the Narrow Land and you English call Cape Cod."

Oldham shook his head in wonder. "And what port do you sail from?"

"From Jeffrey's Creek near Salem. And you?"

"From Boston under the authority of John Winthrop, Governor of the Bay Colony."

"I also sail under His Excellency's authority."

"Not after I inform him that I've found you trespassing in a region where trade has been allotted to me."

"Allow me to wish you well in your complaint," said Squeteague, with a smile.

"I've a mind to teach you a lesson for your insolence," Oldham growled, and pointed to a Narragansett seaman, who crouched behind a gunwale, aiming a pistol at Squeteague.

"Any lesson you may wish to teach will be returned in double measure," Squeteague assured him, as a pair of his Saugus crewmembers stepped forward with muskets at the ready.

As the two ships drifted slowly apart, Oldham shouted, "You haven't heard the last of me!" Squeteague made no reply, but he wondered what harm Oldham might do when he returned to Boston and sought an audience with Governor Winslow.

As it turned out, he had no cause for concern because Oldham, whose crew consisted of two Narragansett seaman and two English boys, would be dead within a week. While trading with the Manissean, a tributary people of the Narragansett living on Manisses—known to Europeans as Block Island after the Dutch explorer Adrien Block who had landed there in 1614—he made the mistake of arguing with a sachem over how much wampum should be exchanged for tobacco. Matters escalated to the extent that Oldham lost the temper for which he was famous and struck the sachem a blow to the chest. At that point, an enraged Manissean warrior dispatched him by splitting his skull open with a hatchet. Having witnessed their captain's execution, the terrified English boys and the Narragansett sailors were bundled into a canoe, taken to the mainland, and turned over to the Eastern Niantic, a tributary tribe of the Narragansett.

As chance would have it, a small bark was sailing in Block Island Sound that day under the command of John Gallop, a trader from Boston, who became curious when he spotted Oldham's pinnace wallowing in swells two miles from the island. Drawing near, Gallop saw a number of Manissean on the deck of the pinnace, but no sign of Oldham. When he hailed the Manissean and received no reply, he became suspicious that they had taken over the ship, so he rammed the pinnace amidships, driving several Manissean over the rail and into the sea. He and his crewmen then boarded the pinnace and made prisoners of two Manissean who surrendered, binding both of them and throwing one into the sea to ensure that they might not contrive to untie each other.

When Gallop and his men searched the pinnace, they found the still warm corpse of Oldham lying under some fish net in a pool of blood and brains. They also discovered two Manissean in the hold whom they kept prisoner by battening down the hatch. After burying Oldham's body at sea, Gallop took the pinnace in tow but was forced to set it adrift when the wind came up and the ocean turned rough. The boat fetched up the following day on the shore near the mouth of Narragansett Bay, where its imprisoned passengers were given sanctuary by the Eastern Niantic, who released the English boys so they could return to Boston.

Squeteague learned what had happened to Oldham when he returned to Boston in early August. By that time, Puritan ministers from one end of Massachusetts Bay Colony to the other were summoning up the deaths of him and Captain Stone as text for sermons warning that the Pequot and their allies, whom they denounced as "Satan's horde," were planning to carry out a massacre such as the one that had taken place fourteen years earlier at Jamestown, Virginia. Fears that such an event might be imminent were further inflamed by Uncas, sachem of the Mohegan and bitter rival of Sassacus, who sent word to Plimoth that the Pequot were preparing to attack and plunder one of the colony's trading ships in the Connecticut River.

Upon consulting with Puritan clergy about whether reprisal should be taken for the deaths of Oldham and Stone, Governor Henry Vane, who had succeeded Winthrop, was assured that the Lord would approve a merciless revenge. He then designated Squeteague to act as scout and interpreter for a force of ninety militiamen and three pinnaces under the command of Captain John Endecott. Vane led Squeteague to believe that Endecott and his soldiers would be sailing to Block Island to make a show of force aimed at persuading the Manissean to desist from further hostile acts against English ships. In fact, Endecott had been given orders to take possession of Block Island, kill all of its adult male inhabitants, and enslave their women and children. Afterward, he was instructed to sail to a Pequot village near the mouth of the Pequot River and demand that the tribe surrender the killers of Captain Stone, pay a thousand fathoms of wampum in damages, and turn over a number of children as hostages for future good behavior.

Endecott had come to Boston in 1628 as one of the original patentees of the King's grant for the Massachusetts Bay Colony and had served a term as temporary governor. Squeteague had seen him occasionally while fetching the *Nauset* from Jeffrey Creek, and knew him to be a zealous Puritan who called for women to be veiled when attending church. Endicott wore curled mustaches that sprouted sideways from his upper lip and a narrow pointed beard that dropped from his lower lip like a tail, thus forming a furry "T" below a pair of sunken, mirthless eyes. He believed Native People to be inferior heathens and undertook the punitive mission he had been assigned by Vane with an eagerness that bordered on relish.

At dusk on August 22, 1636, Endecott and his men—among them Squeteague and Captains John Underhill and Nathaniel Turner—rowed in small boats through heavy surf toward a sandy beach at the northern end of Block Island. As they disembarked and struggled through pounding breakers, fifty Manissean warriors rose from behind the sand dunes and unleashed a hail of arrows that inflicted no serious injuries. Acting on Squeteague's advice, the soldiers moved inland, made camp for the night, and posted sentinels.

On the next day, the Englishmen explored the interior of the island, which was so overgrown with underbrush that they were forced to march single file along narrow trails as they searched for Manissean. Proceeding in noisy fashion, they came upon two deserted villages, each containing more than fifty wetu and surrounded by large fields of corn, which they put to the torch. At daylight on the second day, Underhill and forty men attacked a third village, believing that it might be filled with sleeping Manissean. The village was deserted, however, except for a few dogs that a frustrated Underhill ordered his men to slaughter before setting the place and its surrounding cornfields ablaze.

Squeteague found the wanton killing of the animals and destruction of the corn unsettling because it provided a hint of the true purpose of the expedition. Helpless to intervene, he could only wish that he had refused the role he had been assigned by Governor Vane. However, the mismanaged raid provided him with a valuable example of the English vulnerability to ambush—a weakness that could be exploited in any Native uprising that might occur in the future. Endecott and his soldiers spent the rest of the day searching in vain for the Manissean, who had vanished into the undergrowth like ghosts, leaving the baffled Englishmen with no other course than to board their ships and sail away.

No sooner had they embarked than Endecott proceeded to take out his frustration upon his guide. "A poor job you did of bringing us to grips with the savages," he told Squeteague. "If you hadn't been recommended by Governor Vane I'd be tempted to suspect you had been in league with them."

After leaving Block Island, Endecott's expedition sailed to a fort at Saybrook at the mouth of the Connecticut River, which had been built some months earlier by Lieutenant Lion Gardiner, a thirty-six-year-old engineer who had served in the English army in Flanders and been sent to Saybrook by Governor Winthrop. A tall man with blond hair, Gardiner was not happy to learn that Endecott intended to demand that the Pequot hand over wampum and child hostages. He had been provided with less than half the soldiers he had been promised to defend the fort, and his wife had recently given birth to the first European child to be born in the newly established Connecticut Colony. "You're going to raise a cloud of heathen wasps around our necks," he told the Puritan commander. "Then you'll sail away leaving us to be starved into submission and roasted at the stake."

When the obstinate Endecott refused to postpone confronting the Pequot, Gardiner approached Squeteague. "Can't you talk some sense into this dunderhead? He's going to leave me in an untenable position here."

Squeteague felt sympathy for the young lieutenant's predicament. "I fear that Commander Endecott is not only unskilled in warfare but also convinced of the wisdom of his own ignorance," he replied.

Gardiner gave a grim laugh and held out his hand. "From now on I'll count you as a friend."

A few days later, Endecott and his men set sail for a Pequot village situated at the mouth of a river of the same name. When they arrived late in the afternoon, they were hailed by a crowd of Niantic and Pequot who believed at first that the English had come to trade "Do you come for furs?" they shouted from the shore. When the English made no reply, they became anxious "Do you come to fight? Will you try to kill us?"

Once it grew dark, the Pequot and Niantic lit fires on both banks of the river and made woeful cries that Squeteague interpreted as calls to gather forces in case the English were preparing to attack them. In the morning, they sent a canoe carrying a tribal elder to Endecott's vessel to ask the purpose of his visit. "We English do not allow murderers to live," Endicott replied, and informed the emissary that the Governor of the Bay Colony had sent him to demand the heads of the persons who had killed Captain Stone and his crew. He went on to say that if the Pequot valued their peace and welfare they would give up the heads without delay.

Speaking in a mixture of broken English and Algonquian translated by Squeteague, the Pequot ambassador acknowledged that warriors loyal to Sassacus had killed Stone and his crew, but claimed it was in revenge for the death of Sassacus's father, Tatobem, who had been murdered even though his people had paid for his freedom with a ransom of a bushel of wampum. He then posed a question whose complex reasoning contained a plea for exoneration: "Can you blame us for avenging so cruel a murder when we cannot distinguish the Dutch from the English but take them to be one and the same people, and therefore do not believe that we wronged you for their having killed our king?"

After some discussion about whether the Pequot should have been able to tell Dutchmen from Englishmen, an impatient Endecott told the ambassador, "Either give us the heads of those who murdered Captain Oldham or prepare yourselves to do battle."

"I ask that you allow me to go ashore and inform my people of your intent," the ambassador replied.

As soon as he had departed, Endecott landed his forces and deployed them on a hill that lay close to the Pequot village. When the ambassador returned to say that Sassacus had gone to Paumanok (Long Island), Endecott declared that he knew him to be nearby, and ordered him to be brought forth. "Otherwise, we will destroy your village and burn your corn."

Endecott waited for more than an hour for his demand to be met. He then ordered Captain Underhill and his men to set the Pequot wetu and cornfields on fire, and to shoot any Indian who came within musket range.

"Tell your men to aim above their heads?" Squeteague advised Underhill. "Otherwise, there'll be needless deaths for, as you can see, the Pequot are armed only with bows and arrows."

"We must teach them the lesson we failed to teach the Manissean," Underhill replied, and gave the order to fire upon a group of Pequot who were standing between their village and the hill. When the smoke cleared, two Pequot lay dead on the ground, several others had been wounded, and the rest had fled. As Underhill's men strode among the injured, dispatching them with their swords, Squeteague imagined Captain Hunt advancing with cutlass raised upon his hapless father, and the terrible slice of the blade as it cut through flesh and bone. Only the realization that he would be committing suicide prevented him from drawing his knife and severing Underhill's jugular vein.

After destroying and plundering the Pequot village, the English soldiers returned to their ships for the night. The next morning, they landed on the opposite shore of the river and torched a village inhabited by the Niantic, as well as the cornfields surrounding it. "None of the Indians dared come near," Underhill boasted. "They ran from us as deer from dogs."

Once the Puritan militia had laid waste to everything they could set afire, they left the two smoldering villages, embarked on their ships, and sailed back to Boston. Squeteague did not accompany them. Appalled by the senseless destruction, he notified Endecott that he had business in the interior and returned to Boston on foot through Pokanoket and Nipmuck territory. Along the way, he informed the inhabitants of each village he passed through about the havoc the English had wrought.

To his chagrin, the reaction of the Pokanoket and Nipmuck mirrored that of his fellow Nauset when he had tried to rally them a decade earlier, following Standish's murderous foray at Wessagussett. Fear of the firepower of English muskets outweighed apprehension that the colonists might be planning to deprive them of their land. A disappointed Squeteague consoled himself by remembering the advice of Corbitant, who had counseled patience until the Native inhabitants of the region had become sufficiently armed to achieve parity with the invaders. He also realized that, as the captain of a sailing ship and fur trader, he occupied an ideal position from which to become a supplier of weapons that would even the balance.

No sooner had he arrived in Boston than he was called before Governor Vane, who had received word of the tidings he had delivered to the Pokanoket and Nipmuck during his overland journey, and demanded to know why he had shown disloyalty to the Bay Colony.

Squeteague knew that his head hung in the balance. "Your Excellency, word was bound to spread of Commander Endecott's attack on the Pequot and Niantic," he replied. "If I had not spoken as I did, I would have been suspected of being beholden to the English—something that would have destroyed my usefulness to you as your scout."

Mollified, the governor decided that Squeteague was a clever man who would prove valuable as the colonists extended their reach into the hinterlands.

For Squeteague, it was his first real test in the precarious endeavor upon which he had embarked.

Chapter Five

Endecott's raid convinced Squeteague once and for all that the English were bent on intimidating the Native People as a prelude to depriving them of their ancestral lands, and that Massasoit had been mistaken to make peace with them. At the same time, he realized that if the Puritan and Pilgrim invaders were to be stopped, it would be essential for sachems pursuing vendettas against each other to settle their differences and unite against their common enemy. It was one thing for him to arrive at this conclusion, however, and another to act on it. Opportunity for doing so resided in the fact that the trading commission granted by Governor Winthrop allowed him to act as a double agent—on the one hand, a putative informant for the English; on the other, a real one for his fellow Natives with whom he now increased trading muskets for furs. It was a potentially fatal balancing act because a false move with his brethren could result in his being flayed and roasted alive, while a similar misstep with the Puritans might see him hanged and beheaded, or, worse, drawn and quartered while still drawing breath.

In early September, he sailed the *Nauset* to Pettaquamscutt

Cove on the western shore of Narragansett Bay to trade with the Narragansett and assess the intentions of their sachems—the seventy-four-year-old Canonicus and his nephew, a tall and commanding warrior named Miantonomo, who appeared to be in his early thirties. What he learned proved disheartening to his plan of encouraging the formation of an alliance against the colonists.

"We assured the English we would not oppose their raid against the Manissean," Canonicus told him. "We also promised we will not ally ourselves with Sassacus and the Pequot in the event of war."

Squeteague wondered if Canonicus and Miantonomo might be hoping to incite a conflict between the Puritans and the Pequot in order to gain ascendancy in the region, and ventured to point out potential consequenses. "If the English should vanquish the Pequot, they and their Pokanoket allies will control the territory on either side of you."

Canonicus reacted to the suggestion with disdain. "We don't fear your English friends, or your Pokanoket allies."

"I haven't come as a friend of the English. I've come to understand why you favor them in their hostility toward the Pequot."

Miantonomo explained the complications of the feud that had developed between the Narragansett and the Pequot. "We don't trust Sassacus," he declared. "Warriors led by his father, Tabotem, broke the treaty with the Dutch by killing some of our people who wanted to trade furs at the House of Good Hope. The Dutch retaliated by killing Tabotem, thus earning the enmity of his son Sassacus, whose men then killed an English captain and his crew, thinking they were Dutch. Now the Pequot are seeking our help against the English whom they fear will make war against them because they killed the English captain. But why should we help those who killed our people?"

Squeteague found himself confronting a prime example of the ever-proliferating enmities between sachems that must be overcome if the Native People were to unite against the English invaders. "Have you considered how much territory the English have acquired since they came to our shores?"

"You can thank Massasoit for that," Canonicus growled. "He's given away some of his best land to the colonists at Plimoth. As for Sassacus, he tried to persuade us that the English have designs on our territory, and to join him in a war against them. However, we know his real ambitions are against the Narragansett, so he doesn't fool us."

This old sachem blows one way in the wind and then the other, Squeteague decided. He was comparing the Canonicus of the moment with the Canonicus who, shortly after the Pilgrims arrived at Plimoth, had sent a challenge to Governor Bradford in the form of arrows wrapped in a rattlesnake skin.

Miantonomo endeavored to end the meeting on a friendly note. "You should visit our friend the Reverend Williams to whom we have given land in our midst. He has great affection for us, as we for him, and he knows that we intend to remain friends with the English."

The man Miantonomo referred to was Roger Williams, a preacher who had been banished from the Bay Colony a year earlier for espousing beliefs in freedom of religion that Winthrop and the Puritans considered to be heresy, and for proposing the radical idea that territory occupied by the Native People was rightfully owned by them and should not be expropriated but paid for. How can the Puritans claim territory by right of discovery when it is already inhabited? Williams had asked. To which Governor Winthrop had responded, "If we leave them enough for their use, we can lawfully take the rest, since there is more than enough for both of us."

The land given to Williams by Canonicus and Miantonomo lay at the uppermost reaches of Narragansett Bay, where Williams had established a plantation he named Providence because he considered it a gift from God. Squeteague arrived there a day after leaving Pettaquamscutt, and called on Williams to whom he presented a letter affirming the trade commission he had been granted by Governor Winthrop. He was promptly invited to share a dinner of duck breast and squash, and to spend the night. It did not take him long to realize that Williams harbored a deep suspicion of Sassacus and his Pequot followers, whom he described as the "Devil and his Lying Sorcerers." Moreover, he learned to his surprise that, in spite of his banishment from the Bay Colony, Williams had been providing the Puritans with intelligence about the Pequot.

"After the killing of the trader Stone, I warned Bay Colony officials that the Pequot had found out about Captain Endecott's expedition," Williams said. "I told them that the Pequot planned to sink Endecott's pinnaces by diving under water and making holes in their hulls. In this way, they hoped to acquire muskets to use against the Puritan soldiers. Unfortunately, Endecott and his men failed to punish them sufficiently, so that they and their Niantic allies are now determined to make war. Not long ago they sent envoys to the Narragansett to warn that the English are over-spreading the country and will in time deprive them of their land."

Squeteague found himself surprised by Williams's bias and naivete. Could the man be unaware that Endecott had orders to slaughter the Manissean men and enslave their women and children, kill Pequot and Niantic villagers, and put their wetu and crops to the torch?

"To be sure, it's difficult to know how any of these Native sachems may react," Williams went on. "Canonicus remains suspicious of his ancient enemy Massasoit, who has kept peace with the English settlers at Plimoth. Canonicus is also suspicious of the English, who rescued Massasoit when Canonicus attacked him at Sowams. On the occasion of my first encounter with him, he insisted that the English had sent the plague against his people. When I explained that smallpox and other sicknesses come from God, who strikes down Englishmen and Indians alike for their sins, he pretended to be satisfied, but never doubt that old Canonicus keeps counsel to himself."

"From what Canonicus and Miantonomo have told me, it doesn't seem likely they will join the Pequot in war against the English," Squeteague replied. And more's the pity, he thought, because a union between the Narragansett and the Pequot would give the colonists pause for thought before continuing their aggression.

Williams nodded in agreement. "Miantonomo has promised that, in the event of war, the Narragansett will furnish guides to lead English militiamen into Pequot territory."

Squeteague realized that an attack on the Pequot could have a devastating effect on any possibility of forming a confederation among the Native People. "I hope there'll be a way to prevent such a confrontation," he said.

"I don't see any," Williams replied. "The Pequot and their Western Niantic allies have resolved to die rather than yield. With that in mind, I've provided the Bay authorities with Miantonomo's advice that any attack should take place when the Pequot are asleep in their forts so they can be taken by surprise."

This minister speaks in ways that are baffling, Squeteague decided. At one moment, he sounds like a man of peace, at another like an apostle of vengeance. I must warn Sassacus of the danger that threatens him.

After a two-day sail aboard the *Nauset*, Squeteague arrived at the mouth of the Pequot River and sailed upstream to the fortified village of Weinshauks. There, he disembarked and asked for an audience with Sassacus, whom he had never met. Like Canonicus of the Narragansett, Sassacus was a man in his middle seventies, with a deeply lined face and a stern mouth. His very name meant "fierce" and he regarded Squeteague with suspicion before asking him where he had come from and on whose behalf.

Squeteague realized that he must answer truthfully because Sassacus probably knew very well where he had come from, as well as with whose permission. "I've come from the home of the Reverend Roger Williams at Providence," he replied. "Before that

I traded with the Narragansett and conferred with the sachems Canonicus and Miantonomo. I sail under a commission granted to me by the Governor of the Massachusetts Bay Colony."

"All of them are enemies of the Pequot," Sassacus declared. "The Narragansett sachems have refused to make an alliance with us against the English, the preacher Williams has encouraged them in this, and the Governor of the Bay Colony has sent soldiers who attacked us."

"What you say is true."

"Then why shouldn't I suspect you of being a spy?"

"Because I've come to give warning that the English are preparing to attack you again."

Sassacus's mouth curled into a baleful grimace. "Do you imagine I am without knowledge of this or unaware that you served as an interpreter for the captain named Endecott when his soldiers killed my people and burned our villages?"

Forced to confront the ambiguities attending his dual role, Squeteague took a deep breath. "I acted as an interpreter for the English in order to gain information that might help us prevent them from taking more of our land," he said. "I've come here in the hope of convincing you that the best way to bring this about is for the Native People of the region to unite against them."

"How can you talk of unity when you know full well the enmity of the Narragansett against the Pequot?"

"Perhaps it would be wise to make peace with the English until you can settle your differences with the Narragansett on your one side and the hostile Mohegan on the other."

The cloud that passed over the sachem's face made Squeteague wish he had not brought up the subject of the Mohegan, whose leader, Uncas, had married Sassacus's sister and become involved in a bitter dynastic feud with his brother-in-law over which of them had had the right to succeed Tatobem following his murder by the Dutch.

"Who are you to counsel me?" Sassacus demanded. "Are you a warrior? Have you killed any English?"

Squeteague replied by telling Sassacus about his participation in the encounter between the Nauset led by Aspinet and the soldiers commanded by Standish. He also informed the sachem about the death of his father at the hands of Captain Hunt, as well as his meetings with Corbitant and Epenow.

The sachem's expression softened. "Then it happens I've heard of you already," he said, in a milder tone of voice. "Epenow, who was my friend, told me of meeting you when I saw him some years ago."

"Epenow believed it would become necessary for us to arm ourselves with muskets before rising up against the English," Squeteague said.

"A wise man, Epenow, but I fear he is no more. I think he died last season of the foreign sickness that invaded the island where he and his people had thought to have refuge from it."

"I'm sorry to hear it."

"And since we haven't able to make an alliance with the Narragansett, we'll fight the English by ourselves."

"But they're armed with muskets. How can you defeat them with bows and arrows?"

"We don't intend to fight them in the way of their choosing. We will ambush any soldiers who set foot outside their fort at Saybrook. We will attack their settlements along the Quinnehtukqut. We will kill their men and cattle, capture their women and children, and set fire to their houses as they have set fire to ours. In this way we will drive them from our land."

"Perhaps I can help," Squeteague told him. "My commission to trade for the Bay Colony gives me access to Dutch merchants at Nieuw Amsterdam who can supply me with muskets that I'll deliver to you in exchange for beaver pelts. Within a short time, you'll be as well armed as your enemies."

"I want nothing from the Dutch who killed my father," Sassacus declared. "Nor from anyone who trades with them."

The scorn and irony of Sassacus's words pierced Squeteague like the shaft of an arrow. In this mood, the vow Massasoit had imposed upon him and the agreement he had reached with Governor Winthrop provided frail excuse for his failure to avenge his own murdered father in a manner commensurate with the honor of a warrior. At the same time, he realized that the Pequot sachem would not be deterred from answering the challenge of the Puritans at Massachusetts Bay before he and his people were sufficiently armed to meet it, and that rash action could only lead to his defeat.

"Allow me to wish you well," he said.

But pride and anger bid fair to undo you, he thought.

Sassacus made good on his threat by laying siege to Fort Saybrook within a week, and Pequot warriors harassed Lieutenant Gardiner and his men for the rest of the autumn and the whole of winter. During that time, Squeteague made several voyages from Boston to Hartford and Wethersfield to trade beaver pelts for muskets. In February, however, the *Nauset* became trapped when the Connecticut froze over and he was unable to sail downriver until the ice broke up at the end of March. When he stopped at Saybrook, he encountered a Lieutenant Gardiner who had become furious with both his English superiors and his Pequot enemy.

"Since you were here last, six of my soldiers have been killed," he declared. "The newly reelected Governor Winthrop claims that Pequot arrows aren't capable of doing any great harm, so I sent him the rib of a dead man that had been split apart by a shaft that had passed completely through the poor devil's torso. Even worse, two of my men were captured by the heathen and tortured to death in view of the fort. As was a trader named Tilly, who was foolish enough to ignore my order not to anchor his ship close to the riverbank or go ashore. He and a companion not only went ashore, but also decided to go hunting. They were seized by some Niantic who killed Tilly's shipmate on the spot and carried Tilly downriver to a place in full sight of us. There, they tied him to a stake, embedded hot embers in his flesh, and amputated his hands and feet before putting him to death. Do you wonder I would rather die on the field with honor than have a sharp stake thrust into my belly and my flesh flayed off and thrust down my throat as these savages will do to hundreds of us if God should deliver us into their hands?"

Squeteague could not imagine any way in which hundreds of Englishmen armed with muskets might be delivered into the hands of the Pequot whose chief weapons remained bows and arrows. As a guest of Gardiner, however, he maintained a tactful silence. By the time he sailed the *Nauset* to Saybrook again, Pequot warriors had attacked Wethersfield, killing several men and women, and making captives of two young girls—the daughters of an English settler named Abraham Swain. Gardiner had become further enraged when the Pequot taunted him by parading the Swain girls past the fort in a war canoe festooned with bloody clothes stripped from the bodies of people they had killed.

"I was angry enough to fire our cannon at them," he admitted, sheepishly. "It took the bow off the canoe carrying the girls, but fortunately neither of them was injured. Equally fortunate is that they've been ransomed by the captain of a Dutch trading ship."

When Squeteague stopped at Saybrook on his way back to Boston, he told Gardiner why the Pequot had attacked Wethersfield. "They acted at the request of the Wangunk, who had sold land to the settlers there in return for the promise that they would be allowed to live on it under English protection. However, the settlers claimed they'd bought the land outright and drove the Wangunk away."

At this time, the same Captain Underhill who had participated in Endecott's raid on the Manissean, Pequot, and Niantic arrived at Saybrook with reinforcements raised by the Bay Colony. He was joined by Captain John Mason, whom the magistrates of the newly founded Connecticut Colony had chosen to lead an expedition against the Pequot consisting of ninety English soldiers and sixty Mohegan warriors under the sachem Uncas.

"The presence of Uncas and his Mohegan troubles me,"

Gardiner told Squeteague. "When I asked Mason what evidence he had for trusting them, he replied that his men wouldn't be able to find their way into Pequot territory without Indians to guide them. As for myself, I've informed Uncas that he must prove himself to me by fetching six Pequot, dead or alive, whom we saw passing by canoe last night into the cove at Bass River."

"I've traded with Uncas and his people at Shantok," Squeteague said. "He's a man of great physical strength and an appetite for women that he's been known to satiate with the wives of his subjects. He's also a crafty and malevolent leader who pursues his aims with clever stratagems. He'll not hesitate to use the English to gain advantage in his ancient quarrel with Sassacus."

"Then we shouldn't ally ourselves with him?"

"Making an alliance is one thing," Squeteague replied. "Trusting the ally is another."

The Pequot are about to find themselves caught up between the pride of Sassacus, the muskets of the English, and the ambitions of Uncas, he told himself. Still, the fortunes of war were never certain and the Pequot would be defending themselves in territory they knew as intimately as any living thing that inhabited it.

"To think that all this trouble and bloodshed stems from the killing of a renegade ship captain," Gardiner mused.

Squeteague knew he was referring to the revenge Sassacus's followers had taken upon Captain Stone. "A weak excuse," he agreed.

Later that day, Uncas returned to Saybrook with the heads of five Pequot and a captive named Kiwas, who was considered to be a spy because he had been observed lingering near the fort, and was believed to have participated in the killing of some of Gardiner's men. In spite of this, Gardiner was reluctant to turn Kiwas over to Uncas because he knew that the Mohegan sachem would proceed to torture him. However, when the captive taunted Gardiner with a show of bravado, shouting that he "dared not kill a Pequot," Gardiner had little choice but to relinquish him to the Mohegan to avoid losing face before Uncas. At that point, several Mohegan laid hold of Kiwas and tied one of his legs to a post and the other to a long length of rope.

"I'd rather not be required to witness this display of barbarity," Gardiner muttered.

"Nor I," Squeteague replied. He was tempted to explain that torturing a captive was the way in which Mohegan and other Native People sought to limit warfare by venting their anger against an individual, thus avoiding the wholesale slaughter that resulted when battles were fought in the style of the English, whose strategy was to inflict as many casualties as possible. But he decided to remain silent when he saw Kiwas spread-eagled on the ground and realized that a hideous torment was about to begin.

Twenty Mohegan warriors now grasped the end of the rope attached to Kiwas's leg and, at a command from Uncas, began to pull on it. As the limbs of the hapless captive were stretched apart to full extension, Uncas signaled for the gruesome process to proceed at an even slower pace. With a grimace, Kiwas refused to give his tormentors the pleasure of hearing him cry out, but fainted from pain as the tendons in his crotch were torn apart and a geyser of blood poured from a huge wound that extended upward to his pelvic arch. At this point, the Mohegans let the rope go slack and one of them roused the captive by pouring a bucket of water on his head. Then the rope tautened and the torture resumed until the victim's legs broke away from his pelvis with a sound like that of tree limbs snapping, and a slimy pile of intestines spilled out of a gaping hole in the lower portion of the victim's trunk, filling the air with the stench of excrement.

Seeing the eyes of Uncas fixed upon him, Gardiner forced himself to watch, as did Squeteague, who sensed that his dislike for the Mohegan sachem was reciprocated in full.

Then, as Kiwas's mutilated torso writhed on the ground, John Underhill stepped forward and put the Pequot out of his misery with a pistol shot to the head.

Chapter Six

Puritan ministers reacted to the Pequot attack on Wethersfield with the usual calls for vengeance. The Reverend Thomas Hooker, who had founded Hartford a year earlier, recommended that the colonists undertake a punitive war against the Pequot or risk being considered cowards by other Indians who would "turn enemy against us." In similar fashion, the Reverend John Higginson, who was the chaplain at Fort Saybrook, warned that if the insolent Pequot were not quickly punished, "we'll have all the Indians in the country about our ears."

Thanks to his friendship with Gardiner, Squeteague found himself invited to dine with the lieutenant and his guests, and thus learned about the plan of action devised by Captain Mason, who had been designated to lead the attack against the Pequot. Knowing that Pequot warriors kept guard night and day at the entrances to the Pequot and the Missituck Rivers, where their forts were situated, Mason decided not to risk landing his soldiers by boat, but to bypass both rivers and sail west to Narragansett Bay. There, he would disembark his men, march overland, and surprise the Pequot from the rear. "At worst we'll find ourselves on the same firm ground as they," he reasoned, before requesting Higginson to ask a blessing for the success of the mission.

Lieutenant Gardiner had orders to defend Fort Saybrook. As a result, he did not accompany the expedition but lent support by equipping its soldiers with supplies and by sending his surgeon to assist them. "Mason and Underhill will be marching deep into Pequot country," he told Squeteague on the day the expedition departed. "May God prevent them from being ambushed by an enemy who exceeds them so greatly in number."

Gardiner's invocation to the English deity was noted by Squeteague, who found himself bemused that both the lieutenant and Mason should have sought divine intervention for the invasion.

"Will you join me in a prayer that our soldiers be successful?" Gardiner inquired.

"I'll join you in hoping that they won't shed the blood of innocent people."

"What the Pequot fiends have done here this past winter has caused me to steel my heart against them," Gardiner said.

"But not, I trust, against their women and children."

For a moment, Gardiner remained silent. Then he shook his head in a way that Squeteague could not interpret as either an affirmative or negative response.

"Tomorrow, I'm going to set out for Boston," he told Gardiner. "On the way, I'll stop at the country of the Pequot to see for myself what's happened."

"But won't that put you there before Mason and Underhill?"

Let's hope so, Squeteague told himself. Let's hope I arrive in time to warn Sassacus that they're planning to attack him from the rear. He was thinking, that if the Pequot were to suffer defeat, it would seriously damage the chances of forming a confederacy of Native People to oppose the colonists.

A powerful gale delayed Mason and Underhill from disembarking their troops at Narragansett Bay, and also prevented Squeteague and the *Nauset* from departing from Saybrook. It took a day before the wind died down sufficiently for the English soldiers to begin their overland march, and for the *Nauset* to arrive at the Pequot River. It was early in the evening when the ship came to anchor and Squeteague rowed ashore in a dinghy, where he encountered a party of warriors who had been stationed there to give warning of any invasion from the sea.

"I come with important news," he announced. "Go to Weinshauks and tell Sassacus that the English have landed in Narragansett country and are marching overland to take him by surprise."

"The English are afraid to fight with us," one of the Pequot replied. "Two days ago they sailed past us and continued east without coming ashore."

"Tell Sassacus that the English soldiers intend to attack him from the rear."

When the sentinel returned a short while later, he was accompanied by one of Sassacus's subordinate sachems. "Sassacus wishes to know how you have learned of this English plan," the sachem demanded.

"I learned of it at Saybrook where the English forces assembled."

"Then you must be a spy for the English or you would not have been at Saybrook to begin with."

"Why would I risk coming among you if my intent were not to your benefit?"

"Sassacus believes you have come to play a trick on us. He says for you to leave or he'll put you to the fire."

"Tell Sassacus he can test my words by sending scouts to discover that the English are advancing upon him."

"Sassacus orders you to leave," the sachem repeated.

Squeteague returned to the dinghy, climbed aboard, and pushed off into the river "Tell Sassacus to send out his scouts!" he shouted. "That way he'll know I speak the truth."

By way of reply, one of the Pequot warriors drew his bow and released an arrow that knifed into the water short of its mark.

Darkness had fallen by the time Squeteague returned to the

Nauset. After posting a guard to give warning if the Pequot should attack by canoe, he lay down in his cabin and spent a restless night. In the morning, he debated whether to go on shore and make a final attempt at persuading Sassacus of the danger he faced. But members of the Pequot party he had encountered the evening before were standing at the river's edge, brandishing their bows and shouting taunts. Reluctantly, he gave the command to weigh anchor and sail east along the coast to the Missituck (Mystic) River, where the Pequot had their second fort, and where he hoped to find more receptive ears for his warning. The tide was running against him when he arrived at its mouth, so he decided to anchor for the night off an island that Adrien Block had named for his mate, a man named Vischer, and would come to be known as Fishers Island.

Just before daybreak on May 26, Squeteague steered the *Nauset* upriver past some slumbering Pequot sentries until he arrived within sight of Fort Missituck, where he heard the barking of a dog followed by the cry,

"Owanux! Owanux!"

"Englishmen! Englishmen!"

What followed was a volley of musket fire that echoed across the water as the soldiers commanded by Mason and Underhill shot a volley of lead balls through the palisades and into dozens of wetu that crammed the interior of the fort.

The silence that accompanied the reloading of the English muskets was broken by a moan that came from the residents within, most of whom had just awakened from their last living sleep.

To begin with, Pequot warriors fought valiantly to defend their palisaded stronghold, shooting arrows at the English soldiers who were clearing away branches and brush that blocked the entrances. The defenders were quickly overwhelmed, however, as the soldiers broke through and rampaged among the wetu, wielding their swords at close quarters as they hacked away at anyone—man, woman, or child—they came upon. Mason soon decided that swords alone would not be the most efficient way to destroy the many Pequot still trapped inside. "Let's burn them!" he shouted, and, taking a smoldering firebrand from one of the wetu, set fire to the woven reed mat with which it was covered.

The resulting blaze spread quickly and was joined by a second fire that Underhill had set with a trail of gunpowder on the southern side of the village. With the entire fort about to become an inferno, the two commanders ordered their men to stand outside the palisade and prevent those inside from escaping. In spite of the conflagration, Pequot warriors continued shooting arrows at the Englishmen until fire burned through their bowstrings or they perished in the flames. More than five hundred men, women, and children who remained inside died agonizing deaths in the fire. Most of those who managed to escape the blazing fort were put to the sword by the soldiers, who had surrounded it, or tomahawked to death by Mohegan warriors, who had formed a second circle behind them.

Squeteague's view of the holocaust was obscured by a dense pall of smoke that cloaked the fort shortly after the attack began. However, his ears rang with the anguished screams of hundreds of people roasting to death in flames, and his nostrils were filled with the smell of burning flesh. He remained a hapless bystander until he saw several women and children run through the smoke and throw themselves into the river in an attempt to escape from some pursuing Mohegan who had been posted around the periphery of the fort to intercept anyone who tried to flee. At that point, he jumped into the dinghy, rowed into their midst, and began pulling them from the water.

The few women and children who managed to reach the safety of Squeteague's dinghy were imperiled by Mohegan who swam after them and grasped at the boat's gunwales in an attempt to tip it over and spill its terrified passengers into the water. Pandemonium followed, with Squeteague raising an oar above his head and bringing it down upon the shaved skulls of a succession of warriors until its blade had been shattered and half a dozen of the attackers were floating lifeless on the river in pools of blood. After ferrying the women and children he had rescued to the *Nauset,* he and his crew returned to the riverbank, where they proceeded to gun down several Mohegan whose deaths would subsequently be deplored by Roger Williams as having been caused by misdirected English musket fire. In the end, Squeteague and his men were able to rescue more than a dozen women and children who had managed to escape the conflagration. Some of them were badly injured. Indeed, one infant was so horribly burned that Squeteague released it from its agony by holding it underwater until bubbles ceased rising to the surface from its tiny lungs.

John Underhill would look back upon the carnage he and his mens had inflicted as ordained by the Almighty, declaring that even though the massacre was a sickening sight for young soldiers, "we had sufficient light from the word of God for our actions."

Captain Mason would suggest that in setting the fort ablaze he had acted as the instrument of God, who had expressed His displeasure with the Pequot by "making them as a fiery oven."

Governor Bradford of Plymouth Colony would write, "It was a fearful sight to see them frying in the fire and horrible was the smell of it, but our soldiers praised God who had given them so speedy a victory over so proud and insulting a foe."

Roger Williams was said to have been revolted by the massacre, but his ambivalence showed through in a letter he wrote later to Governor Winthrop congratulating him on God's having placed in his hands "another drove of Adam's degenerate seed."

In the end, no one came away from the scene of butchery more appalled than the Narragansett, who, though ancient enemies of the Pequot, were unaccustomed to warfare of such brutality, and complained bitterly to Mason and Underhill about its consequences.

"It has been too furious," they protested. "You have killed too many people!"

As things turned out, the killing had not ended, for when Pequot warriors from Weinshauks arrived at the funeral pyre Fort Missituck had become, they stamped the ground in rage and, according to Mason, "tore the hair from their heads." They then charged after the English soldiers, who were retreating toward the Pequot River with the intention of embarking their wounded on some pinnaces that had arrived there from Narragansett Bay. Bows and arrows were no match for muskets, however, and the Pequot suffered dozens of additional casualties in the running battle that followed.

Afterward, many of the surviving Pequot gave themselves up to the Narragansett, while others made their way by canoe to Long Island, where they placed themselves under the protection of the Montaukett. As for Sassacus, he and his second in command, Mononotto, decided their best course of action lay in abandoning Weinshauks and retreating west along the Connecticut shoreline with the hope of joining the Mohawk in New York.

In the end, Squeteague decided that Mason and Underhill may have had a closer call at Fort Missituck than anyone suspected. Only two of their men had been killed in the attack, but twenty of them had been wounded by Pequot arrows. Some of the injured had been shot in the face and head, such as Lieutenant Robert Seeley, from whose eyebrow Mason had pulled an arrowhead. Others had been pierced in the body, shoulders, and arms, and still others in the legs. Many could not walk. As a result, only fifty men were on hand to cover the retreat to the pinnaces at the Pequot River, because the rest were required to carry the wounded.

Squeteague decided that, if Sassacus and his warriors had arrived from Weinshauks sooner, they might have been able to break through the outer circle provided by the Mohegan and fallen upon the English from the rear. Just as he would always believe that, if he and the Nauset had charged into Standish and his soldiers during the skirmish at First Encounter Beach, they could have driven the invaders of the Narrow Land into the shallows of the bay and slaughtered them with their tomahawks.

Chapter Seven

Following the massacre at Fort Missituck, Squeteague sailed the *Nauset* to Long Island, where he arranged for the women and children he had saved to be given protection by Wyandanch, sachem of the Montaukett. Wyandanch had little love for the Pequot, who had exacted tribute from the Montaukett for years in the form of wampum that served as currency throughout the region, and he drove a hard bargain. "In return for granting protection to these Pequot you have brought, I ask that you arrange with Lieutenant Gardiner at Saybrook for us to trade along the Quinnehtukqut River. Tell the Englishman that, if he agrees, I'll send him the heads of some Pequot warriors who have taken refuge here."

When Squeteague met with Gardiner, he relayed Wyandanch's request for trade but not the sachem's promise to send him the heads of Pequot warriors in return. Gardiner informed him that Sassacus and Mononotto, accompanied by several hundred Pequot warriors, women, and children, were in full flight along the Connecticut shoreline, harried by the combined forces of Mason and Uncas, and hampered by the slow pace of their children, as well as the necessity of foraging for clams and other food on coastal mudflats. He also said that fresh troops had arrived from the Bay Colony and captured a hundred Pequot warriors who had sought refuge in a swamp north of Weinshauks known as the Owl's Nest.

Squeteague soon learned that an English captain had ordered thirty of these captives to be bound and put on the bark owned by John Gallop, who had then taken them out to sea and thrown them overboard to drown. Other Pequot men and boys were being transported to the West Indies to be sold as slaves. As for the women and children, some were parceled out to the Mohegan and Narragansett, while others were sent to the Bay Colony to work as indentured servants."

Sickened by the atrocity Oldham had committed and aware that Native People quickly succumbed to the heat of the tropics, Squeteague sent a messenger to Roger Williams at Providence, asking him to intervene with the Puritan authorities in behalf of the remaining captives. Some weeks later, Williams sent back a copy of a letter he had written to the magistrates of the Bay Colony in which he had reacted to the execution and enslavement of Pequot captives with curious ambivalence:

> If any of them deserve death, then it's a sin to spare them, but if they don't deserve death, what punishment other than slavery is suitable? I am convinced that captives can lawfully be deprived of wife and children, but I ask you to consider whether, after a reasonable time of imprisonment, they ought to be set free as long as there is no danger that they will rejoin the enemy.

Meanwhile, Squeteague had sailed the *Nauset* west along the shoreline, shadowing the English and Mohegan forces, and taking on board as many Pequot women and children as he could find. East of the Quinnipiac River, some of his crewmen who had gone ashore on a promontory to look for stragglers came across the head of a Pequot sachem lodged in the fork of an oak tree. An elderly Pequot woman told them that the sachem had been captured by the Mohegan, and that Uncas had shot an arrow through his heart, cut off his head, and placed it in the tree to remind passersby of his power.

At the mouth of the Quinnipiac, Squeteague came upon a large group of women and children who had become too weak from hunger and fatigue to cross the river and were waiting to be overtaken and put to death by advance elements of the pursuing Mohegan. After anchoring the *Nauset* as near to shore as possible, he and his crewmen began ferrying the desperate refugees to the ship in the dinghy. By the time they completed the rescue, several large canoes manned by Mohegan warriors came around a point of land and surrounded the ship. Though outnumbered, Squeteague and his crew had the advantage of firing down upon the canoes, sinking some of them with musket shot and maneuvering the *Nauset* to ram others. Within a few minutes, most of the attackers had either been killed or drowned.

Squeteague now sailed past the mouth of the Housatonic River, where he learned from a Native fisherman that the main body of Pequot led by Sassacus and Mononotto had taken refuge with some local Sasqua in a nearby swamp. "It's a quagmire so thick with bushes that men can scarcely enter it," the fisherman told him. "The first English soldiers who tried were driven back by a hail of arrows. They then surrounded the swamp and sent an interpreter to assure the people there that those who had not killed Englishmen would be spared death. As a result, nearly two hundred Pequot and Sasqua men, women, and children have surrendered—among them Wincumbone, the wife of Mononotto, and her two children." The fisherman went on to say that the Sasqua had been released, but that the Pequot men were being held so they could be sold into slavery. As for Wincumbone, Governor Winthrop had ordered her to be well treated because she was said to have saved the Swain girls from harm during their time of captivity. She and her children, as well as other Pequot women and children, were sent to the Bay Colony to work as servants for

English families.

Unable to be of assistance to the beleaguered Pequot in the swamp, Squeteague and his crew anchored the *Nauset* offshore and awaited the outcome of what they knew would be an attempt on the part of the remaining Pequot warriors to break out of the encirclement. The next day, under the cover of a heavy fog, the Pequot made a desperate attack against Mason's soldiers, who killed many of them with musket fire and executed the wounded on the spot. While the battle raged, Sassacus and Mononotto escaped with twenty followers and traveled forty miles northwest until they arrived at the Taconic Ridge overlooking the Hudson River Valley. There, they took refuge in a cave where they were discovered by Mohawk warriors, who, instead of granting them the sanctuary they hoped for, put them to death.

The destruction of the Pequot that took place first at Fort Missituck, then at Owl's Nest, and finally during their desperate retreat along the Connecticut coast did not satiate the colonist's thirst for vengeance, even though most of the survivors offered to become vassals of the English in exchange for their lives. Governor Winthrop of the Massachusetts Bay Colony, Governor Edward Winslow of Plymouth Colony, and representatives of the colonies at Hartford and New Haven dictated a peace treaty that called upon Uncas and Miantonomo to execute all Pequot warriors who had fought against the English, and to send their heads to the colonial authorities. The remaining Pequot were forbidden to return to their villages or to call themselves Pequot. The Pequot River was renamed the Thames, the fortified village of Weinshauks became Groton, and a settlement at the mouth of the river became New London.

Thus did the colonists expunge the identity of what had once been a powerful Native nation.

The slaughter of the Pequot at Missituck had a profound effect on the consciousness of the Native People of the region. They not only realized they could no longer live with the English in peace, but also that the cruelty of the English in burning to death hundreds of Pequot men, women, and children meant that their future existence was threatened with extinction. For the time being, they had no choice except to lie low, but now they knew deep down that one day they would have to rise up against the invaders if they were to continue to maintain a presence in their ancestral land.

Meanwhile, Squeteague had returned to Narragansett Bay, where he released the second group of Pequot women and children he had rescued into the protection of Miantonomo, who had succeeded his aging uncle Canonicus as chief sachem of the Narragansett. Like many other Native leaders of the region, Miantonomo had been appalled by the slaughter at Fort Missituck and had begun to reassess his relationship with the colonists.

"Canonicus and I should have listened to Sassacus when he tried to warn us that the English intended to overrun our country," he admitted to Squeteague. "Instead, we foolishly helped in his downfall. We were wrong to assume that the good will of our friend Roger Williams would be shared by the English at Plymouth and those of the Bay Colony at Boston."

"Since the first colonists came to our land thousands have followed," Squeteague replied. "They now outnumber us by more than two to one."

"To avoid the fate of the Pequot we must put aside our ancient quarrels and unite against them," Miantonomo declared. "I will now make peace with the Pokanoket with whom my people have long been enemies, and with the Nipmuck and Massachusett who live to the north. I will go to Long Island and ask Wyandanch of the Montaukett to join me. I'll seek alliance with the Pocumtuck, the Paugusett, and Mattabesic to the west, as well as with the Mohawk, Mahican, and Wappinger, who live near the Dutch. In this way, I will form a confederacy of Native People strong enough to convince the English to cease their expansion into our lands."

"Your chief obstacle will be Uncas and his Mohegan," Squeteague observed. "He's made alliance with the English in return for permission to expand into your territory. You will be well advised not to trust him."

"It's no longer a matter of not trusting him," Miantonomo rejoined. "I'm of a mind to kill him."

When Squeteague returned to Boston, he was summoned before the Council of Magistrates by Governor Winthrop to answer Uncas's accusation that one of his warriors had seen someone from a sailing ship killing Mohegan warriors and rescuing Pequot who were fleeing the conflagration at Fort Missituck. Fortunately for Squeteague, the warrior had been slain during a skirmish with Sassacus's retreating forces, so an eyewitness no longer existed. However, sufficient question had been raised that Winthrop ordered him to answer the charge.

Squeteague attended the meeting dressed in a pair of simple deerskin leggings and the beaded shirt Wianna had given him. He was now a man of thirty-three, with a handsomely sculptured face, an erect carriage, and a confident manner.

"You have been accused of aiding the enemy at Fort Mystick," the Governor informed him. "What have you to say?"

"The accusation is untrue," Squeteague replied.

"Do you deny being present at Fort Mystick?"

"I do not deny it. I had sailed my ship into the river and anchored near the fort to gather information—a task Your Excellency may recall he had previously charged me with."

"Do you deny having helped some Pequot escape?"

"I don't deny that either," Squeteague responded, coolly. "I rescued some unarmed Pequot women and children who had thrown themselves into the river to escape being tomahawked by Mohegan warriors."

One of the council members leapt to his feet. "But these were heathen enemy," he protested. "Hundreds of them were slain at the fort, so why not in the river?"

Squeteague looked at the man with disdain. "The burning of innocent women and children at the fort was an act unworthy of men," he said. "I wish I had been able to prevent it. Unfortunately, I was only able to save a few women and children who escaped the flames."

"Is this not treason?" the council member cried.

"No," Winthrop declared, "it's the testimony of a man who will not barter his conscience."

Admonished, the council member sat down.

"You're free to go," Winthrop told Squeteague. "On condition, of course, that you remain loyal to the Bay Colony. This means that you'll continue to curry favor with Miantonomo and inform us of any evil intentions he may entertain toward us."

Squeteague bowed his head to acknowledge the command. "I'm the loyal scout of Your Excellency," he said, and left the room.

But he knew that Winthrop had rejoiced over the fiery massacre of the Pequot at Fort Missituck, and felt no loyalty to him whatsoever.

Squeteague now became one of Miantonomo's chief counselors. In this capacity, he accompanied the Narragansett sachem to Long Island, where Miantonomo urged Wyandanch and the Montaukett to stop paying tribute to the English and join a coalition that would oppose the encroachments of the colonists. "We must become one people like the English are and treat each other as brothers," he declared. "Otherwise we'll soon be overwhelmed as they cut down our grass for their cows and horses, chop down our trees for their cabins, and empty our forests and rivers of the deer, turkey, and fish that our fathers enjoyed. Believe me when I say that it's best for you to join us, because we Narragansett and our other brothers east to west, including the Mohawk, are resolved to fall upon the invaders at a time that will soon be at hand."

Squeteague told Miantonomo that he had been rash to talk of attacking the English with the aid of the Mohawk, whom the English feared above all other Native People, and advised him not to do so in the future, because it might provoke military reaction on the part of the colonists. He was troubled when Miantonomo rejected his counsel, and even more so during the coming months when the Narragansett sachem became implicated in several plots to assassinate Uncas, who was the leading Native ally of the colonists.

Might Miantonomo be succumbing to the same hubris that had led to the undoing of Sassacus?

When word of Miantonomo's exhortation to the Montaukett reached the magistrates of the Bay Colony, they summoned him to Boston, where he proclaimed himself to be "innocent of any ill intentions." Squeteague assured Winthrop and his colleagues that he believed this to be true, and they decided there wasn't sufficient ground for them to take action against the Narragansett sachem. The enmity between Miantonomo and Uncas kept escalating, however, until Miantonomo came under suspicion of hiring a Pequot to shoot an arrow at the Mohegan leader under cover of darkness. The arrow grazed Uncas's arm and the wound soon healed, but the Pequot archer fled to the Narragansett for protection. When the authorities of the Bay Colony ordered Minatonomo to turn him over to Uncas for punishment, the Narragansett chief ordered him put to death. This led Governor Winthrop to conclude that Miantonomo "had stopped the Pequot's mouth by cutting off his head."

Meanwhile, Squeteague continued to supply the Narragansett with muskets obtained from Dutch traders at Fort Orange (later Albany). Unfortunately, an overconfident Miantonomo soon came to believe that he had acquired enough guns to overcome Uncas, and when the Mohegan sachem burned down the village of a Connecticut River sachem named Sequassen, who was one of Miantonomo's allies, the Narragansett chief decided to go to war.

By this time, the sachems of a number of lesser clans in the region had become weary of Mohegan and Narragansett demands for tribute, and made plans to place themselves under the protection of the Massachusetts Bay Colony. Miantonomo feared that Sequassen might follow suit, and decided he must come to the aid of his ally or lose face before the sachems he had been encouraging to join his confederation. He then assembled a force of nearly one thousand warriors to invade the territory of the Mohegan.

When Squeteague learned of Miantonomo's preparations for war, he tried to convince him to delay attacking Uncas until he could equip his forces with enough muskets to guarantee overwhelming firepower and victory. What he really feared was Uncas's reputation for stealth and subterfuge. The crafty Mohegan chief, whose name meant fox, had outwitted his enemies at almost every turn, and Squeteague worried that Miantonomo might not fare any better against him

Fortunately for him, he was unable to accompany the invasion army because Governor Winthrop had ordered him to attend a ceremony scheduled to take place in Boston to receive submission from a group of sachems who had requested protection from the Bay Colony.

Chapter Eight

Ignoring Squeteague's advice, Miantonomo marched into Mohegan territory at the head of a thousand Narragansett warriors in early August, 1643, and confronted Uncas and four hundred Mohegan warriors at a place that came to be known as Sachem's Plain, which was situated near the junction of the Shetucket and Quinebaug Rivers. There, Uncas challenged Miantonomo to personal combat, proposing, "If you kill me, my men shall be yours, but if I kill you your men shall become mine." Whereupon Miantonomo replied, "My men have come to fight and they shall fight." At that point, Uncas dropped flat upon the ground—a prearranged signal to his warriors to let loose a volley of arrows—then leapt to his feet with a war cry and led the Mohegan in a tomahawk charge against the surprised Narragansett, who fled the field in confusion.

According to Mohegan legend, Miantonomo and some companions took a wrong turn during their flight and came to a gorge on the Yantic River (afterward known as Indian Leap), where the Narragansett sachem injured himself as he jumped across. More accurate no doubt is an account that described Miantonomo as hampered by an armored corselet he was wearing and being overtaken by a fast-running young warrior named Tantaquideon, who held him until Uncas arrived. Uncas took his prisoner to the Mohegan village at Shantok, where he accepted wampum from the Narragansett for the ransom of their chief. After accepting the ransom, however, he marched Miantonomo to Hartford, where he handed the Narragansett sachem over to the colonial authorities.

By this time, colonial officials at Massachusetts Bay, Plymouth, and Hartford had become alarmed that war between the Mohegan and the Narragansett might spread across the region, and had formed a coalition called the United Colonies of New England, under which the General Court of each colony would appoint a delegation of commissioners to act on its behalf. The first meeting of the commissioners took place in Boston shortly after Uncas delivered Miantonomo to the authorities at Hartford. According to John Winthrop, a commissioner from Massachusetts, all of his colleagues were agreed that it would not be safe to set Miantonomo free, but "neither had we sufficient ground to put him to death." After seeking the advice of some notable Puritan clergymen, the commissioners concluded that Uncas could not be safe while Miantonomo lived, and that the Mohegan sachem might justly condemn such a "false and bloodthirsty enemy" to death. They went on to rule that, once all of them had returned safely to their homes, the Connecticut authorities would surrender Miantonomo to Uncas, who should proceed to kill him. Having ensured that Miantonomo's execution would not be blamed on them, they proceeded to salve their consciences by urging Uncas "that in the manner of his death all mercy and moderation be shown."

Upon retrieving Miantonomo at Hartford, Uncas, his brother Wawequa, several Mohegan warriors, and a pair of English soldiers who came along to witness the pending execution, marched the prisoner east into Mohegan territory until they reached Sachem's Plain. There, Wawequa walked up behind Miantonomo and drove a hatchet into the back of his skull. Uncas ordered his enemy to be buried where he had been captured and the place marked with stones.

Squeteague was devastated by the news that Miantonomo had been assassinated, because he believed the Narragansett sachem provided the last best hope of forming a Native confederation that might oppose the growing power of the colonists. Alone among the chiefs of New England, Miantonomo had realized the importance of fashioning an alliance between the various bands of Native People, and had shown himself to be capable of raising a large and formidable army. The death of the Narragansett sachem convinced Squeteague that his efforts of the previous decade had largely gone for nothing.

This conviction became all the stronger during the course of the ceremony held to greet the leaders of more than half a dozen Native groups and sub-groups who had decided to submit themselves and their people to the colonial authorities in return for protection. Among them were Nashacowam, sachem of the Nashaway, who occupied the Nashaway (Nashua) River Valley; Papassaconnaway, the venerable sachem of the Pennacook, who lived by the Merrusquamack River; and four sachems of the Massachusett—Cutshamekin of Punkapoag, located in the Blue Hills near Boston; Mascononomo of Agawam (Ipswich); Chickataubet of Titicut, near Middleborough; and, to Squeteague's great surprise, his former lover, the squaw sachem Wianna.

Equally surprising was the presence of Massasoit, leader of the Wampanoag, whom Squeteague had occasionally visited in the decade that had passed since Canonicus had besieged him at the English trading post near Sowams. Past sixty years of age, his demeanor still grave and his posture erect, he was held in an esteem that bordered on worship by the Quabaug, a Nipmuck sub-group he was representing.

Squeteague had expected Massasoit to greet him with his customary warmth and affection. Instead, the elderly sachem regarded him with a mixture of sorrow and recrimination. "You have broken your oath to me by becoming an advisor to Miantonomo who, by defying the English and attacking the Mohegan, has paid for his rash action with his life and brought suspicion upon the rest of us."

Though taken aback by the accusation, Squeteague stood his ground. "Great sachem, I have seen the English murder and enslave the Pequot. I've watched them take away our forests and hunting grounds. And now they've allowed Uncas to execute the one man who might have united us against them had he lived."

Massasoit shook his head, sadly. "There was a time I looked upon you as I might a son, but you have mocked me by undermining my efforts to keep the peace. How can I hold you any longer near my heart?"

Squeteague winced at the thought of losing the surrogate father he thought he had found. "I have too much respect for you, great sachem, to learn of your disapproval without deep regret."

"Is it true that you have been supplying weapons to the Narragansett?"

"It is true," Squeteague acknowledged.

"Then you are engaging in activity that will bring the wrath of the colonists down upon all our heads. Don't you understand that the English will soon become powerful enough to enforce the peace I made with them on their terms not ours?"

"I understand that if we don't rise up against them they'll divide the rest of us, use us against each other, and do to us what they've done to Sassacus and Miantonomo."

"Going to war will be the end of the Wampanoag and all the Native People of the region."

"And if we don't go to war?"

"Time will be the judge of that and all things," Massasoit replied, and turned away.

Squeteague looked after him in dismay. But time is against us, he was thinking.

Under the terms of submission, the sachems were required to pledge allegiance to the Bay Colony, to make tribute payments to the colony, and to obey its civil and religious laws, including those that forbade sins such as fornication and adultery. They were also required to place their lands under the jurisdiction of the Massachusetts Bay Colony, which they took to be the same as submitting them for common use, unaware that the colonial authorities viewed them as property that could be disposed of as they saw fit.

As Squeteague listened to the reading of the terms of submission, he found himself once again remembering the early warnings of Corbitant and Epenow, who had bitterly opposed Massasoit's giving land and food to the settlers at Plimoth Plantation at a time when the Wampanoag had been capable of finishing them off with ease. His estimation of Massasoit rose, however, when the elderly sachem informed Governor Winthrop that, under no circumstances would he allow the Quabaug or any other people over whom he exercised influence to be instructed in the Christian religion—another term of submission required by the Bay Colony.

"My people have many gods and spirits," he told Winthrop. "They have gods of the sun, the moon, the water, and the animals. What need have they to worship the one and only God of the English?"

"We don't wish to levy an undue burden upon you," Winthrop said. "All we desire is that you consent to learn our ways."

"Let the burden upon us be that we live together in peace," Massasoit replied.

Except for Massasoit, all the other sachems agreed to obey the Ten Commandments, which were read to them by the magistrates of the General Court, who explained them in such ponderous detail as to diminish the attention of anyone who might be listening. As for Wianna, who could scarcely take her eyes off Squeteague, she paid them so little attention that even as they were being intoned she arranged with an aide to have her powwaw husband sent on a healing mission to the Pawtuckett, whose members were said to be suffering from some unspecified illness. Following the submission ceremony, she sat next to her former lover at a celebratory dinner of roast pig and acorn squash washed down with goblets of cider.

No sooner had the feast begun than she reached across his lap with a hand that knew exactly what it wished to find, and commenced to prepare him for a violation of one of the commandments she had just agreed to abide by.

Squeteague found himself aghast at her boldness. "It won't go well for the Puritan magistrates to discover us at this," he whispered. "Last year, they whipped two young lovers of their own people for the sin they call fornication. Imagine what they might do to you and me!"

"Look upon it as your punishment for not having come to see me for so long," Wianna murmured, smiling flirtatiously at the Reverend William Gates from Watertown, who was sitting on the other side of her.

"Surely you don't expect anything to come of this while we're having dinner," Squeteague protested.

"Just so long as you remember what comes afterward," Wianna replied.

When Squeteague entered Wianna's wetu an hour later, he found her reclining on her otter-pelt mat with her deerskin skirt rolled high around her thighs. Motioning him to sit beside her, she commanded him to give her an accounting of his escapades since they had been together.

At first, he found himself embarrassed to do so and unsure of where to begin.

"Begin at the beginning," she suggested. "When you sailed away to trade for furs on the Connecticut River, did you not find a woman there?"

"Yes," Squeteague recalled, "a Niantic girl who came with me when I sailed upstream."

"Were you her first man?"

"I think so."

"Do you mean you don't know?"

"Yes, I was the first."

"Did you please her?"

"I believe so."

"You don't know?"

"She cried out during her spasms of pleasure."

"Then you must have pleased her. How many spasms did she have?"

"I didn't count them," Squeteague replied.

"A man should give his woman the pleasure of many spasms," Wianna said. "What became of this girl?"

"Her cries aroused the members of my crew to look for women among the river people."

"So your ship became a vessel echoing many cries of pleasure."

"No, the river people threatened to withhold their beaver pelts and trade with the Dutch if I didn't control the lust of my crew, so I returned the girl to the Niantic when I sailed back to Boston."

"Necessity before pleasure," Wianna sighed. "I know it well for being married to Webcowit—a powwaw who can't cure himself of impotence. What sweet torment to hear of your adventures!"

Squeteague was aware that the space between them had become heavy with the scent of female arousal.

"Continue," Wianna demanded. "Who came next?"

"A Pequot woman whom I rescued from death at the hands of the Mohegan."

"She must have been exceedingly grateful."

"She took pleasure in pleasing me," Squeteague said.

"I shall want the details later when you have done pleasing me and it becomes my turn to reply in kind to your—what the Englishmen call their 'yard.'"

"Is that not a unit of measure?" Squeteague inquired.

"In their case, it is an empty boast. Believe me, slippery one, no Puritan yard I have yet encountered has the measure of yours." Wianna gathered her skirt around her hips and shifted position.

"You still have some time to account for," she continued.

"There was an Englishwoman in Providence whose husband had gone back to London and been kept there on business."

"An Englishwoman!" Wianna exclaimed. "What is it like to be with one of them? Do they give cries of pleasure?"

"The first time she forced herself to be quiet, having come to my room when I had been a guest in the home of her sister and her sister's husband."

"Lovemaking with the risk of discovery is a double pleasure. Was there a second time during which your lady felt less constraint?"

"When she had a servant row her out to my ship," Squeteague replied. "There, she gave vent to a year's worth of longing with spasms and cries I thought might never end. Unfortunately, her husband returned and it was the last time we met."

"Delightful rogue," Wianna said. "Have you finished?"

"Except for some encounters with women I rescued from the Mohegan along the Connecticut coast."

"Were they grateful like your earlier Pequot?

"Equally," Squeteague replied.

"Some women take pleasure in bestowing their favors freely. Others, like some of my Massachusett girls, have taken to granting them in return for gifts. This doesn't sit well with our young men who resent the colonial males for buying what they consider to be theirs. In any case, my nearness to the English at Shawmut, as well as their great superiority in numbers, has required me to tread a careful line. Since you went away, I've managed to keep the peace by deeding the colonists large tracts of land at Menotomie and near the Mystic Lakes."

"And today you've kept more peace today by agreeeing to the English terms of submission."

With a shrug, Wianna squirmed out of her deerskin skirt with the ease of a snake shedding its skin. "The only terms of submission I wish to hear about now are those I require of you," she told Squeteague, as she lay back upon her bed of pelts. "So kindly set about to please me with the same ardor you have addressed your lovers since we were together.

Which is how Squeteague came to remain in the wetu of the Squaw Sachem Wianna for several more days and nights.

Chapter Nine

Following his sojourn with Wianna, Squeteague made several ventures into Nipmuck country to deliver a new type of musket to the Nashaway, Quinebaug, Wabaquassett, and other Nipmuck sub-groups whose members were arming themselves to increase their ability to procure beaver pelts. By this time, he had become aware that the cumbersome, slow-firing matchlock muskets carried by English settlers and soldiers, which required their users to ignite a priming charge with a smoldering taper, were not only slow to reload, but also highly inaccurate. The new muskets were called flintlocks because they employed a piece of flint to create a spark that fired the powder charge. Far easier to use than matchlocks, they were immediately popular with Native hunters to whom Squeteague introduced them after acquring them from Dutch arms traders at Fort Orange. As a result, he became acquainted with and trusted by many Nipmuck sachems in a relatively short period of time.

During one of these trips, he encountered a beautiful Pequot woman named Alawa, who, as a young girl, had escaped from the Owl's Nest following the holocaust at Fort Missituck, only to be captured by some Mohegan warriors, who wished to curry favor with Uncas by presenting her to him as a gift for the appeasement of the carnal appetite for which he was notorious. Alawa had escaped from the Mohegan by feigning sickness, and, left unguarded while her captors fashioned a litter to carry her, had fled north to the territory of the Quinebaug, where she had become a servant of the wife of Moas, one of the sachems with whom Squeteague had been trading flintlocks for furs. Squeteague first saw her when she served him venison in Moas's wetu, and was struck by her beauty and grace. He then asked and received permission from Moas and his wife to speak to her. Their first encounter proved less than successful because Alawa had been traumatized by the carnage at the Owl's Nest, where she had seen her mother and sister hacked to death by English soldiers, and from which her father had escaped only to be overtaken and killed by the Mohegan. As a result, she could scarcely look at Squeteague or speak to him above a whisper.

"The past can't be forgotten," he told her. "You and I have suffered at the hands of the English in similar fashion. I've seen my father dragged away by them and my mother succumb to one of their diseases. Yet one must live on. One must find the courage to endure."

"How can one find such courage when the English are so powerful?" Alawa asked.

"Our fathers have lived on this land for generations. It is ours and for this reason we shall prevail."

"Warriors believe they can prevail by making war. I know it from my own father and other Pequot sachems. But look what happened to them and to my people."

Squeteague had no ready answer for this rejoinder, nor was he inclined to argue with this beautiful woman for whom he felt an overwhelming tenderness and need to protect. Instead, he told her that he hoped she would consent to see him again.

At their second meeting, he started out by attempting to reassure her. "I'm the captain of a ship that allows me to travel far and wide. If you would agree to be my woman and there should be another war, I promise to take you someplace safe."

Alawa gave an unexpectedly playful laugh and a toss of her head. "If safety were the most important thing to me, I'd do better to find myself a Mohegan sachem or an English soldier."

Once again, Squeteague found himself at a loss for words. A moment later, his silence became unbearable. "Can't you see I've lost my heart to you?" he blurted.

"If that's true it's far more important than safety," Alawa murmured, and reached out to touch his arm.

"It's true." Squeteague declared.

"Then I'm happy to know it."

Little by little, Alawa began to trust him and to believe that he did love her and would be kind and protective. This led to meetings that lasted long into the night, and finally to a night of lovemaking in which he proved to her that he could be both gentle and ardent. After a week of fervent courtship, he persuaded her to accompany him back to Narragansett territory, where they began living together in a wetu he had built on the shore of Pettaquamscutt Cove, where the *Nauset* lay at anchor.

Soon afterward, Alawa discovered she was pregnant. When she told Squeteague, he found himself of two minds. At forty years of age, it was past time for him to become the father of children. Orphaned since childhood, however, he had become accustomed to a life of freedom that would now of necessity be circumscribed. In the end, all other considerations were overwhelmed by his love for Alawa and the knowledge that an unmarried pregnancy might result in her disgrace.

Squeteague took her in his arms and stroked her braided hair. "With your consent, I would have you be my wife," he said

Alawa looked into his eyes. "Then I'll ask Nokomis, mother of earth and moon who has made me fertile, that I may present you with a son."

"If it should be a daughter who would become a woman like you, I'd be equally pleased."

"First a son and then a daughter," Alawa told him.

Unlike the way many Narragansett men treated their wives, Squeteague would not allow Alawa to undertake heavy work as she grew large during the winter. Instead, he encouraged her to stay inside the wetu during cold weather, made a warm blanket for her from the hides of beaver he trapped in nearby streams, and fed her partridge—her favorite food—that he shot out of trees with his bow when they had become drowsy after eating fermented berries. In the spring, he brought her trout tickled by hand from under the banks of brooks, eels speared in the mud of the inlet, and fat oysters gathered in the shallows.

In July, she bore a healthy baby boy whom they named Epenow after the sachem whose exploits he had admired as a young man.

Squeteague was overjoyed to hold his son in his arms. "This is the happiest day of my life," he told Alawa. "I'll never forget it." He was thinking that the arrival of a son conferred new responsibility upon him as the protector of his family, which, in turn, caused him to question the wisdom of continuing his dangerous role as a double agent and gunrunner. However, the realization that his own father would never hold his grandson reminded him of the oath he had taken to avenge Pocassonet's death at the hands of Captain Hunt. So there could be no question of turning back. He would continue to work for an uprising against the English invaders no matter how dangerous it might prove to be or how long it might take to bring about.

By this time, Miantonomo's younger brother, Pessacus, had become supreme sachem of the Narragansett. He retained Squeteague as his chief advisor and sent him to Boston to seek permission from Winthrop to avenge the killing of Miantonomo by going to war against Uncas. "Remind the governor that Uncas absconded with the wampum we paid him to ransom Miantonomo," he told Squeteague.

When Squeteague undertook to carry out this instruction, an exasperated Winthrop informed him that under no circumstances would he or the commissioners allow the Narragansett to attack their Mohegan ally.

Squeteague found himself faced with a delicate task of diplomacy. "Pessacus and his people suspect that the commissioners sanctioned the execution of Miantonomo," he said. "I must warn Your Excellency that the Narragansett believe their honor to be at stake and are determined to avenge themselves upon Uncas."

The last thing Winthrop wanted was a war that would threaten the growing settlements on the frontier. "What do you advise?" he inquired.

"I suggest a compromise in the form of a delay that could result in a cooling of passions," Squeteague replied. "A requirement that the Narragansett put off attacking Uncas until the spring."

As a result of Squeteague's advice, the commissioners of the United Colonies made a treaty with Pessacus that obliged the Narragansett to defer making war until after the following year's planting of corn.

When the agreed-upon delay ran out in May, Narragansett and Niantic warriors led by Pessacus and Ninigret, a Niantic sachem and uncle of Miantonomo who had become an important leader in Narragansett affairs, fell upon the Mohegan at Fort Shantok on the Thames River, seriously wounding Tantaquideon, who had run down Miantonomo two years earlier, and besieging Uncas and a large number of his men behind the palisades of their stronghold. By now—thanks in large part to Squeteague—the Narragansett and Niantic had acquired a significant arsenal of guns, and were inflicting heavy casualties on the Mohegan, who, armed by their Connecticut Colony allies, were doing the same to the Narragansett and Niantic.

According to an alarmed Roger Williams, "War is raging next door to us with both sides plunged into barbarous slaughter!"

In order to save Uncas further casualties, the commissioners of the United Colonies sent messengers to Pessacus, ordering him to cease the attack. Furious with their interference, the Narragansett sachem told Squeteague to take a message back: "Tell them that if they persist in meddling in my affairs, I will enlist the aid of the Mohawk, in which case no Englishman will dare stir out of his house to piss for fear of being killed."

When Squeteague delivered Pessacus's threat to the commissioners, he could tell from their expressions that it had aroused both anger and anxiety. After a brief consultation with his colleagues, Winthrop asked him whether he thought the Narragansett sachem was boasting or serious when he threatened to join with the Mohawk in hostile action against the colonists.

"The Narragansett have obeyed the provisions of the treaty they signed with the United Colonies last year," Squeteague replied. "Whether they'll enlist the Mohawk in their cause may well depend upon how Your Excellencies respond to them."

When the cry of consternation that greeted Squeteague's response had died down, Winthrop regarded him with unaccustomed skepticism. "For many years I have depended upon you to provide information about the intentions of our Indian neighbors," he said. "Yet you now appear to be taking their side with a suggestion that we placate them. In any case, here's our answer. Tell Pessacus and Ninigret that we will deal harshly with them if they should undertake to disobey our commands, let alone raise arms against us with or without the Mohawk."

The siege of Shantok was lifted a week later when an Englishman from Fort Saybrook sailed up the Thames and delivered provisions to the desperate Mohegan. However, the Narragansett raids continued until the colonial commissioners raised an expeditionary force of three hundred men commanded by Edward Gibbons, a veteran of the Fort Missituck massacre, who was ordered to march into Narragansett territory and subjugate the inhabitants. Remembering how the English had annihilated the Pequot, Pessacus and Ninigret wasted little time in traveling to Boston, where they signed a peace treaty that obliged them to pay the United Colonies two thousand fathoms of wampum, return all captives and canoes they had taken from the Mohegan, and maintain a lasting peace with the Colonies.

Squeteague observed the capitulation of the Narragansett and Niantic sachems with despair. Without the strong leadership of a warrior such as Miantonomo, he could no longer expect to assist in the formation of a confederacy that might stem the expansion of the colonists into the interior of New England. If any alliance among the Native People were possible, it would occur as the result of events he could no longer foresee.

Meanwhile, the business of trading flintlocks for furs was booming.

The reading of the Ten Commandments at the ceremony celebrating the decision of the sachems to submit themselves and their subjects to the protection of the Bay Colony symbolized a policy that encouraged the spreading of the Gospel among the Native People. In 1646, the magistrates of the Massachusetts General Court forbade them to commit blasphemy under pain of death, or to worship their own gods—an infraction punishable by fines. The magistrates also ordered them to observe the Sabbath by attending mandatory worship services, or pay a fine of five shillings for each absence. Power to enforce these edicts was given to the chief sachem in each of the Native communities that lay within the domain of the colonial government.

By this time, the Reverend John Eliot, who had come to New England with the first Puritans, had been appointed by the General Court as "Apostle to the Indians," and was conducting religious services at Nonantum (later Newton), a small village on the Charles River near Boston, whose leader was a sachem named Waban. During the next ten years, Eliot preached to Native People throughout the Bay Colony and established half a dozen mission towns for converts to Christianity, who were known as "Praying Indians." Funds for this endeavor were authorized by an act passed in 1649 by the English Parliament that created a foundation called the Society for Propagation of the Gospel in New England.

Squeteague considered Eliot's proselytizing as another form of subjugation designed to bring Native People into towns where they could be more easily controlled by the colonial authorities who remained fearful of an uprising. "Why do you welcome the English preacher?" he asked Waban, whom he encountered on one of his journeys into Massachusett territory. "Don't you realize that his religion will destroy our way of life?"

Waban looked at him with alarm. "The God of the English has made them too powerful to resist."

"You're not afraid of the Englishman's God as much as his muskets," Squeteague declared.

"God has made the English powerful by giving them muskets."

"Then why shouldn't we arm ourselves with muskets and become equally powerful?"

"I've heard rumors that this may be happening," Waban replied. "Surely, it's a temptation to be resisted."

Squeteague remembered the dying Iyanough uttering similar misgivings about the power of the English God at a time when the Pokanoket and other Wampanoag could have overrun Plymouth Plantation and annihilated its inhabitants with ease. How foolish Massasoit had been to welcome the invaders at such a time! How weak of Waban and the so-called "Praying Indians" to embrace their religion! And how arrogant of the preacher Eliot to be spreading it among them!

Meanwhile, tensions had escalated once again on the frontier when the Mohawk threatened to come to the aid of the Narragansett in their conflict with the Mohegan, and a bellicose Uncas warned them that, if they intervened, he would "cover the ground with gobs of their flesh." Such pronouncements alarmed the commissioners of the United Colonies, who summoned Pessacus and Ninigret to explain their presumed alliance with the Mohawk.

Speaking in behalf of the two sachems, Squeteague assured the commissioners that neither of them had made alliance with the Mohawk and that they intended to pay the entire amount of the heavy fine that had been levied against them. "They want you to be aware, however, that one day they will require satisfaction for all the wrongs Uncas has done them."

"Inform them that any attack upon Uncas and the Mohegan will occasion an immediate reprisal on the part of the United Colonies," one of the commissioners replied.

This threat had its desired effect for a short time, but the situation soon heated up again when a Narragansett named Cuttaquin ran a sword into the breast of Uncas as the Mohegan sachem and some of his men boarded an English trading vessel at anchor in the Thames River near Shantok. Uncas's wound turned out to be a minor flesh cut and healed quickly, but not until his followers had seized Cuttaquin and cut off the index fingers of both his hands as a way of preventing him from ever holding a sword again.

When Cuttaquin confessed that Ninigret had hired him to kill Uncas, the commissioners summoned him and the Niantic sachem to Boston to answer questions regarding the assassination attempt. Squeteague accompanied them as their interpreter. "Ninigret denies hiring Cuttaquin to kill Uncas," he told the commissioners. "He asks you to consider Cuttaquin's amputated fingers. Don't they suggest to you that his confession has been obtained through torture?"

The commissioners chose not to believe this explanation, however, and ordered Cuttaquin to be taken to Shantok and turned over to Uncas.

John Winthrop, perennial governor of the Bay Colony and Squeteague's longtime champion, had died a few weeks earlier, and one of the commissioners who had been present when Winthrop had defended Squeteague against the charge of treason following the Pequot War took the opportunity to question his present allegiance. "I recall the day our Governor commanded you to remain loyal to the Bay Colony," he declared. "Yet you now appear before us as a counselor for Indians who have shown themselves to be insolent and defiant. I'm of a mind you should be held accountable for your association with these villains."

"Let me remind you that I appear here under a guarantee of safe conduct," Squeteague replied.

"Do you still consider yourself bound in service to the

Colony?"

"I consider myself to be in the service of no one but myself."

"So you have betrayed the trust our Governor placed in you."

Squeteague responded with quiet fury. "As you and your fellow commissioners betrayed Miantonomo to death at the hands of Uncas," he said. "And as you now betray Cuttaquin. As you pretend to care for our spiritual lives while stealing our lands. And as you have made lawful the selling of our people into slavery."

The commissioner turned an outraged face to his colleagues. "Hear how this wretched heathen presumes to pass judgment on the decisions of this body and its magistrates!"

"You have the makings of a fine interpreter," Squeteague informed him, before turning on his heel and leaving the commissioners in stunned silence.

On the one hand, he found himself relieved that the double game he had been playing for so many years was finally over. On the other, he was under no illusion that from now on he was anything but a marked man.

Chapter Ten

Squeteague would ordinarily have made the voyage from Pettaquamscutt to Boston in the *Nauset*, but on this occasion he had accompanied Ninigret and his bodyguards overland. So he was obliged not only to return the same way, but also by himself because he had business dealings to conduct with a Dutch arms dealer whose ship had put into Salem, and Ninigret and his entourage had preceded him by several days. From a cluster of rude log huts and wharves on the waterfront, he followed a cart path that led to Cambridge, then along the south side of the Charles River to Nonantum, where forests were falling to the metal axes of the settlers, and from there to the recently established Praying Town of Natick. From then on, habitation ceased except for an occasional cabin and cornfield as the trail, which had been carved deep into the soil by generations of moccasin-clad feet, led south through stands of white pine, hemlock, ash, and oak tall enough to plunge the path into shadow at midday.

Squeteague had passed this way traveling north, when he had accompanied Ninigret to Boston a few days earlier. The trail was criss-crossed with dozens of other paths leading east and west and he soon found himself uncertain about which one led to Providence and from there south into Narragansett territory and his home at Pettaquamscutt. Moreover, at some point he found himself overtaken by the sense that he was being followed. He could not have specified the precise time at which this suspicion first occurred to him. Perhaps it was in the late afternoon when, pausing to rest, he felt a tremor in the path beneath his feet. Certainly it came at twilight while he was descending from a ridge to the ford near the junction of the Titicut (Taunton) and Nemasket Rivers, and saw fleeting shadows cross the moon that was rising through the treeline behind him. Whoever it might be was not attempting to overtake him, which meant that if he was being followed with evil intent the ambush would occur at the ford where he would be waist-deep in flowing water and helpless to defend himself since, under the terms of the safe conduct, he was traveling unarmed. At this point, Squeteague left the path he had been following and crawled through a stand of alders in wetlands that bordered the river, until he drew close to the wading place. There, half a dozen Mohegan wearing warlocks that traversed the crowns of their shaved skulls were holding a parley to determine what had become of their quarry.

Squeteague had stepped off the trail so close to the ford that his stalkers knew he must be nearby. Accordingly, three of them returned along the path to look for signs where he had left it, while the other three began to patrol the river by canoe in case he should try to swim across. The first three were lucky, the canoers not so fortunate. Crouching on top of an overhanging bank, Squeteague hurled himself upon them, upsetting the craft and throwing its occupants into the river, where he proceeded to drown one of them by scissoring his neck between his legs and holding the man's head under water. A second Mohegan swam poorly enough to be overtaken and dispatched in similar fashion. The third had reached the riverbank and was crawling through tall grass when Squeteague caught up with him and silenced him forever by pressing his face into a thick layer of muck.

The commotion had been heard by the Mohegan who were combing the alder swamp. Soon they would reach the river and find the body of their companion lying in the grass. With no time to lose, Squeteague swam to the opposite shore and hauled himself from the water. He was scrambling up a steep bank toward the forest when he felt a sharp sting in his side, saw a flint arrowhead protruding from the fleshy part of his midriff, and ducked behind a screen of trees as another arrow struck a trunk beside his head. Falling to his knees, he placed both hands on the shaft that had pierced his side, pulled it forward and free, and came close to fainting from the pain. Casting the arrow away, he looked about for something to staunch the blood flowing from his wounds and chanced upon a pine tree with resin exuding from its trunk. After applying the resin as poultice to the punctures in his side, he raced off into the forest, hoping he was not leaving a trail of blood that would enable the Mohegan to run him down.

The ford near the juncture of the Titicut and Nemasket had been frequented for centuries by Native People of the region, who set weirs in the shallows to catch herring, shad, and tomcod during their spawning runs. For this reason, it was called "place of many fish" and approached from all directions by footpaths. The trail Squeteague had been following led south from Natick to the crossing place; another led west to Providence; another southeast into the territory of the Pocasset; and still another known as the Nemasket Trail—the one he ended up taking—followed the Titicut until it flowed into Narragansett Bay. There, he encountered a Pokanoket fisherman who, seeing that he was injured, took him across the water by canoe to a promontory dominated by a rocky hill called Montaup (lookout place) that lay close to the village of Sowams, the home of Massasoit. It was here at dawn on the following morning that an ashen-faced Squeteague arrived.

Some Pokanoket women led him into a wetu, where they cleansed his wounds, applied new poultices of elm bark to prevent infection, and fed him bowls of fish soup to help him regain his strength. On the morning of the second day, he awoke to find himself looking up at the tall, imposing figure of Massasoit whom he had last encountered at the submission ceremony when the sachem had voiced displeasure with him for supplying the Narragansett with weapons.

"We meet again," Massasoit said, solemnly.

Squeteague did not need to be asked what the sachem wanted to know. "I was ambushed by some Mohegan at the ford on the Titicut River," he explained.

"Mohegan are rarely seen in that part of our country."

"I'm certain they were Mohegan. Some were following me, while others were waiting at the ford."

"And what were you doing there?"

"I had been in Boston interpreting for Ninigret before the Bay Colony commissioners. I was on my way back to Pettaquamscutt where I've been living with my wife and child."

"So you're are still consorting with the Narragansett," Massasoit observed. "Everyone knows they and the Mohegan to be bitter enemies, but it seems strange that the Mohegan would come such a long way to ambush you if it's true that you are merely an interpreter."

"I suspect they were persuaded to do so by the English, who consider me a traitor."

"And what reason have the English to consider you a traitor?"

"They know that I despise them for burning Pequot women and children at Fort Missituck, for drowning captives, for selling others into slavery, for forcing their religion upon us, and for taking and spoiling our land."

Massasoit regarded him, gravely. "We will discuss these matters when you are better recovered from your wounds."

A few days later, Squeteague was conducted to Massasoit's wetu—a large dome-shaped structure adorned with decorative strips of birch and chestnut bark. "You have admitted supplying guns to Pessacus and his kinsman Ninigret," the sachem declared. "Both are enemies of the Pokanoket. Why should I not consider you to be my enemy as well?"

"I have come here wounded and in need of healing," Squeteague replied. "I am too grateful for your help and kindness for you to consider me your enemy."

Massasoit regarded him askance. "Except for the alliance I made with the English, the Narragansett might have turned the Pokanoket into slaves. You know this because you were present when Standish and his soldiers came to my assistance. Earlier, when I had fallen ill, Edward Winslow came from Plimoth to attend me. He saved me from death. When I recovered I had proof the English loved me and were my friends. I told my sachems that while I lived I would never forget the kindness they had showed me."

"As I will not forget yours," Squeteague declared.

"I have returned the love of the English by pledging them my loyalty," the Sachem continued, "and by granting them land at Patuxet and other places on which to settle. I have not only repaid them, but also acted for the benefit of my people who, as I've said from the beginning, must learn to live among them if there is to be peace."

Squeteague remembered Massasoit expressing these same beliefs when they had met for the first time a quarter of a century earlier. Can nothing that has happened in the meantime have changed this great sachem's way of thinking, he wondered, or is he too old and set in his beliefs to acknowledge that the English greed for land can only bring doom and devastation to his people?

"You once told me you couldn't dwell on every evil done in the past, but must consider what was best for the future. Have you considered how much of our land the English have acquired and what this means for our future?"

"No one knows better than I how the English have multiplied and spread," Massasoit replied. "When they first arrived it took a whole day of walking to reach them. Now they are so close I can see smoke rising from their chimneys from the summit of Montaup."

Squeteague detected a note of resignation in the sachem's voice. You see smoke rising from English chimneys because you've given them land, he told himself, knowing that the sachem had deeded hundreds of square miles of Pokanoket territory to the settlers from Plymouth who were establishing settlements in their newly acquired domains.

"The colonists are also spreading their religion among us," he said, aware that Massasoit had held out the hand of friendship to them in every way but that.

"This troubles me," the sachem acknowledged. "However, the English say their God obliges them to do it and will not give it up."

"So we can't do anything to prevent them from taking our land and forcing us to accept their God?"

"We don't have to accept the English God, but it's wise to accommodate their need for land. Their guns have proved superior to our bows and arrows. We can only benefit by living in peace with them."

"And at the cost of becoming their tributary?"

Massasoit bridled at the question, but replied in a measured voice. "After the death of Sassacus, I went with my eldest son before the court of the English at Plimoth to renew the treaty I had made with them. At that time, I declared myself once again to be a subject of the King of England and so I shall remain."

Remembering the savagery of the Puritan attack on Fort Missituck, the dense smoke filled with the smell of burning flesh, and the screams of terrified women and children, Squeteague decided he would rather choke to death on a fish bone than submit allegiance to any English king.

Massasoit was scrutinizing him intently. "Since you are living among the Narragansett, you know that many of their warriors burn with the desire to rise up against the English. It's the same with warriors of the Pokanoket as well as the Nipmuck. But if these men wish to see their sons grow to manhood they will not join in fighting the colonists. I have warned my own sons that, if they engage in war with the English, they'll meet with certain defeat and death."

"I've listened carefully to your words and I will keep them in my heart," replied Squeteague, who wondered how Massasoit's sons—Wamsutta and Metacom—felt about the increasing English incursions into Wampanoag territory.

"Do more than keep them in your heart," the sachem advised. "Share them with Pessacus and Ninigret. Tell them that if they're foolish enough to think they can overcome the English in war they'll lose everything—their villages, their cornfields, their canoes, their wives and children, and most certainly their lives."

At this point, Massasoit raised his hand in a gesture of farewell. "This may be the last time we shall meet," he said. "I've arranged for some of my men to take you by canoe to Pettaquamscutt. Return to the Narragansett in peace."

Squeteague left Sowams before the puncture wounds in his side had fully healed. After crossing the two arms of Narragansett Bay that flanked Aquidneck Island, he arrived exhausted on the shore of Pettaquamscutt Cove and entered his wetu to find Alawa fast asleep beside their five-year-old son, Epenow. Taking care not to awaken them, he crawled unto the mat that provided their bed and was welcomed by Alawa, who reached across the child and enfolded him in a drowsy embrace.

Tired though he was, he found himself unable to fall asleep. Instead, he considered the events of the past several days and, in spite of his skepticism about gods, gave thanks to Kitcki Manitou, the Supreme Being of the Wampanoag, for having saved him from death at the hands of the Mohegan, and for delivering him to the village of Massasoit, the surrogate father who had provided him with succor. He also mulled over the warning the sachem had delivered against going to war with the English.

That night, he dreamed that the Mohegan had captured him at the ford and taken him to Uncas, but before the Mohegan sachem could begin to torture him, he was released through the intervention of Webcowit, the husband of Wianna, with whom he had committed the mortal sin the Puritans called adultery. Dreams were important to the Wampanoag. They warned of danger, revealed opportunities, and explained strange happenings. They spoke to the intimate relationship that existed between humans and the supernatural, and provided the way in which the gods and spirits made their will known to man.

When Squeteague awoke, he found himself puzzled by his dream. Many of his fellow Wampanoag would have gone to a powwaw to have it interpreted and learn how to ward off any malevolent consequences that might attend it. However, Squeteague disliked the local powwaw—a charlatan who invariably sought to curry favor with the Narragansett sachems, Pessacus and Ninigret—and decided he would interpret the dream himself. For this reason, he went off into the forest and, after a period of reflection, came to the conclusion that his rescue from Uncas by Webcowit signified that the spirit of the medicine man had forgiven him for lying with Wianna in his absence, and that this forgiveness had tided over to his deliverance from the Mohegan at the ford.

But might the dream also signify that the gods disapproved of his amorous adventure with the squaw sachem, and had allowed him to escape his Mohegan assassins so they might punish him later? Squeteague considered this to be possible, but he did not believe for a moment that he would be subject to the penalty imposed by the followers of the Puritan God, who had passed a law declaring, "if any man should copulate with another man's wife they should both be punished by death." Still, he was aware that sleeping with a married woman was frowned upon by his own people, which caused him to reevaluate his escapade with the married Wianna in light of his escape from the Mohegan and his good fortune in having a loving wife in Alawa and a healthy son in Epenow. Unlike the Puritans, who were constantly harangued about sin by their ministers, Squeteague and his fellow Wampanoag had little concept of guilt, but held themselves to rigorous standards of courage, manliness, and sacrifice. Consequently, by the time Sque-teague emerged from the forest, he had made a solemn decision to remain faithful to Alawa—his loyal wife and the mother of his son.

For her part, Alawa had witnessed too much carnage at the hands of the English and their Mohegan allies to be comfortable with Squeteague's gunrunning activities, let alone with his aim of arming the Native People of the region so they might one day mount an insurrection against the invaders. Like women through the ages, she feared war and the catastrophe it inevitably brought to families. Her loved ones had become paramount in her exis-tence and she regarded any threat to them with abhorrence. She made her feelings known to Squeteague without regard for the traditional subservience a Native woman was expected to provide her warrior husband.

"You and I have been happy here among the Narragansett," she told him. "We live in a land of plenty. We have a beautiful son who looks like you. We abide in peace with the English, who live on Aquidneck and in Providence. Why is it necessary to anger them and turn them into enemies?"

"They're our enemies already," Squeteague replied, knowing she would never forget that English soldiers had murdered her mother and sister at the Owl's Nest. "Sooner or later they'll drive us from our land just as the sachem for whom Epenow is named predicted many years ago."

"But we live in Nokomis's earth and under her blessing and protection. She won't be pleased with us if we bring trouble to it."

"There's already trouble," Squeteague replied, "and more in the offing. If we don't prepare for it, we'll be overwhelmed by these English whose greed for our land has no bounds."

Alawa reached out and caressed the scars that had formed over the puncture wounds in his side. "I'm afraid for you and our son. I'm afraid for the three of us. I can't bear the thought that harm may come to our family."

Squeteague took her in his arms. "I'll protect you and our son," he declared. "It's my solemn vow and duty."

During the next few years, he continued to venture to sea in the *Nauset* to buy and trade for muskets, which he then delivered to the Narragansett, Pokonoket, Nipmuck, and other Native People in the interior, who were becoming restless in the face of growing expansion into their territory by the colonists. Aware of Alawa's anxiety, however, he began to spend more time at Pettaquamscutt, helping her till their fields and care for their plantings of corn and beans, and teaching Epenow how to hunt and fish. The boy had already become expert with a small bow and arrow Squeteague had carved from the branch of a hickory tree. Now he watched his father fashion a larger one from a piece of ash, rub bear grease on it, and hang it in their lodge to season and make supple. Over time, he learned how to make bowstrings from the sinew of a deer's leg, to fashion arrows from straight branches of dogwood trees, to split turkey feathers and glue them with spruce gum to arrow shafts, and to shape arrowheads by chipping flintstone.

In addition, Squeteague taught Epenow how to set snares for rabbits and deer and built deadfalls for bear. In the spring and fall, they made weirs of stakes interwoven with branches to catch smelt, shad, and alewives as they swam up nearby streams to spawn. During the winter, they speared eels through holes in the ice, and in other seasons flounder in salt ponds, striped bass in creeks and estuaries, and salmon at the waterfalls of the Kittacuck (Blackstone) River to the north. Together, they cut down a chestnut tree, and fashioned a sea-going dugout by rounding three sides of the trunk with hatchets, and hollowing it out with fire and quahog shells.

Such was young Epenow's education at the hands of his father. As a consequence, the two of them often came home to their dome-shaped wetu fatigued from the day's efforts and glad to have the supper of broiled rabbit and maize cakes, or partridge and squash, or whatever other fare Alawa had prepared for them. In the evening, they told stories of what had happened to them during the day—Alawa describing how she had set a coat and hat on a pole to scare blackbirds from the corn plants, Epenow how he had speared two flounder at once, and Squeteague how he had come across a black bear in a berry patch. Sometimes they told stories from the past—Epenow remembering the first rabbit he had killed with his bow and arrow, Alawa meeting Squeteague when he visited the Quinebaug, and Squeteague the encounter between the Nauset and the soldiers of the red-bearded Captain Standish, who, but for the fearsome fire and noise of their muskets, might have been overwhelmed and driven into the sea.

Part Three

PRELUDE

Chapter Eleven

By mid-century, the Commissioners of the United Colonies were summoning Pessacus and Ninigret to appear before them on a wide variety of pretexts—failing to pay tribute for wrongs they were alleged to have committed, storing guns and powder, negotiating with the Mohawk, plotting rebellion with the Dutch, harassing Puritan missionaries, and making inter-tribal marriages to increase the number of warriors who might some-day be raised against the English. The two sachems complied with these summons because of a grudging respect for colonial military power. Neither of them did so willingly, however, nor would either of them allow his people to be converted. When asked to join the ranks of the righteous by the Reverend Thomas Mayhew, Jr., who was in the process of Christianizing the Indians on Martha's Vineyard, Ninigret advised him to "go and make the English good first." Even Uncas, a strong ally of the English, demanded to know how long he and his Mohegan should be required to pay tribute, and whether their children and grandchildren would be subject to it.

During the winter of 1653, when England was at war with the

Netherlands, the colonial commissioners in Hartford learned that Ninigret and Squeteague had spent time in the Dutch colony of Nieuw Amsterdam, where they were rumored to have purchased guns with the intention of attacking English settlements in Connecticut. As a result, the commissioners demanded that the Niantic sachem respond to the charge of plotting to mount an insurrection. Ninigret's reply—a series of questions drafted by Squeteague—tweaked the commissioners for trying to intimidate him:

> *Do the English believe we imagine them to be so sleepy*
> *as to think ourselves capable of doing them harm? Haven't*
> *we learned that the English are not a sleepy people?*
> *Do the English think we're foolish enough to sell*
> *our lives and the lives of our wives and children and*
> *all our kindred and have our country destroyed for a*
> *few guns, powder shot, and swords? What good would*
> *those do us when we're dead?*

When England's war with the Netherlands ended a year later, the commissioners learned that Ninigret was denying that the United Colonies had jurisdiction over him, and summoned him to Hartford to explain himself. Ninigret declined the invitation, demanding that the English "let him alone." At that point, the commissioners raised an army of two hundred and seventy foot soldiers and forty cavalry under the command of Major Simon Willard, of Groton, and sent it to Rhode Island to force Ninigret to accept English authority, pay a heavy additional fine of wampum, and turn over any Pequot living under him. When Ninigret objected to these demands, Willard told him that the alternative was to have "his head set upon an English pole." Having little choice, Ninigret signed a coercive peace treaty.

After the signing, Willard's interpreter—a Montaukett named Cockenoe—took Squeteague aside. "There's something you should be aware of," said Cockenoe, who had been captured as a boy during the Pequot War and indentured to the family of a Massachusetts Bay militiaman named Callicott. "Uncas has received permission from the colonial authorities to track you down and cut you off for killing three of his warriors at the ford on the Titicut River."

"How do you know this?" Squeteague asked.

"Through a Massachusett named Wassausmon, an interpreter for the English, who call him Sassamon. I know Sassamon because he lived with the Callicott family when I became their servant. He served as an interpreter for the Puritans in the Pequot War, and he can read and write English as well as speak it. He has studied at Harvard and been a schoolmaster. For these reasons, the colonists use him to write deeds for Native lands they wish to acquire. I saw him a week ago when Major Willard was mustering his soldiers."

"But why would Sassamon give you warning that I was in danger?"

"That wasn't his intention. Sassamon believes that Uncas plans to kill you when you're away on a mission for Ninigret. Since he knows that I often interpret for the English on such occasions, his intention was to advise me of the danger, not you."

Squeteague did not tell Alawa about Cockenoe's warning because he didn't wish to alarm her. He did, however, tell her about the requirement in the treaty that obliged Ninigret to turn over any Pequot being harbored by the Narragansett. "From now on, we must keep the *Nauset* in readiness to leave," he said.

By this time, the imposition of heavy fines for various offenses and the subsequent seizure of land for failure to pay them on time had become a favorite method of the English for acquiring large tracts of territory from the Native People of the region. Other stratagems included getting a Native person drunk and inveigling him to sign a deed he could neither read nor understand; recognizing the false claim of a Native who did not own the land and then "purchasing" it from him; driving Native People off the land by allowing cattle and hogs to trample and devour their crops; or simply "persuading" them to relinquish land at gunpoint.

Dispossessing the original inhabitants through fraud and force originated by and large with the land-hungry offspring of the first settlers at Plymouth and Boston, most of whom were now dead. Elder Brewster, the spiritual leader of the Separatists who landed at Plymouth in 1620, had died in 1644. Edward Winslow, the savior of Massasoit, had returned to England in 1646, and subsequently succumbed to yellow fever in the Caribbean. John Winthrop, the first governor of the Massachusetts Bay Colony, had died in 1649. The pugnacious Myles Standish had died in 1656 at his home in Duxbury on land that Massasoit had given him. And William Bradford, the revered Governor of Plymouth Colony, had died in 1657. In that year, Massasoit signed the last of many land deeds he made with the colonists, and went to live out his remaining days with the Quabaug in Nipmuck territory west of Boston. He died in 1661 and was succeeded as sachem of the Pokanoket by his eldest son, Wamsutta.

By 1660, a changing of the guard had taken place among the colonists, and in its wake came multiple attempts by the children and grandchildren of the first settlers to increase their land holdings by jurisdictional maneuvering, by playing off one group of Native People against another, and by encouraging the depredations of the Mohegan under Uncas, who had by now had learned the whereabouts of Squeteague and his family. Not one to deny himself revenge, Uncas sent three of his most able warriors along the coast in a seagoing dugout until they came to Pettaquamscutt Cove, where the *Nauset* was anchored. Disembarking at the mouth of a nearby creek, the Mohegan made camp some distance from Squeteague's wetu and spent several days hiding in the forest while they determined his habits and those of his wife and son. On days when Epenow did not accompany his father to hunt game, the boy could be seen in the offshore shallows, gathering oysters, clams, and lobsters, or spearing eels and flounder. Alawa could be found tending beans, corn, and squash in her garden or performing chores, such as weaving reed mats and mending clothes inside the wetu. As for Squeteague, he either took to the forest and marsh to hunt deer and ducks, or paddled his canoe into Narraganett Bay to fish for bass and salmon.

Based on these observations, the Mohegan devised a plan. Guns would be left behind and replaced with bows and arrows so as not to alert any Narragansett who might be in the vicinity. The boy would be dispatched while wading, the woman taken in her garden or wetu, and Squeteague ambushed as he returned to camp through the woods, became isolated on an expanse of marsh, or landed his canoe on the shore.

Uncas had promised a handsome reward of wampum for the scalps of the man and boy, and the capture of the woman for himself.

Success would depend upon stealth and patience.

The Mohegan bided their time. Several days after arriving, two of them waded into the cove from different places along the shoreline and made their way toward Epenow, who was feeling for quahogs with his toes before plucking them from the mud and dropping them into a reed basket which, together with a fish spear, was tied around his waist with a sinew. At the same time, the third Mohegan came up behind Alawa, who was tilling beans in the garden, clamped a hand over her mouth to stifle any sound, and wrestled her to the ground. An osprey's eye view would have presented a tableau in slow motion—a woman squirming desperately beneath the straddling figure of a man, and two other men converging silently upon a boy who remained unaware of their approach.

All this changed in an instant as Epenow, always alert for the chance to spear fish, heard some mullet splashing behind him and turned to find himself confronting the fierce-looking Mohegan, who, faces painted and warlocks bifurcating shaved skulls, had come within close range. His first instinct was to find refuge in deeper water by swimming out into the bay, towing the basket and the fish spear behind him, but he soon realized that this maneuver would at best provide a delay because the two Mohegan were swimming after him with knives clamped between their teeth. At that point, he grasped his fish spear, set the clam basket free, and, taking a deep breath, dived underwater and swam behind the nearest of his pursuers. When he came to the surface, he was gasping for air—a sound that alerted the Mohegan warrior who turned toward him, knife in hand, on the assumption that Epenow was unarmed. A moment later, he paid for that mistake with his life as Epenow drove the fish spear into his throat, causing a death gurgle heard by the second warrior, who removed the bow he had strapped over his shoulder, nocked an arrow, and made ready to let it fly.

Because his aim was impeded by having to tread water, the Mohegan's first missile skimmed across the surface wide of its mark. The second arrow came closer, however, and Epenow dived again and swam off to one side to deprive the Mohegan of a target. When he came up for air, he saw that the warrior had lost track of him and was looking in a different direction, so he took another plunge and swam toward the man until he found himself looking up at a trail of bubbles made by a pair of scissoring legs. At this point, Epenow thrust his spear into the midsection of the Mohegan, who cried out as he thrashed on the surface in death throes that were accompanied by a pink cloud of blood.

As Epenow swam and then waded toward shore, he caught sight of his mother pinned beneath the third Mohegan, who was peering toward the bay, his painted face swiveling from side to side as he tried to locate his companions. Seconds later, seeing Epenow running full tilt toward him through the shallows, he leapt to his feet, lifted Alawa to hers, and started dragging her into the forest. With a scream of terror, Alawa struggled to free herself as Epenow gained solid ground and ran after them. He had made up half the distance when the Mohegan, realizing that he was going to be overtaken, flung Alawa aside and continued on alone. Epenow paused by his mother long enough to assure himself that she had not been hurt, and then continued the chase, pursuing the Mohegan toward the camp where he and his companions had hidden their canoe.

The Mohegan proved to be a wily tactician. Knowing that he would be delayed at the camp by the necessity of launching the canoe, he hid behind the trunk of a large oak and lay in wait until Epenow came abreast of him, at which point he felled the boy with a blow to the head that laid him unconscious on the ground. For a moment, the warrior was tempted to take the scalp of the young pursuer who had so violently turned the tables on him and his companions, but the speed with which their plan had gone awry had unnerved him and he was in a hurry to be gone.

Half an hour later, he had loaded the dugout with enough provisions to reach the Mohegan settlement at Shantok without having to take the chance of landing in Narragansett territory. At that point, he launched the craft and paddled from the mouth of the creek and out into the bay, where, to his surprise, he encountered Squeteague who had heard Alawa's terrified cry, learned from her what had happened, and was waiting in his canoe with his bow and arrow resting across the gunwales. The Mohegan reached into the bottom of the dugout for his musket, but Squeteague had already drawn his bow and released an arrow whose shaft pierced the warrior's breast bone, passed through his chest cavity, and exited halfway through the rib cage in his back.

After towing the dugout and its dead passenger to shore, Squeteague returned to his wetu where he found Alawa in a high state of anxiety over the fate of their son. With a heavy heart, he set out to follow the trail that the Mohegan and Epenow had left in the forest and came across the prone figure of Epenow who, to his vast relief, was beginning to stir. Helping his son to his feet, he draped the boy's arm over his shoulder and half-carried, half-walked him back to the wetu, where he laid him down on a bear hide to rest, while Alawa pressed a mud poultice to a nasty wound that had matted the hair on the back of his head with coagulating blood.

A day later, Epenow had recovered sufficiently to help his father and mother weight the bodies of the Mohegan by tying stones around their feet and consigning them to the bottom of the bay. That night, the three celebrated their deliverance from

Uncas's assassins with a feast of oysters, roast rabbit, and beans. Afterward, they told each other stories of what had happened. Alawa recalled her fright as she lay pinned to the ground beneath the Mohegan, who had clamped his hand over her mouth. Epenow described how his ability to hold his breath while swimming underwater had allowed him to dispatch his would-be assassins with his fish spear. Squeteague told of shooting quickly and accurately before the third Mohegan could raise his musket. However, his own exploit paled in comparison with the victories in close-quarters combat of his son, whose bravery and resourcefulness at an age even younger than he had been at the confrontation on the beach with Standish's soldiers filled him with pride.

Before retiring for the night, Squeteague embraced his fourteen-year-old son and handed him a trophy—a bone-handle knife carried by one of the Mohegan assassins he had killed with his fish spear.

"You have become a warrior," he said

Chapter Twelve

Squeteague knew that the disappearance of the Mohegan assassins would infuriate Uncas and result in his sending more of them to hunt him and his family down. As a result, he, Alawa, and Epenow spent the next few days breaking camp, gathering vegetables that had ripened in the garden, and ferrying their belongings to the *Nauset*. Once the sloop was loaded, they raised sail, headed east past Aquidneck Island, and then north up Buzzards Bay to Mattapoisett. There, he anchored a short distance offshore and, leaving Awala and Epenow on board, paddled by canoe to land, where he was met by a group of Pocasset men. They wasted no time in conducting him to the wetu of Weetamoo, the daughter of Corbitant, who had become squaw sachem of the Pocasset following the death of her father.

In addition to Alawa and Wianna, Squeteague had encountered some beautiful women in his life, but nothing had prepared him for the beauty and poise of the young, full-breasted queen he found himself confronting. After a moment's hesitation, he told her his name, the reason he had come, and requested that he and his family be given refuge.

When Weetamoo inquired why he had elected to seek sanctuary among the Pocasset, he told her that he had met her father soon after the English landed at Patuxet.

Weetamoo regarded him with a flirtatious smile. "You must have been very young."

"Not even twenty."

"Yet my father consented to see you?"

"He knew I had witnessed the arrival of the English and taken part in an attempt to repel them."

"My father believed that the foreigners had come to take our land and destroy our people. He taught me when I was just a girl to be suspicious of them."

"He told me the same" Squeteague replied, "but also warned that it would be futile for us to make war on them before arming ourselves with muskets. He sent me to Noepe, where I met Epenow who also believed that one day it would be necessary to rise up against the English."

"You and your family are welcome among us," Weetamoo told him. "Here you'll be safe from the Mohegan, and tonight you'll dine with me and my husband, Weequequinequa"

When Squeteague returned to the *Nauset*, Alawa took the news of the dinner invitation without remonstration, as befitted a Wampanoag wife who was not permitted to question her husband's conduct. As for Squeteague, he was not long in Weetamoo's wetu before he realized that she was bored with Weequequinequa, an older man she had apparently married to forge a relationship with a tributary group. For a while, he strove to maintain decorum in spite of his hostess's insistent rubbing of an inviting foot against his, but when Weequequinequa excused himself to retire, he came face to face with the choice of rejecting her and thus risking the refuge she had offered him and his family, or succumbing to blandishments that were rapidly reaching a point from which there could be no return. Finally, he pleaded that, because his son had recently been wounded by a Mohegan warrior, his presence was needed on the *Nauset*. At that point, Weetamoo bade him a reluctant goodnight with a look that let him know she would have preferred not to spend it alone.

Fortunately for Squeteague's peace of mind and his vow to remain faithful to Alawa, Weetamoo soon became a widow and moved her headquarters west, to an area near a fast-flowing stream called the Quequechan (leaping waters) that formed spectacular rapids before entering the Titicut River at Montaup Bay, where the city of Fall River would one day be founded. There, she married Massasoit's eldest son, Wamsutta, thus forging an alliance between the Pocasset and the Pokanoket—two of the most powerful groups in the Wampanoag Confederation. The alliance would become even stronger when her younger sister, Wootonekanuske, became the wife of Wamsutta's younger brother, Metacom. The two brothers then petitioned the Court at Plymouth Colony to take English names and were given those of Macedonian kings— Wamsutta becoming Alexander and Metacom becoming Philip.

A year after Weetamoo left Mattapoisett, Squeteague became involved in a dispute with a Pocasset sub-sachem over the rights to a shellfish bed, and he and his family were forced to leave their place of refuge. Sailing the *Nauset* south through Buzzards Bay, he followed the route he had taken by canoe to Noepe thirty years before, until he arrived at Poocuohhunkkunnah (Cuttyhunk) the outermost of the Elizabethan Islands that Gosnold had named for his queen, in 1602. There, he put in for the night before sailing to Noepe, where he and his family were greeted by friendly Aquinnah, who gave them food and shelter. Two days later, they proceeded along the southern coast of the island until they came to Great Harbor, home of the Reverend Thomas Mayhew, Jr, whose father had purchased Noepe from Sir Fernando Gorges.

Mayhew Junior had set out to Christianize the Native People living at Chappaquidick (separate island). One of his first converts was a man named Hiacoomes, who had become a preacher himself and had sent his orphaned nephew, Samuel to live with Mayhew Senior so that the boy could learn how to read and write and guard against the wiles of Satan. By the time Squeteague and his family arrived, however, young Samuel had discovered the joys of carnal knowledge with several of Mayhew Senior's female servants, and, unforgivably, with the young daughter of one of Mayhew's most devout English parishioners. This sort of conduct engendered deep disapproval on the part of the Mayhews, elder and younger, who threatened to banish Samuel from the Praying Town they had established. Greatly distressed, Hiacoomes came to Squeteague shortly after his arrival in the hope that a person of substance, such as the captain of a ship, might talk some sense into a boy who had committed such folly.

"What has he done that you should want me to remonstrate with him so severely?" Squeteague asked.

Hiacoomes could scarcely bring himself to describe his nephew's transgressions.

"He has lain with women," he said, in a whisper

Squeteague gave a shrug. "Isn't that the way of young men?"

"One of them was an English girl," Hiacoomes replied in a scandalized tone of voice.

Squeteague smiled and shook his head. "I fear I can't help you," he told Hiacoomes. "I once lay with an Englishwoman and enjoyed her fully."

Mortified, Hiacoomes scurried away. The next day, Squeteague received a visit from one of Mayhew's deacons, who advised that it might be best for him to leave Marthas Vineyard.

"We're devout followers of the Lord," he announced, "and cannot countenance anyone among us who would espouse the ways of Satan. However, the Reverend Mayhew believes in forgiveness and grants you permission to stay on condition that you earnestly repent and take instruction in the righteous teachings of the Bible."

Are we going to keep sailing from place to place?" Alawa asked, when they pulled anchor that afternoon, "or are we going somewhere to spend the winter?"

"We're going somewhere to spend the winter," said Squeteague, who, as evening arrived, steered the *Nauset* through an opening between two sand spits and into shallow water. "This is Popponessett Bay," he told Alawa and Epenow. "The bottom is alive with eels in the spring."

"How do you know this?" Epenow asked.

"I came here once with my father to spear them."

The territory around Popponesset Bay and adjacent Waquoit Bay was called Massipee (place near great ponds) and the people living there were called "South Sea Indians" by the colonists, because they inhabited a region on the south shore of the Cape. In fact, they were mostly remnants of the Nauset, Payomet, Cummaquid, and other Cape Cod bands whose members had been pushed from their lands by English settlers. They had retreated to Massipee (later Mashpee) where they had managed to carve out a tract of some ten thousand acres and keep it free of white encroachment thanks to becoming Christianized.

When Squeteague and his family arrived, the residents of Massipee welcomed them as kinfolk and helped pull the *Nauset* out of the water and onto a log cradle on the shore so it would be free of the ice that choked the bay each winter. They also helped build a sturdy wetu for the newcomers in a nearby hollow to withstand the cold winds that blew from the northeast. As things turned out, Squeteague, Alawa, and Epenow could not have found a better place to spend the winter. The two bays teemed not only with eels, but also with flounder, oysters, lobsters, soft-shell clams, quahogs, scallops, and waterfowl. Several rivers, all of them conduits for sea-run trout and alewives, emptied into the bay through fresh-water wetlands that provided home for muskrat and beaver. Raspberries, huckleberries, gooseberries, and strawberries grew in profusion along their banks. The ponds from which the rivers flowed provided habitat for bass, pickerel, perch, and bluegills. The forests held an abundance of deer and smaller game.

In the spring, Squeteague and Epenow cleared ground so that Alawa could plant corn, beans, and squash that helped sustain the family while the two men fished and hunted. In this way, two more years passed during which Epenow met a girl named

Chepi, whose parents, like many other people at Massipee, had been converted to Christianity by a preacher from Sandwich named William Leveridge, and were not pleased to discover that their daughter was going off into the forest with a boy. Indeed, the girl's father, a prominent man named Poponet, came to Squeteague to demand that he put an end to the affair.

"Your son is leading our daughter into the path of sin," he said.

Squeteague tried to humor the upset parent. "Since when do boys and girls their age not experiment with each other in the ways of love?"

"Since we received instruction in the ways of the Lord who forbids us to indulge in fornication at the risk of eternal damnation in a place of burning called hell."

"Let's not judge these children of ours too harshly," Squeteague replied. "They're only doing what young people have done since ancient times."

"These are new times," Poponet told him. "The Lord has come among us to spread His holy word and we must obey Him."

Squeteague realized there was no point in trying to reason with someone so rigid in doctrine and belief. "I'll talk to my son," he said, "but I can't command him to stop seeing your daughter. He's already a warrior who has killed enemies in combat. He's a man."

"I'll seek counsel from our preacher," Poponet declared. "Perhaps he can determine what should be done."

"Chepi and I wish to make our lives together," Epenow announced, when Squeteague told him about Poponet's visit.

"Are you willing to accept her religion?"

"We haven't talked about that," Epenow replied.

How like young people in the throes of passion not to consider the problems facing them, Squeteague thought. "Christianity is full of rules," he said. "Your life will be proscribed by them. The God of the Christians declares thou shalt not do this and that and a multitude of things. You'll be required to attend long church services on the day they call the Sabbath. You'll have to spend much time in prayer. You should talk about all this with Chepi.

That way there'll be no misunderstanding between you."

That night, Squeteague discussed the matter with Alawa. "But they're so young," she protested. "Why can't they wait a little longer?"

"Poponet and his wife believe that Epenow has led their daughter into sin. They want to put an end to it but, of course, they may agree to a marriage. For my part, I've told Epenow what to expect if he becomes a Christian. I've suggested he talk things over with Chepi so they can come to a decision about it."

The next day, Epenow went to Poponet and his wife to ask for their permission to marry Chepi. He told them that he was an experienced hunter and fisherman, who would be able to provide for their daughter in a manner that would satisfy them. When Poponet asked whether he would consent to become a Christian, Epenow replied that he and Chepi had discussed it as a possibility and promised to keep an open mind about it.

"I've consulted with our preacher," Poponet said. "He tells me I musn't agree to a marriage until you're converted to the ways of the Lord."

Crestfallen, Epenow and Chepi came before Squeteague and Alawa to tell them about Poponet's decision. "We've decided to run away," Epenow declared.

"You're too young and have no place to go," Squeteague pointed out. "It's best that you and Chepi stay with your mother and me."

"But we can't remain here in Massipee."

"That being the case, we'll find another place to live."

Alawa was reluctant to leave Massipee, where they had been so warmly welcomed, but she agreed that Epenow and Chepi should remain with the family until they found a suitable place to live. A few days later, they loaded the *Nauset* with their belongings and sailed from Waquoit Bay across the Sound to Nantucket (Faraway Island) where they learned that the inhabitants, like those in Massipee, were being converted to Christianity. As a result, they anchored for one night before proceeding north the next day past the treacherous shoals at Monomoy and up along the backshore of Cape Cod to the inlet at Nauset, which afforded the only safe anchorage in the long stretch of shoreline between the elbow of the Cape at Monomoy and its curled fingers at Meeshawn. Here, large combers broke upon a sandbar that lay across the entrance to the inlet, which required Squeteague to catch and ride consecutive cresting waves until the *Nauset* was deposited in calm water beyond their reach. At that point, he steered the sloop up a channel and past a vast expanse of salt marsh before coming to anchor opposite a headland covered with oak trees, which stood above a huge boulder that sat on the shore.

"This is where I was born and grew up," he told his wife and son. "Beyond the boulder lies a midden and a sacrifice heap. Out on the marsh is where the English captain and his men set upon my father and took him captive. When he shouted at me to run, I dodged some sailors who tried to catch me and raced through soft mud where they couldn't follow. Once I reached solid ground, I ran past the boulder and the brush heap and into the forest at the top of the hill. When I looked back, my father had disappeared. I never saw him again."

Seeing her husband filled with emotion, Alawa placed a hand on his arm. "If the sacrifice heap is still there, Epenow and I will throw sticks on it in thanks that you were able to save yourself," she said.

A short distance to the north Squeteague could make out the sand cliff Aspinet had stood upon when he had instructed him to run along the beach after the *Mayflower* as it sailed parallel to the coast. At that time, the peninsula had been covered with deep forest, but Squeteague could see that much of the land had now been cleared of trees. Cattle roamed in pastures that had replaced the woods. Ox-drawn wagons were making their way over a cart path that followed the ancient foot trail along the edge of the cliff to the Pamet River. Smoke curled into the sky from the chimneys of log cabins.

Squeteague had planned to sail as far as Meeshawn and to anchor in the same cove that had sheltered the *Mayflower* when it had made land, but at the sight of so much English habitation at the place where he had spent his childhood he decided not to venture farther north. On the next day, he sailed the *Nauset* out of the inlet and headed south to Monomoy, where he steered it across the same treacherous shoal that Champlain had navigated almost half a century earlier and into the harbor in which the French explorer had anchored. There, he encountered the elderly sachem Mattaquason, who remembered a dying Tisquantum telling Squeteague what had happened to his father.

"You have returned in a different time," the sachem said. "The English are now living everywhere among us."

"How did it happen so quickly?" Squeteague inquired.

"Their laws have made it easy for them to buy our land."

"But did their laws require you to sell your land?"

"They have rewarded us with things of value."

Kettles, hoes, and trinkets, Squeteague thought, and asked Mattaquason what he considered his land to be worth.

Mattaquason considered the question at some length, before telling his visitor that he had just sold four square miles of territory in Monomoy to an Englishman named Nickerson for the price of a rowboat.

Chapter Thirteen

As Squeteague pondered where to go next, he found himself in a quandary. Cape Cod was fast being taken over by colonists from Plymouth, and Boston remained out of the question because of the hostility he had provoked among the Puritan authorities there. Farther to the north lay the territory of the warlike Abenaki, allies of the French. In the other direction, Nantucket, Massipee, and Marthas Vineyard had fallen under the sway of English ministers preaching Christianity. The only remaining choice was a return to Narragansett territory.

Squeteague and his family had been gone from Pettaquamscutt Cove for more than two years and, by the time they returned, the danger posed by Uncas had diminished because the Mohegan sachem was beset with problems of his own caused by the growing number of English settlers who were pushing into the land surrounding the Thames estuary and the Connecticut River Valley. Meanwhile, colonists from Plymouth Colony had been making similar incursions into Narragansett and Pokanoket territory, prompting Pessacus and Ninigret to employ Squeteague's services again as a gunrunner, and to hold parleys with Alexander, who had become sachem of the Pokanoket upon the death of his father, Massasoit. A crisis occurred when the magistrates at Plymouth summoned Alexander to appear before them to explain why he had sold land without their permission. When he failed to show up, Governor Prence ordered him brought before the Court.

By a consummate combination of fate and irony, the man sent to fetch the son of Massasoit was none other than Major Josiah Winslow, the thirty-three-year-old son of Edward Winslow, who, forty years earlier, had nursed a dying Massasoit back to life and become his treasured friend. Winslow set out from Plymouth on a hot July morning, in 1662, accompanied by ten armed militiamen on horseback, and found Alexander, his wife, Weetamoo, and his interpreter, John Sassamon, eating breakfast at a fishing camp on Monponsett Pond. Through Sassamon, Winslow reminded the Pokanoket sachem that he had failed to appear in court when summoned, and informed him that he must now comply with the court's order. When Alexander objected to being treated in such an insulting manner, Winslow pointed a pistol at him and told him that if he refused to go he would be a dead man.

Winslow then marched Alexander and his entourage under a broiling sun to Marshfield, where the sachem fell ill. Indeed, Alexander became so feverish that his attendants were allowed to take him home, carrying him on their shoulders to the Titicut River and then by canoe to Montaup, where he died a few days later. Convinced that Plymouth authorities had poisoned her husband, Weetamoo vowed to avenge him, as did Alexander's younger brother, Metacomet, now known as Philip, who became sachem of the Pokanoket a short time later in the presence of nearly a thousand warriors who had streamed to Montaup from the far corners of the Wampanoag Confederation. A short time later, Philip appeared before the magistrates and denied convening a council of war to instigate an uprising, but made it clear that he considered himself to be on a par with King Charles II and not subject to the commands of Governor Prence. Henceforth, the colonists referred to him with the mocking appellation "King Philip."

Squeteague learned of Alexander's death and Philip's ascendancy to the sachemhood of the Pokanoket upon returning to Pettaquamscutt Cove with a shipload of muskets purchased from Dutch traders on the north shore of Long Island. The outraged reaction of the Pokanoket and other Wampanoag to Alexander's death held promise that the insurrection he had helped prepare for so many years might be at hand, but when he informed Alawa of the possibility that they might be forced to leave Pettaquamscutt if war should break out, she voiced her displeasure.

"Why should we even think of leaving? The hunting and fishing here are good and my garden has renewed itself. Epenow and Chepi are happy and, best of all, she is with child."

"She's told you this?"

"She doesn't need to tell me. I know because I'm a woman. Chepi will give birth when the alewives run."

Within a year of returning to Pettaquamscutt, Squeteague was not only providing guns for the Narragansett, the Pokanoket, and the Nipmuck, but also for an increasing number of tributary clans whose leaders were arming their warriors with view to a conflict that now seemed inevitable. His trips into Nipmuck country allowed him to observe the proselytizing activities of the Reverend John Eliot, who had undertaken strenuous efforts to convert the Nipmuck to Christianity and had established several so-called Praying Towns in their territory. Eliot was assisted in this endeavor by Daniel Gookin of Cambridge, who had been named by the General Court to serve as the first Superintendent of Indian Affairs for the Bay Colony, and to make sure that Praying Towns were situated and fortified in a manner that provided an outer ring of defense for the main Puritan settlement at Boston.

Gookin was empowered to approve the civil and religious leaders who were chosen in the Praying Towns, to make sure that Praying Indians observed the Sabbath, and to preside over a traveling court that settled disputes. It was during a hearing to determine how much land would be allotted for a Nipmuck Praying Town near Quinsigamond (Worcester) that Squeteague decided to confront him.

"Who gives the English the right to claim that they can issue us grants for the purpose of establishing settlements?" he demanded. "Has the land not been ours for the lives of our fathers, grandfathers, and forefathers as long as time can remember?"

Gookin regarded his interlocutor with the authority of the office that had been conferred on him. "This is a new time," he declared. "The present and future well-being of the Indians reqires that they receive land by grant from the English, who are a more powerful people than they."

Squeteague turned to the Christianized Natives who made up most of Gookin's audience. "Listen to how the English regard you," he advised. "Listen to this Superintendent of Your Affairs telling you how grateful you should be to receive from the English what is already yours and has been through the ages!"

Gookin's face flushed with rage. "If there were soldiers here, I'd order you whipped!"

Squeteague laughed with disdain at the blustering official. "Why not carry out the order yourself?"

Some weeks later, he attended a meeting in Rhode Island at which the Reverend Roger Williams, the avowed friend of the Narragansett, was addressing English settlers in Warwick regarding their desire to empty the town of its Native residents. "It's true that most Indians are not only treacherous, but also practice whoredom, witchcraft, blasphemy, and idolatry," Williams told his listeners. "I implore you, however, not to employ violence to rid yourself of their heathen presence. Keep in mind that you may knock out their brains and yet not make them sufficiently peaceable to surrender, just as some oxen will die before they rise, yet with gentle persuasion will rise and draw and do good service."

This was too much for Squeteague, who was furnishing guns to the Narragansett, Nipmuck, Pokonoket, and other Native People at a much faster rate than Williams and his fellow preachers were making converts among them. He had seen firsthand the extent to which the Native inhabitants of the region were smoldering with resentment over the vast land swindle that was taking place, the requirement that they obey English laws and customs, and the heavy fines being levied against them for trivial offenses. Approaching Williams at the end of the meeting, he reminded the elderly minister that they had met before the Pequot War to discuss the volatile situation that existed in the region.

"I remember you well," Williams replied. "What a pity that Sassacus and his Pequot did not desist from their depredations before the soldiers of the Bay Colony and Connecticut were forced to wreak such righteous vengeance upon them."

"Since you have such a good memory, perhaps you'll remember what I'm about to tell you," Squeteague said, through clenched teeth. "Remember that the people you and your English friends have been dispossessing are going to rise, but not to draw like oxen or do good service."

During a meeting between Pessacus, Ninigret, and agents from Plymouth Colony regarding property the colonists wished to purchase on the frontier, Squeteague encountered Philip for the first time, as well as John Sassamon, who had become Philip's secretary and interpreter. Sassamon had developed a reputation as a bridge between two cultures, but he was not trusted by the English, who wondered if his work for Philip might be corrupting him, or by the Pokanoket, who suspected that the colonists wanted him to convert Philip to Christianity.

"You and I would seem to have much in common," he told Squeteague. "We've been orphaned early in our lives, lived among the English, learned to speak their language, and accepted their religion."

"You're mistaken in the last," Squeteague replied. "I'm not a Christian."

"Then God be willing that you may one day see His light and become one."

Squeteague smiled at Sassamon, whom he judged to be at least fifteen years his junior. "At my age conversion becomes less and less of a possibility."

"God's grace can be acknowledged at any age, and the wisdom of the Gospel can be accepted until the very end of life."

Squeteague took note of Sassamon's tendency to pontificate. "Weren't you interpreting for Philip when he told Reverend Eliot that he cared no more for the Gospel than for a button on his coat?"

"Blasphemy must sometimes be overlooked." Sassamon replied.

"Especially when one is translating for a sachem," Squeteague observed, with a smile.

Once the meeting with the English agents got under way, Squeteague realized that Philip, who appeared to be in his middle twenties, depended on Sassamon more than he would have suspected, and that Sassamon was translating with greater bias toward the interests of the colonists than the young Pokanoket sachem seemed to realize. At one point, he flatly contradicted Sassamon when he softened Philip's demand that he be paid more money for a proposed land sale than he had been offered.

"Are you trying to usurp my position as interpreter for the sachem of the Pokanoket?" Sassamon demanded.

"I haven't the least desire to come between you and your employer," Squeteague replied, coolly. "My sole interest is that each of the parties understands with accuracy what the other is saying."

"We differ over a minor choice of words," Sassamon declared.

Squeteague decided not to challenge him further. He had made his point. Moreover, the Plymouth agents were demanding to know whether it was true that the three sachems had been holding secret meetings to form an alliance against the colonists. Philip, Pessacus, and Ninigret denied the allegations and demanded to know who had made them. At that point, Squeteague glanced at Sassamon, saw a flicker of unease in his eyes, and decided that the interpreter was a slippery character—someone engaged in playing both ends against the middle.

"Sassamon bears watching," he told Pessacus on the way back to Narragansett territory. "He's not to be trusted."

"That's Philip's problem," Pessacus replied.

"It could become yours if, as I suspect, he's an agent for the English."

The following year, Squeteague, who had become the grandfather of a three-year-old boy named Quannto, reached the age of sixty. He was still physically and mentally strong—not the swift runner he had once been, but not greatly diminished in stamina as was the case with many Wampanoag, who lived without seriously impaired capacity until they had attained the age of seventy or more.

By this time, Philip had embarked upon a series of land sales, much as his father had done, except for a far different reason—to purchase guns for use in an uprising against the English. In order to raise money for weapons, he sold land near his father's home at Sowams on which English settlers established the town of Swansea. He also sold the English a large tract of land in his wife Wootonekanuske's ancestral home at Mattapoisett, where her sister, Weetamoo, and her father, Corbitant, had lived. Not surprisingly, Sassamon wrote up and witnessed many of the deeds that recorded these transactions.

No one knew better than Squeteague why Philip was selling land. As gunrunner for the Narragansett, he was the most logical purchasing agent of muskets for the young Pokanoket sachem, who wished to acquire a store of them without tipping off the English authorities at Plymouth and Boston. For this reason, Philip invited him to a meeting at Sowams to negotiate the terms of a contract. It was the first time that Squeteague had the occasion to speak alone with the Pokanoket sachem, and his impression of the man was mixed. Shorter in height and slighter in build than his father, Philip did not possess the dignified bearing of Massasoit, but showed himself to be crafty by nature, quick to take offense, and highly suspicious of the English, whom he blamed for having caused his older brother's death. He was also vain. Unlike his father, who had dressed simply, he wore a buckskin cloak adorned with beads and a large belt of the finest wampum, and took pleasure in parading through the streets of Boston, where he drew considerable curiosity on the part of its residents. In addition, he surrounded himself with an entourage of advisors, who addressed him in terms that approached servility. For all that, Squeteague recognized him as a man of intelligence and purpose.

"I want you to provide me with flintlocks," Philip said at the outset. "I'm told they're much superior to the matchlocks with which many of the English settlers and soldiers are armed."

"That's true," replied Squeteague, who recommended flintlocks to his customers because they were faster to load, more reliable to fire, and easier to carry than the older matchlocks.

"I'm also told that you have the ability to procure them in large numbers?"

"I do," Squeteague replied. "The Dutch have recently surrendered Nieuw Amsterdam to the English, but Dutch arms dealers continue to sell flintlocks to the Mahican, Mohawk, and Wappinger in the Hudson River valley, as well as to the Massapequa living on Long Island. I'll be able to purchase them at ports along the river and on the island, and deliver them to you at Montaup Bay."

Philip smiled at the prospect. "The English have no idea that the money they're paying me for the land I'm selling them will one day be returned in the form of powder and shot. Rest assured you'll be rewarded for every flintlock you bring me."

"I do it not only for money, but also for the opportunity of stopping the invaders from taking more of our land."

Philip regarded him intently. "Is that why my father held you in such esteem?"

Squeteague realized that he was being tested in a complicated and roundabout way, because Philip must know about the falling out that had taken place between him and Massasoit. "Your father was a great leader," he replied, carefully. "He believed that peace with the English was in the best interest of his people, especially while his enemy Canonicus was alive. I, however, believed that when the English burned the Pequot fort at Missituck and the helpless men, women, and children inside, their true intent toward us had been carved in stone for all to see."

"That happened before I was born and I never heard my father speak of it. In any event, do you agree that the time is at hand for us to rise up against them?"

Squeteague contemplated his response. "I tried in vain to persuade Sassacus not to go to war with the English before he and his Pequot had made allies among their neighbors and acquired muskets to replace their bows and arrows. I counseled Miantonomo not to attack Uncas and the Mohegan until he was sure of victory. Since then, I have observed Pessacus and Ninigret capitulate time and again to the demands of the English, even to the point of forcing their neighbors to provide wampum to pay the fines the colonists have imposed upon them. What I have not seen during this whole time is a leader who can forge the strong alliance of Native People necessary to ensure a successful insurrection."

Philip stiffened. "You are in the presence of one," he declared. "Or do you think that I, Philip of the Pokanoket and son of Massasoit, am not capable of leading such an uprising?"

Squeteague found himself confronting the Pokanoket sachem's grandiosity head on. "If you can persuade the Narragansett and the Nipmuck to become your allies and resolve to wait until you and they are well armed, you'll have a chance of success. Otherwise, I fear you cannot prevail, because your English enemy is too powerful and numerous."

Philip responded soberly. "I will not be able to control my warriors much longer. They bristle with the desire to avenge themselves against the colonists who humiliate us at every opportunity by taking our land, imposing their laws and religion on us, and allowing their cattle and hogs to graze on our corn and beans."

"I will do my best to supply you with the flintlocks you need," Squeteague assured him. "I will also counsel Pessacus and Ninigret to agree to an alliance in the event of war. Both are cautious men, however, and may require considerable persuasion."

"So you believe in the necessity of an uprising, after all!"

"I believe that it must come soon or that it will never come," Squeteague replied.

Chapter Fourteen

Over the next several years, Squeteague continued to sail the *Nauset* back and forth through Long Island Sound, carrying weapons to the Narragansett at Pettaquamscutt, the Pokanoket at Montaup Bay, and the Nipmuck, to whom he delivered his cargo at isolated coves on the Merruasquamack River, which flowed between Massachusetts and territory to the north. It was during a delivery to the Nipmuck that he encountered a sachem named Mattaump, who informed him that he had become known among the Quabaug for a reason he found disheartening, to say the least.

A fierce advocate for going to war with the colonists, Mattaump related the reason for Squeteague's notoriety with relish. "Massasoit, who lived among us in his last years, grew tiresome by reminding us over and over to keep peace with the English," he recalled. "Then he discovered that, instead of heeding his advice, we had been stockpiling muskets so we could rise up and drive the invaders from our land. He also learned that it was you who had been supplying us with many of these weapons. At that point, he declared that you had betrayed him in spite of his warnings, and called on the Great Manitou to punish you and your descendants forever. Afterward, he took to his wetu and remained there until he died."

Squeteague found himself too dispirited to respond. He had imagined that his differences with Massasoit had been acknowledged, if not resolved, during their final meeting at Sowams when the sachem had afforded him refuge, allowed him to receive treatment for the wounds inflicted on him by his Mohegan attackers, and arranged his return to the Narragansett with a message warning Pessacus and Ninigret not to go to war against the colonists. To learn after all this time that the man he considered his surrogate father had placed a curse on him and gone to his death reviling him struck a bitter blow. With a heavy heart, he ordered the anchor and sails of the *Nauset* to be raised and, hastened by a following wind and current, made for the sea.

Meanwhile, Philip's wife, Wootonekanuske, had borne him a son, and Philip had asked Sassamon, who had become his secetary as well as interpreter, to write a will that would leave his lands to his new heir. However, instead of writing the will as Philip intended, Sassamon contrived to leave the lands to himself, and when Philip discovered the deception, the secretary fled to safety in Plymouth territory, where he became a preacher to Native converts living at Nemasket near Assawompsett Pond.

By 1670, Philip was selling more and more land to the colonists and using the proceeds to enlarge his growing store of flintlocks. During this time, Squeteague witnessed a number of suspect transactions the English were making in Nipmuck territory west of Boston. Under Massachusetts Bay law, colonists were required to petition the General Court for a grant of land and the right to build a settlement on it. If their petition was approved, they were awarded a grant—usually about eight miles square—and were then required to secure and pay for a deed from the sachems owning the property. As usual, when the sachems affixed their marks to such deeds, they did so with the understanding that the land was to be occupied jointly and used in common, not realizing that the English settlers, fur traders, and speculators who signed the deeds considered the land to be theirs. In this way, thousands of acres were transferred to English ownership over a period of twenty years by unsuspecting Nipmucks and other Native People.

Many of these land purchases were approved by Daniel Gookin, who had been named by the General Court to facilitate the establishment of new townships and settlements. In this capacity, he helped to draw up a purchase and sale agreement, in 1674, for an eight-square-mile tract of land at Quinsigamond that was signed by two Nipmuck sachems, John and Solomon. In return, Gookin and some associates agreed to pay the sachems twelve pounds, and make an advance payment of two coats and four yards of cloth valued at twenty-six shillings.

While conducting a tour of Nipmuck territory a few months later, Gookin informed John and Solomon in the presence of Squeteague, who had come there to deliver weapons, that the agreement they had signed amounted to an outright sale of land from which they could be evicted.

"You're a thief!" Squeteague shouted. "Your interpretation of the transaction John and Solomon made in good faith is dishonest!"

Unable, as many of his compatriots were, to distinguish one Native person from another, Gookin seemed to have forgotten that he and Squeteague had confronted each other before. "Are you aware of who I am and the office I hold?" he demanded. "Do you presume to question His Majesty's Superintendent of Indian Affairs?"

"I'm aware of who you are," replied Squeteague, who knew that Gookin had carried out a sentence handed down by the Massachusetts General Court condemning Sarah Aahton, a Praying Indian from Natick, who had taken a lover after being abused by her husband, to be whipped and stand on the gallows in Boston with a noose around her neck. "You're the brave fellow who punishes women by having them beaten and humiliated."

I n March of the following year, tensions rose on the frontier when Philip led a group of warriors from Montaup to the nearby English settlement at Swansea to demonstrate his disapproval of colonial expansion into Pokanoket territory. In an attempt to defuse the situation, the Plymouth magistrates invited him to meet with a group of colonial delegates at the Town of Taunton. Philip, in turn, asked Squeteague, whom he trusted as his gunrunner, to attend the meeting as his interpreter and witness. Things went poorly for the Pokonoket sachem, who was forced to sign a treaty in which he acknowledged fault for intimidating the settlers at Swansea, agreed to surrender all Pokanoket guns, and guaranteed not to sell land or go to war without the permission of the governor of Plymouth. He also agreed to pay a fine of one hundred pounds, to kill and deliver seven wolves each year, and to become a subject of Plymouth Colony.

"Not a single flintlock shall be turned over," he told Squeteague through clenched teeth as he put his mark on the document placed before him. "No permission to sell land will be sought, not a penny paid, nor a wolf killed and delivered. As for these English fools imagining that I might become their subject, it's a wonder their scalps don't itch in anticipation of what I have in store for them."

When Squeteague returned to Narragansett territory, he assured Pessacus and his nephew, Canonchet, the son of Miantonomo, who had by now assumed a leading role in Narragansett affairs, that Philip had signed the treaty to buy time so that he could enlarge his arsenal of guns. He also told them that new decrees issued by the Commissioners strictly forbade English arms dealers from selling muskets to the Native People of the region. As a result, his business began to thrive as never before, and his counsel on military matters was sought by Pessacus and Canonchet as they devised a strategy to defend their homeland in a conflict that now seemed inevitable.

The advice he gave was invariably the same.

"Make an alliance with the Pokanoket and the Nipmuck so that in the event of war they will come to your assistance. At the same time, make sure you have enough flintlocks and gunpowder hidden away so that if the English invade your country you won't run out of weapons or ammunition."

"Why should we wait for them to invade?" a young Narragansett warrior demanded. "Why shouldn't we fall upon them, kill their men, and take their women and children captive?"

"There are many thousands of English now," Squeteague told him. "They outnumber us greatly. They have ships that can carry hundreds of soldiers and provisions to the shores of Narragansett Bay. How can you be sure of defeating them?"

"By filling their hearts with fear," the warrior replied.

Squeteague smiled. "Before you were born, I heard the same thing from a sachem of the Pequot named Sassacus. That was before the English invaded the territory of the Pequot, set fire to their fort at Missituck, and burned up everyone inside—men, women, and children alike."

"Are you suggesting that we not go to war?"

"I'm suggesting that you don't go to war until you have sufficient weapons and a strategy that will give you a chance of winning."

By now Squeteague suspected that Ninigret, the aging sachem of the Niantic, had decided to keep his people out of any conflict that might flare up between the English and the Narragansett. Crafty old Ninigret has opted to wait and see how the wind blows, he thought. Knowing that Pessacus and Canonchet were trying to make up their minds about joining Philip, he asked them what plan they had for defending the Narragansett homeland in the event of an English invasion.

It was Canonchet who answered. Tall, commanding, and confident like his father, Miantonomo, he wore a silver-laced coat, an embroidered mantle of wampum slung over his shoulders, leggings of buckskin fringed with tufts of hair and feathers, and moccasins decorated with beads. "We're building a large fort in the middle of the Great Swamp," he said. "There, we'll shelter our women and children and do battle."

Years of fighting against Uncas and the Mohegan had made Pessacus cautious. "What do you suggest?" he asked Squeteague.

"I recommend building a series of forts that will make it possible to retreat from one to the other, finding muskets and forges for repairing them, as well as gunpowder and food in each. In that way your women and children will be safe while your warriors conduct a series of ambushes to delay, weaken, and ultimately wear down your enemy."

It was Sassamon who informed Plymouth Colony Governor Josiah Winslow that Philip had been meeting secretly with his Narragansett counterparts. By this time—the winter of 1675—Squeteague had turned seventy and Sassamon was in his late fifties. The older man appeared to be living quietly with his wife and family at Pettaquamscutt Cove on Narragansett Bay, and the younger preaching the Gospel to Praying Indians living at Nemasket. In reality, Squeteague was using the *Nauset* to run guns to the Narragansett, Pokanoket, and Nipmuck, while Sassamon was spying in behalf of the authorities at Plymouth.

In late January, Sassamon set out in the snow to the colony, fifteen miles away, and warned Governor Josiah Winslow that Philip was planning to mount an insurrection against the English. He also told Winslow that he believed his life to be in danger and that Philip would have him murdered if his warning was discovered. However, Winslow paid little heed to Sassamon's words because, as the Reverend Increase Mather would later write, "they had originated with an Indian and one cannot believe them even when they speak the truth."

A week or so after his meeting with Winslow, some Natives came across Sassamon's body under the ice at Assawompsett Pond. Lying on top of the ice were his hat, musket, and a brace of ducks. It appeared that, while crossing the pond on his way home from a hunting trip, he had fallen through a soft spot in the ice and drowned. The people who found his body had taken it to shore and buried it. When the identity of the dead man was discovered, a coroner's jury was ordered to conduct an exhumation, which determined that Sassamon's neck had been broken and that his death had not occurred by drowning. Because of Sassamon's previous allegations, Philip was an obvious suspect. However, the Pokanoket sachem appeared voluntarily before the Plymouth court at the end of February and denied that he had anything to do with Sassamon's death, or that he had been plotting to rebel against the colonists. Although unconvinced of his innocence, the court had no firm evidence to disprove his denial and little choice except to let him go.

In April, an Assawompsett named Patuckson, who claimed to be an eyewitness, came forward and declared that he had seen three Pokanoket men kill Sassamon. As a result, the court brought a charge of murder against them, declaring that they had "willfully and with malice aforethought killed John Sassamon by twisting his neck until he was dead, and then attempted to hide the crime by casting his body through a hole in the ice of the pond."

Philip tried to persuade the court to transfer the three defendants to his custody, on the grounds that its members had no jurisdiction to handle a case that constituted an internal problem of the Pokanoket, but colonial authorities insisted on jurisdiction because the alleged crime had taken place in territory claimed by Plymouth Colony.

The trial of the three men began in the first week of June and was attended by Squeteague, who was sent by Philip to witness the proceedings. It was presided over by Governor Winslow and seven assistants and heard by a jury of twelve Englishmen and, according to Plymouth authorities, "six unpredjudiced Indians," from nearby Praying Villages. The first witness to testify was the alleged eyewitness named Patuckson, who happened to owe a large gambling debt to one of the defendants. A second witness had not seen the crime committed but only heard about it second-hand from Patuckson. Additional evidence admitted in the proceedings included the claim that, when the court ordered one of the defendants to stand next to Sassamon's dead body, it began "bleeding afresh, as if it had been newly slain, although it had been buried a considerable time before."

Squeteague could hardly believe his ears as he listened to ghoulish superstition being treated as truth. Indeed, it was all he could do to prevent himself from getting to his feet and speaking out against the mock justice that permeated the proceedings. It would have been a futile gesture in any case. Under English common law, felony defendants were not permitted the benefit of counsel, or the opportunity to cross-examine witnesses, or even to address the jury.

At the conclusion of the trial, the jury unanimously found all three defendants guilty of the murder of John Sassamon and sentenced them to death. This verdict flew in the face of a general principle in colonial law that required a minimum of two witnesses for conviction in a capital case. Nevertheless, the three men were hanged at the end of the week, but only two of them were executed because the rope broke when youngest one was dropped from the scaffold. In a desperate to save his life, he declared that he had merely been an onlooker when the other two defendants had killed Sassamon. However, the ancient English tradition of granting a reprieve to a condemned man after a failed execution was not accorded in his case. A month later, he was shot to death by a firing squad.

Appalled by the injustice of what had taken place, Squeteague told Philip that the trial and its aftermath had been a travesty and a farce.

"It's the worst possible outcome," the sachem said. "It means I will no longer be able to control my warriors who want any excuse to fight the English. I had hoped to delay going to war for a few more months when we might have stored more flintlocks and made firmer alliances with our neighbors, but I haven't any choice now except to carry out the wishes of those I lead."

Squeteague could look back nearly forty years to the time he had warned the prideful Sassacus not to seek revenge against the Puritans until his warriors were better armed, and to a similar warning he had given the impetuous Miantonomo before his ill-fated attack on Uncas and the Mohegan. Since then he had done his best to encourage unity among the Native People of the region and to provide them with the muskets that would enable them to rise up against the English invaders, only to learn now that these preparations might prove insufficient for them to prevail.

In this mood, he reflected on the admonition against going to war that Massasoit had issued from the beginning, the curse the sachem had called down upon him for supplying weapons that would make such a war possible, and the irony of fate which decreed that Philip would now lead the Pokanoket into a conflict that ran directly counter to his father's deepest wish.

Philip was correct in his assessment of the situation that faced him. The execution of the three defendants set the combustible Pokanoket Nation on fire to such a degree that it soon became impossible for him to control his warriors. A week later, he sent emissaries to Awashonks, squaw sachem of the Sakonnet, who lived in the nearby village of Sogkonate (later Little Compton), to ask her to join him in making war against the colonists. Awashonks honored her guests by holding a ceremonial dance in their honor in which she took strenuous part. At the same time, she sent a messenger to inform Benjamin Church, an English neighbor, about Philip's proposal and invite him to attend the dance.

Upon arriving at the festivities, Church found his hostess to be in a "muck of sweat" as a result of her exertions, and proceeded to deny the claim made by Philip's emissaries that Plymouth Colony was planning to attack her. He told Awashonks that the English intended no harm to the Sakonnet, and advised her to keep on good terms with them. For her part, Awashonks told Church to go to Plymouth and inform the authorities there of her good faith. She assured him that her warriors would guard his house while he was gone.

On his way to Plymouth, Church passed through the territory of the Pocasett, where he learned that Philip had held a war dance at Montaup attended by hundreds of Wampanoag warriors. When he arrived at the colony, he relayed this information to Governor Winslow, who promptly sought and received assurance from Governor John Leverett of Massachusetts that he could count on the Bay Colony's support in the event of hostilities.

On June 17, the Quaker deputy governor of Rhode Island, John Easton, and four other men rowed across Narragansett Bay to Montaup to meet with Philip in an effort to persuade him to accept arbitration of his differences with Plymouth Colony. Among the party was Squeteague, who had been asked by Easton to serve as his interpreter. If Philip was surprised to see his gunrunner in the company of some peaceloving Quakers, he gave no sign of it, having come to consider Squeteague as indispensable in his plan to mount an insurrection against the English.

"Our business in coming here is to make sure that you neither suffer nor commit any wrong," Easton declared at the outset. "Our most fervent desire is that your quarrel with Plymouth be decided peacefully and not by fighting, which is the way of dogs."

Philip agreed that fighting was not the best way to resolve differences, but inquired how Easton proposed to bring about justice.

"Through intermediaries," Easton replied. "In this way, the Pokanoket might choose the sachem of a distant tribe and the English might select the governor of New York—neither of them being a direct party to their dispute—who would hear the complaints of each side and act as peacemakers to find fair resolution."

"I haven't heard of this way of settling quarrels," Philip said, "but I think it's too late in any case. When the English first came to our shores, my father was a great man and the English were as a little child. My father made peace with them and gave them corn and showed them how to plant it. He provided them with land to live on. He made every effort to make them welcome. The English should do to us now as we did then when we were stronger than they. Instead, they have replied to our kindness by doing us great harm. When my older brother became sachem, they seized and held him until he took strangely sick and died. Since I became sachem, they have overrun our land with their farms and cattle. You should know that I'm determined not to see the day I have no country."

Squeteague's estimation of Philip soared as he translated words that recounted the history of the previous half century in a manner that was succinct and powerful. For the rest of the morning and much of the afternoon, he continued to interpret as Easton and his Quaker companions pleaded for Philip to accept arbitration, and the Pokanoket sachem insisted that the English could not be trusted.

By way of emphasizing his suspicion, Philip referred to the recent trial at Plymouth. "If twenty honest Indians testified that an Englishman had done them wrong, the English would disregard it, but if a dishonest Indian testified against one of his brothers the English would consider it sufficient."

While rowing back across the bay, Easton wondered aloud why Philip had rejected his offer with such vehemence.

Squeteague looked at him with disbelief. "Do you imagine he has any choice? His warriors are furious because the colonists build settlements on their land, treat them as inferiors, and make them subject to their laws. Now the colonists have executed three of his followers without proof of murder or regard for Wampanoag custom, but only with regard for their own law, to which the Wampanoag are not bound. Didn't you hear his final words?"

"Yes," said Easton, with a sigh, "and we know them to be true."

A few days later, seventy-five-year-old Roger Williams made a final attempt to act as peacemaker. He met with Philip on the shore of Narragansett Bay near Providence, and warned the Pokanoket sachem that he was leading his people to extermination. He compared the Wampanoag to a canoe about to be capsized on a stormy sea of English fury.

"My canoe is already overturned," Philip replied.

Part Four

WAR

Major battles, ambushes,

X Native American Attacks

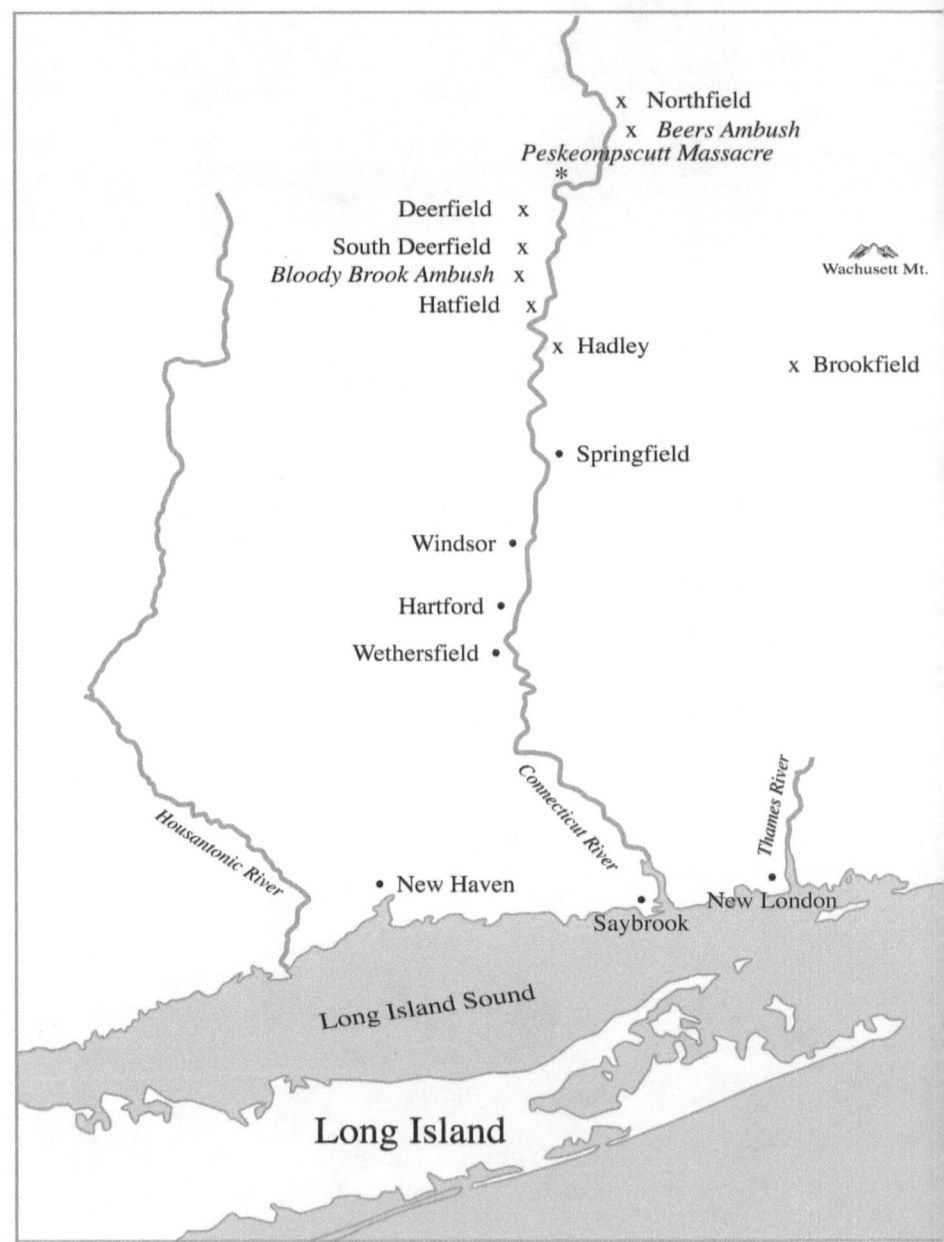

x Northfield

x *Beers Ambush*

Peskeompscutt Massacre

*

Deerfield x

South Deerfield x

Bloody Brook Ambush x

Hatfield x

Wachusett Mt.

x Hadley

x Brookfield

• Springfield

Windsor •

Hartford •

Wethersfield •

Connecticut River

Thames River

Housantonic River

• New Haven

• New London

•
Saybrook

Long Island Sound

Long Island

and massacres in King Philip's War

* English Attacks

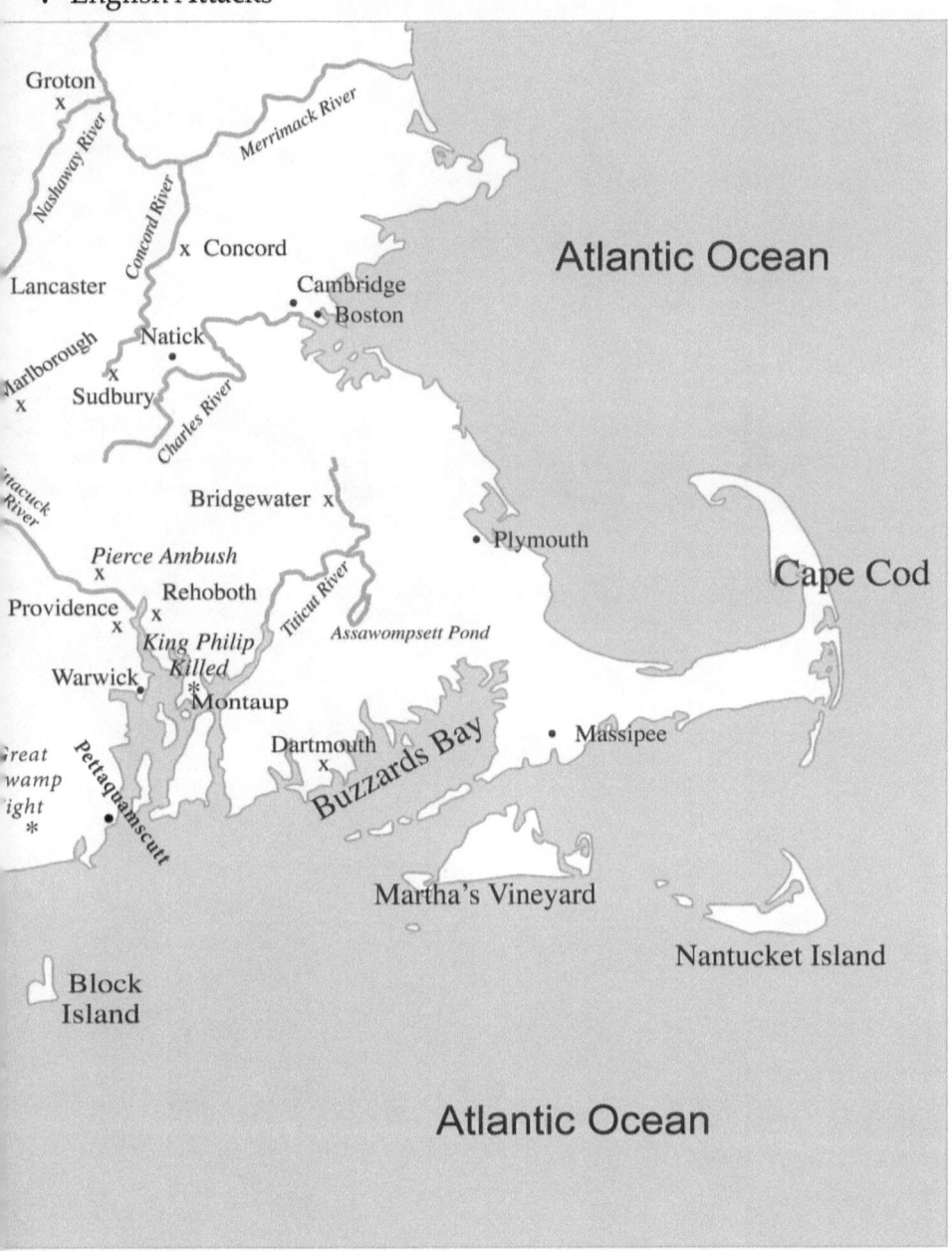

Chapter Fifteen

Squeteague learned that war had broken out from a runner who arrived from Pokanoket territory to inform Pessacus and other Narragansett sachems of the news. John Easton later described the initial event that occurred on June 23 at Kickemuit, a small English settlement near Montaup, which had been evacuated a few days earlier by fearful inhabitants, who had taken refuge in a fortified garrison house owned by the Reverend John Miles:

> Some Indians were seen looting one of the abandoned dwellings by an old man and a boy, who shot at and wounded one of them as he ran away. When other Indians came to the garrison with the news that their companion had died and to ask why he had been shot, the boy shrugged and replied that it was of no concern to him. Some settlers who had taken refuge there tried to explain that these were the idle words of a young and foolish boy, but the Indians were angered and hurried away.

The boy's nonchalant reply had immediate consequences. On

the following day, Pokanoket warriors killed him and the old man, as well as eight other settlers in nearby Swansea. By this time, Benjamin Church, who had been made a captain by Governor Winslow, had led a small force of Plymouth soldiers to the vicinity, but found himself heavily outnumbered by Pokanoket warriors and was obliged to hole up in Miles garrison until reinforcements arrived four days later.

Meanwhile, on June 26, a total eclipse of the moon took place over New England—an event regarded as ominous by Natives and English alike. For the 18,000 Pokanoket, Nipmuck, Narragansett, and other Native inhabitants of the region, it portended a time when war would come and many people would die. For the 60,000 colonial inhabitants of the area, it heightened awareness of divine disfavor. Governor Winslow declared a day of fasting and humiliation in which "we humble ourselves before the Lord for all those sins whereby we have provoked Him to interrupt our peace and comfort." As if to salve a troubled conscience, he also claimed, "before the present troubles broke out, the English did not possess one square foot of land in this colony but what was fairly obtained by honest purchase from its Indian proprietors."

The black night of the eclipse fell upon a column of English militimen who were marching into Pokanoket territory to relieve Church at Miles garrison and provide defense for towns under threat of attack by Philip's forces. Among them was a group of multinational pirates who had been captured off the coast of Maine by a privateer named Captain Samuel Mosley and reprieved from hanging if they agreed to fight in behalf of the Massachusetts Bay Colony. When Mosley and the pirates arrived at Kickemuit, they found eighteen houses burned to the ground and the heads of slain settlers mounted English-style on poles by the roadside. A few miles away, they came upon Philip's village at Sowams and found it deserted. The Pokanoket sachem and his followers had fled by canoe across Montaup Bay and joined the Pocasset, who were led by his dead brother's widow, Weetamoo.

Mosely's presence so close to Narraganset territory posed a

grave concern to Squeteague, who had been sent word by Cockenoe that Puritan authorities had learned of his role as gunrunner for the insurgents, placed a bounty on his head, and assigned Mosely and his pirates to kill him. Knowing that Mosely harbored a visceral hatred for Native People, Squeteague decided to deal with him before he could bring harm to his family at Pettaquamscutt. Without telling Alawa, he traveled north to a large swamp near the mouth of the Titicut River, where Philip and Weetamoo had taken refuge with several hundred Pokanoket and Pocasset warriors and their women and children. There, he persuaded the Pokanoket sachem that he could bait Mosely and his pirates into making a frontal assault on the swamp, thus giving his warriors a chance to inflict heavy casualties on them. On the evening of July 18, he approached Mosely's hilltop camp and announced his presence.

"Heeyaa, Mosely! Come out of your filthy hole and find the heathen Squeteague, who's twice your age yet can't be killed by any such vermin as you!"

As Squeteague expected, Mosely and a giant Dutch pirate named Cornelius Anderson, accompanied by two dozen companions and a pack of ferocious dogs, came boiling out of the encampment like a swarm of angry hornets. They pursued Squeteague to the edge of the swamp, where he turned and, raising his tomahawk, gave a piercing whoop of derision before plunging into it. As he had predicted, the pirates followed him and soon lost a number of men to a withering fusillade as they tried to come to grips with an enemy armed with flintlocks who used the swamp and the thick leaves of its trees as shelter and camouflage. Realizing that he had been tricked, Mosely gave the command to retreat, thus ensuring that he and Anderson would live to fight another day.

A few days later, Philip and Weetamoo, together with their warriors, women, and children, forded the Titicut River at low tide and escaped into the forest. The two sachems and their followers were pursued by other English soldiers accompanied by fifty Mohegan under the command of Uncas's son, Owaneco, who caught up with them in the Nipsachuck swamp northwest of Providence. During the ensuing fight, thirty Pokanoket and Pocasset warriors were killed and fifty surrendered. Among the dead was Nimrod, one of Philip's chief captains. While the Mohegan were looting the possessions of the slain warriors, Weetamoo led two hundred of her followers south to sanctuary among the Narragansett, while Philip and the remnants of his forces straggled north into Nipmuck territory.

When Alawa found out why Squeteague had left their home, she remonstrated with him. "Haven't you done your share in this war? You're too valuable to your family to pretend that you're still a warrior. From now on leave the fighting to younger men."

Meanwhile, Philip's brother-in law Tuspaquin, better known as the Black Sachem, attacked and destroyed the English settlement at Middleborough, just north of Assawompsett Pond, while Totoson, another sachem loyal to Philip, burned houses at Dartmouth on Buzzards Bay, killing six of its inhabitants. And on July 14, Nipmuck warriors led by the sachem Matoonas, whose son had been falsely accused of murder by the English and hanged on Boston Common four years earlier, fell upon the town of Mendon, thirty miles southwest of Boston, killing another six people.

Squeteague learned of these raids from Pokanoket and Pocasset refugees who fled to Narragansett territory seeking asylum. With conflict spreading across New England, he decided to keep his family with the Narragansett, the most powerful people of the region, but was disappointed to discover that Pessacus and Canochet had failed to heed his advice on how to defend themselves in the event of invasion, and were limiting their military options by building a single and supposedly impregnable fortress in the confines of the Great Swamp, which lay ten miles inland from Squeteague's home at Pettaquamscutt Cove.

That the war would be fought to the bitter end and without quarter he had little doubt, especially on being told by the captain of a Dutch ship he encountered while sailing in Long Island Sound that, after being assured of their safety if they surrendered, one hundred and fifty Pocasset men, women, and children had been taken to Plymouth, transported from there to Cadiz, in Spain, and sold into slavery.

Cadiz—the same place his father would have been sold had he not been slain at sea by his English abductor, Captain Thomas Hunt.

Worried about the safety of his family, Squeteague continued to keep a close watch on the progress of the war and especially on the whereabouts of Mosely. Following the raid on Mendon, Governor Leverett of the Bay Colony demanded that the Nipmuck hand over Matoonas and his accomplices, and sent Captain Edward Hutchinson deep into Nipmuck territory with twenty-five mounted troopers to force compliance. Hutchinson was told by the residents of Brookfield that the Nipmuck had gathered at a place called Menemesit on the Ware River, about ten miles away. When he approached Menemesit the next day, he and his men were ambushed by more than a hundred warriors led by Matoonas and Mattaump, the Nipmuck sachem who had told Squeteague about the curse Massasoit had laid on him. Eight Englishmen were killed and five others were wounded, including Hutchinson, who later died of his injuries. Native guides led the survivors back to Brookfield, where they and more than sixty inhabitants of the town barricaded themselves in a tavern and endured a two-day siege until help arrived in the form of Mosely and his band of pirates.

Squeteague and other advocates of the insurgency took heart from the events of September, word of which spread quickly among the Native People. On September 2, warriors of the Nipmuck and River People attacked the town of Deerfield and killed seven men from nearby Northfield who were working in fields outside their fort. Two days later, they ambushed Captain Richard Beers and thirty-six soldiers who were on their way to evacuate the garrison at Northfield, killing Beers and twenty-one of his men.

Two weeks after that, a group of five hundred Nipmuck and Po-kanoket waylaid Captain Thomas Lathrop and eighty troops as they were fording a stream called Muddy Brook while escorting grain carts from Deerfield to Hatfield. Lathrop and sixty-three of his men were killed. Muddy Brook ran red with their blood and was known from then on as Bloody Brook.

During October, the colonists abandoned their settlements at Deerfield, Northfield, and Brookfield. By the end of November, the Nipmuck, Pokanoket, Nashaway, Quabaug, Wabaquasset, and other bands retired to remote camps in the forests near Wachusett Mountain, where they prepared to spend the coming winter. Meanwhile, Canonchet and Cornman, a Niantic sachem representing Ninigret, were summoned to Boston, where they signed a treaty requiring them to hand over Pocasset refugees. The authorities of the Bay Colony were especially interested in making a captive of the squaw sachem Weetamoo.

The deadline passed with not a single Pocasset surrendered. By now, the Puritans had become suspicious to the point of paranoia regarding the intentions of the Narragansett, whom they suspect-ed of preparing to enter the war on the side of the Nipmuck and the Pokanoket. Indeed, sentiment against the Native People was running so high among the colonists that they interned several hundred Praying Indians on Deer Island and Long Island in Boston Harbor. There, during the bleak winter of 1676, deprived of shelter and blankets, the hapless Natives struggled to survive by digging clams on frozen windswept mudflats, and died in droves of starvation, disease, and exposure to the elements.

Captain Mosely personified the attitude of many English set-tlers toward the insurgents. On one occasion, he allowed his dogs to tear apart an elderly squaw captive. On another, he disobeyed orders and destroyed the wetu of some friendly Pennacook who lived by the Merruasquamack River. He also arrested a group of fifteen Praying Indians, who had committed no offense, roped them together by the neck, and marched them to Boston to be tried on suspicion of having attacked an English settlement. All of the defendants were acquitted. Not surprisingly, Mosely was feared and hated by both Praying Indians and the Native warriors he encountered on the battlefield.

Squeteague, of course, had reason to be especially wary of him. During the autumn, he made several voyages in the *Nauset* to the western end of Long Island Sound to procure muskets from Dutch traders for Pessacus and Canonchet, who were stock-piling weapons in the fortress they had built in the Great Swamp. In the middle of November, he learned that authorities of the United Colonies were not only demanding that the Narragansett turn over Pokanoket and Pocasset refugees, but were also rais-ing a large army in which Mosely would serve as a commander. At that point, Squeteague decided the time had come for him to move his family to safety.

"I'm taking them to Noepe," he told Canonchet. "The Aquin-nah have offered us sanctuary there."

"You'll find yourselves among Christianized Indians who love the Englishman's God," Canonchet said, with contempt.

Squeteague gave a shrug. "If Mosely and his pirates or the En-glish and their Mohegan allies find us in your country, we'll be as good as dead."

"You're welcome to join us at our fort in the Great Swamp."

Squeteague shook his head. "I fear that your fort cannot with-stand the assault of a large army."

After a moment of silence, Canonchet said, "I won't try to per-suade you further. You were a friend of my father and have always shown yourself to be a friend of his people. Go to Noepe in peace and with the respect of your Narragansett brothers. However, I have a final request to make of you. I ask that you make one more trip to Long Island so we can be sure to have enough muskets if the English decide to attack us in the swamp."

That evening, a twisting ribbon of smoke curled from a fire that warmed the wetu of Squeteague and Alawa, who were sharing a meal of roast pheasant, squash, and corn with Epenow,

Chepi, and Quannto. Important decisions affecting the families of the Wampanoag were usually made by the eldest male, but Squeteague had always involved Alawa in such matters, and he was now also seeking the counsel of Epenow and Chepi, who did not need to be reminded of the danger that could attend an English and Mohegan invasion of Narragansett territory. Alawa opposed the idea of leaving her home at Pettaquamscutt and moving to Noepe, where many of the inhabitants had been converted by the Reverend Mayhew. Chepi seemed undecided. Epenow, who, at the age of thirty continued to resemble Squeteague, agreed with his father.

"The present troubles will have an end," he said. "Our stay with the Aquinnah needn't be permanent."

"But what if they require that we convert to Christianity?" Alawa asked.

Chepi reminded Epenow that her father's insistence on conversion was what had led them to leave Massipee.

Epenow looked to Squeteague for support.

"We don't need to accept the English religion," Squeteague declared. "Neither do we have to reject it out of hand."

"Are you suggesting we should *pretend* to worship their God?" Alawa said.

Squeteague gave a laugh. "Better that than staying here to run the risk of being chopped up by the Mohegan."

"I hear the Narragansett are building a secret fort in the Great Swamp," twelve-year-old Qannto ventured.

Ordinarily, the boy would have been reprimanded for speaking out of turn, but Squeteague merely smiled. "If you have heard about the hideaway it can't be much of a secret."

"Perhaps it's not a secret but it's said to be impregnable," Alawa observed.

Squeteague shook his head. "The English are rumored to be raising an army to invade Narragansett territory. If Canonchet and Pessacus allow themselves to be surrounded in the swamp, things will end badly for them."

"If it isn't safe for us to take refuge there, we should leave," Chepi told Alawa.

"Not without me," Alawa replied, with a sigh

"Then it's decided," Squeteague declared. "All that remains for us is to load our possessions in the *Nauset* and take refuge with the Aquinnah. But first, I have to make a last trip to the Dutch on Long Island."

"Why must you go there now of all times?" Alawa asked.

"The Narragansett have been kind to us. Canonchet's father, Miantonomo, gave us sanctuary when we needed it. Now his son has asked me to do him and his people a final favor. I can't refuse him."

Squeteague had heard rumors that the colonists were raising an army, but he didn't know that the Commissioners of the United Colonies had already met in Boston, where they had decided to raise a force of more than a thousand soldiers under the command of Plymouth Colony Governor Joshua Winslow to launch a preemptive strike. This army would include five hundred and seventeen men from the Massachusetts Bay Colony, one hundred and fifty-eight from the Plymouth Colony, and four hundred and sixty-five from the Connecticut Colony, including one hundred and fifty Mohegan warriors under the command of Uncas's son, Owaneco. Among the Plymouth contingent was Captain Benjamin Church, who had been designated by Governor Winslow as his aide-de-camp. Serving as a company commander with the Bay Colony force was the infamous Captain Mosely. The excuse the colonists would make for attacking the Narragansett was that Pessacus and Canonchet had failed to turn over Weetamoo and the Pocasset who had sought shelter with them. The real reason was their fear that the Narragansett—far and away the strongest group of Native People in the region—might join forces with Philip.

On December 2, a day of prayer was declared throughout New England so that, in the words of Reverend Increase Mather, the colonists could "fall upon their knees before the Lord, the God of

Armies, entreating His favor and gracious success in the under-taking."

That same day, Squeteague set sail in the *Nauset* for Manhasset at the western end of Long Island Sound, where he planned to meet Dutch arms dealers. On December 8, Winslow and the soldiers from Plymouth and Massachusetts Colonies, who had gathered at Dedham, marched southwest toward Narragansett territory. A few days later, they reached the Seekonk River at Providence, where Winslow ordered Church and Mosely to sail with their men to Smith's Landing at Wickford, a few miles from Pettaquamscutt, and prepare for the bulk of the army that would be marching overland to join them. Soon after the two captains arrived at Smith's Landing, Mosley captured a renegade Narragansett named Peter, who agreed to lead the English to the fort in the Great Swamp, where more than two thousand warriors, women, and children had gathered to defend themselves.

After the main army arrived at Smith's Landing, English soldiers pushed south along the coast toward Pettaquamscutt, killing every Narragansett and burning every wetu they came across, until the sound of nearby musket fire alerted Epenow to the danger that threatened his family. He was aware that his father had little confidence in the impregnability of the fort in the Great Swamp, but decided that he had no other choice than to send Alawa, Chepi, and Quannto to seek refuge there while he stayed behind to delay the marauders as best he could. After picking off a pair of soldiers who had come running toward him through the forest, he was reloading his flintlock when he found himself facing combat with the giant Dutch pirate Cornelius Anderson, who had a reputation for killing Wampanoag captives with his bare hands. Having shot at Epenow and missed, Anderson swung the butt of his flintlock at Epenow's head, but failed to make contact because of an intervening tree branch. Then, flinging the weapon aside, he wrapped Epenow in a powerful bear hug that Epenow broke by bringing his heel down on the arch of his opponent's foot and his knee into Anderson's groin. He was about to finish off the

Dutchman with his knife when shouts announcing the arrival of additional soldiers forced him to flee.

Before nightfall, he caught up with Chepi, Quannto, and Alawa. An hour later, a Narragansett scout led them to the fort—a massive structure built on a four-acre hillock in the middle of the swamp—which was surrounded by a palisade made of tall tree trunks planted vertically in the ground, and a sixteen-foot-thick inner wall of mud and brush that had been woven together to form an almost impenetrable barrier. At strategic places in the perimeter of the breastwork, Narragansett engineers had built blockhouses and flankers that would enable defenders to pour enfilade fire on attackers trying to breach its walls. In a further attempt to make the fort impregnable, they had provided it with a single entrance—a tree trunk felled to form a bridge across a ring of the ice that surrounded the hummock of high ground in the frozen swamp. When Epenow and his family passed over the trunk, they entered the fort through the opening in the palisade and found themselves in a vast interior filled with hundreds of wetu.

Within a few days, the nights turned bitterly cold and two feet of snow had fallen. On December 18, Winslow's men were forced to sleep out of doors on the outskirts of the swamp. They awoke chilled to the bone. Many of them were suffering from frostbitten hands and feet. Nevertheless, at five o'clock Winslow gave the order to march into the swamp and attack the Narragansett fort. He had little choice. The supply ships carrying food for his army were becoming locked in the ice that was covering the harbor at Smith's Landing, and the food in their holds was freezing solid.

A hundred miles to the west, Squeteague and his crew found themselves in a similar predicament and were desperately chopping the ice from the decks and rigging of the *Nauset*, which had been surrounded by floes congealing in the waters of Manhasset Bay.

Chapter Sixteen

It was one o'clock in the afternoon on one of the shortest days of the year, when Narragansett sentinels posted at the flankers and blockhouses on the perimeter of the fort saw hundreds of English soldiers materialize out of a light fog that infused the snow-covered cedar swamp in which they and their compatriots had taken refuge. The sentries were not surprised by the appearance of the long-coated colonial troops because scouts had been tracking them since early morning, and from time to time picking them off with their flintlocks. Expected though it was, the approach of the English had an ominous quality, as if the very fact that they had managed to make their way through the swamp—something they would not have been able to do had it not been frozen over—portended an unfavorable outcome to the siege that was about to begin

From within the palisades, Epenow watched the English ranks fan out a hundred and eighty degrees around the perimeter of the fort and congregate at the entrance, as well as at a place where the palisade and inner wall had been only partly finished. He had offered his services to Canonchet as soon as he arrived, but the Narragansett sachem had declined, knowing that Squet-eague would have wanted Epenow to guard his mother, wife, and son. For this reason, he had assigned Epenow and his family to a wetu that had been fortified against musket shot by bags filled with corn stacked against its sides.

Alawa was shaking with fear—more for Quannto, Chepi, and Epenow than for herself. "Your father was right," she told her son. "Better for us to have gone to Noepe than be trapped in this for-bidding place."

Epenow placed a hand on her shoulder. He was thinking that when the English militiamen had come to Pettaquamscutt, he should have directed the family to strike out into the forest, rather than take refuge at the fort, but there was nothing to do now except offer words of reassurance. "We'll be safe here," he said. "There are hundreds of warriors to defend us."

No sooner had the words left his mouth than the English un-leashed a fusillade of musket fire against the perimeter of the fort as they continued to mass their forces before the log entrance and the unfinished portion of the rampart. The first onslaught was not long in coming. One company of soldiers rushed two abreast across the log bridge entrance, while another company attempted to breach the incomplete section of the palisade. Both were driven off by fierce volleys that killed their captains and inflicted heavy losses. More soldiers took up the charge, only to be decimated by intense fire from within the fort.

For a time, Epenow was heartened by the turn the battle had taken, but then a large column of militiamen stormed the outer perimeter of the fort, breached the breastwork, and fought their way inside. At that point, he joined the fray, shooting down several soldiers who were attacking wetu near the perimeter and killing another by splitting his skull with his tomahawk. The Nar-ragansett rallied and for a time seemed to be on the verge of driv-ing the invaders away. However, Winslow ordered an attack by soldiers he had been holding in reserve and, in spite of a hail of musket fire that killed four of their captains within minutes, these fresh troops managed to gain a new foothold inside the fort and, together with other soldiers, engaged the Narragansett defenders in savage hand-to-hand combat.

Loading and reloading his flintlock, Epenow took a heavy toll of the English attackers who were advancing between the fortified wetu, firing into them at random and bringing their pikes and swords down upon the women and children who ran from them in terror. At the door of the wetu where Alawa, Chepi, and Quannto were hiding, he made a final stand, firing his musket until the bodies of dead soldiers lay all around him and his weapon no longer functioned. Wounded in both legs, he fought on with his tomahawk until a point-blank blast caught him full in the chest and flung him backward against a grain bag that lay beside the doorway. In the fading light, he looked into the face of the Englishman who had shot him, heard screaming and smelled smoke and burning flesh coming from wetu that had been set on fire. As he died, the cries of women and children came fainter and fainter from all around him.

With the fort ablaze, most of the defending Narragansett abandoned it and began to fire at their attackers from hiding places in the surrounding swamp. By now the battle had been raging for three hours and taken a heavy toll on both sides. More than a hundred Narragansett warriors had been killed and many wounded. Hundreds of Narragansett women and children had perished in the flames or been hacked to death by English swords. Night was falling and, fearing ambush, Winslow ordered what was left of his army to retreat to Smith's Landing at Wickford. Eight hundred English soldiers carrying more than one hundred dead and wounded struggled through deep snow. Twenty of their dead were left at the fort. Twenty-two of the wounded died during the march. A day later, thirty-five soldiers were buried in a mass grave at Smith's Landing. Others died of their injuries during the following weeks.

Three captains from the Massachusetts contingent had perished in the attack. Four of the five captains in the Connecticut contingent had been killed by Narragansett musket fire. One of the dead captains was John Mason, son of the John Mason who had given the order to set Fort Missituck ablaze, incinerating hundreds of Pequot women and children. Another was Nathaniel Seeley, son of the Robert Seeley who had served under Captain Mason at the Missituck massacre, and from whose eyebrow Mason had plucked an arrowhead. Among the dead from the Bay Colony contingent was John Gallop, Jr., son of the John Gallop who had rammed the murdered John Oldham's boat, thrown one of his bound Manissean captives overboard to drown, and would later do the same to thirty bound Pequot who had been taken prisoner at the Owl's Nest.

The retreat of Winslow's army from the fort in the Great Swamp, where hundreds of Narragansett women and children died in the same fiery agony that had been inflicted on hundreds of Pequot women and children thirty-eight years earlier, was made easier in its early stages by flames from the burning wetu.

Puritan chroniclers would ascribe this light to the Blessed Illumination of Divine Providence.

Sailing through the night in Long Island Sound, Squeteague had a fearful premonition He imagined that the ice that had nearly trapped him at Manhasset Cove had covered the world and frozen everything in place. Nothing moved. Even the *Nauset*, which was beating into a cold wind from the northeast, had lost momentum. In this mood, he tacked the sloop back and forth, willing it ahead as if his mind could propel its hull through troughs between high waves that were breaking over its bow. Late the following day, he entered Narragansett Bay and anchored in Pettaquamscutt Cove.

His wetu and that of Epenow and Chepi had been burned to the ground. Footprints in the snowcover indicated that it had been trampled over by soldiers, and blood on the trail leading toward the Great Swamp showed that some kind of furious encounter had taken place, with at least two booted bodies dragged away. Windblown drifts of snow obscured the rest. The onset of darkness prevented him from learning what might have happened. With a sinking heart, he returned to the *Nauset* to spend the night.

With daybreak, he strapped on a pair of snowshoes he found hanging from a tree and resumed his search. At a place on the trail where wind had scoured the snow cover, he came across the moccasin prints of Alawa, Chepi, and Quannto. Later, he found the larger footprints of a man he assumed to be Epenow, who kept turning around to look behind him. Pressing on, Squeteague entered the vast swamp where he encountered a band of Narragansett women and children who fled as he approached. Fearfully now, he broke into a run until he came upon the remnants of the fort whose twisted and blackened palisades loomed above the swamp like the spine of a great dead beast.

The interior of the fort had been reduced to ash and cinder. A pall of smoke and the smell of burnt flesh hung over the place. Hundreds of corpses lay singly and in heaps covered by a thin blanket of new snow that cloaked the agony of their final moments. Here and there, small groups of Narragansett wandered in a daze as they searched for possessions and food that had not been destroyed by flame. No one took any notice of Squeteague or replied to his questions regarding the whereabouts of his family. He found himself hoping that they had escaped the conflagration, like the band he had encountered in the swamp and the people who were scavenging among the ruins. But his heart was heavy as he blamed himself for leaving them at Pettaquamscutt. He had taken the *Nauset* away just when it would have provided the best way to escape a danger he should have known was approaching. He had left his wife, son, daughter-in-law, and grandson to fend for themselves at a time when he should have remained to protect them.

Now he began searching among the blackened piles of rubble to which row on row of wetu had been reduced, turning frozen bodies over and dusting the snow off the faces of the dead in an effort to identify who had once inhabited them. An hour later, he came upon the corpse of Epenow, whose chest wound had bled a bright red stain into the snow. His hand clutched the bone-handled knife Squeteage had given him to celebrate his victory over the Mohegan assassins. Beside him lay his tomahawk and the bodies of Chepi and Alawa. All three of them had been slashed by swords and scorched by flame.

There was no sign of Quannto.

For a long time, Squeteague sat beside the stiffened bodies of his loved ones, reproaching himself for not having stayed at Pettaquamscutt and wondering if the curse Massasoit had invoked could account for the tragedy that had befallen him. But could he blame the sachem who had wanted to keep the peace with the English from the beginning, and had repeatedly warned against going to war? No, far more just to find fault with himself—he who had spent years supplying the Native People of the region with the weapons that had made it possible for them to rise up. Still, the Narragansett had not attacked the colonists but had simply taken refuge in the Great Swamp and defended themselves against an invading army. In this mood, the questions Squeteague and the doubts he entertained became riddles as seemingly impenetrable as the swamp the English soldiers had ended up infiltrating with ease.

Squeteague pried apart the frozen fingers of Epenow and took the bone-handled knife he had given him the day he had shown himself to be a warrior. Then, getting to his feet, he staggered through snow, carrying the corpses of his son, Alawa, and Chepi several hundred yards from the fort to an isolated hummock in the swamp. There was no possibility of digging a grave in the frozen earth, so he laid them side-by-side and covered them with rocks until he had built a large stone cairn that would afford protection from the predations of animals. When the weather warmed, he would return to bury them properly. After he had finished constructing the cairn, he hailed an elderly Narragansett and asked if he had seen a boy of Quannto's description. The old man shrugged and waved a hand to indicate the dozens of snow-covered bodies that lay around them. Then he told Squeteague that Pessacus, Canonchet, Weetamoo, and her Narragansett husband, Quinnapin, had escaped from the fort and fled with several hundred warriors into the forested interior. If the boy were alive, he could be with them. Or, of course, he might have been taken prisoner by the English.

Squeteague made his way out of the swamp and back to Pettaquamscutt where he was in time to see an English frigate making off with the *Nauset* in tow. He had nothing now except the clothes on his back, his flintlock, Epenow's tomahawk and knife, the pair of snowshoes on his feet, and a heart filled with despair. At this point, he set out to follow the boot tracks left by Winslow's soldiers as they retreated to Smith's Landing at Wickford. The soldiers had a twenty-four-hour head start, however, and most of them had reached the garrison before he did, except for a pair of wounded stragglers who had not been able to keep up with the main force. Coming up behind them, Squeteague used his dead son's tomahawk to kill both with blows to the skull.

During the next few days, he preyed on sentries who had been deployed to guard the perimeter of the garrison, stalking them silently by snowshoe and executing them in the same manner. Because of hunger, cold, and disease, the morale of the men at Smith's Landing began to deteriorate. It was not helped when word circulated that someone leaving a strange, circular pattern of snowshoe tracks around the bodies of his victims was killing sentinels at the rate of one or two a night.

Canonchet soon learned of Squeteague's depredations from his scouts, who were also following the English army. At that point, he sent a messenger to Squeteague, inviting him to join the Narragansett who were hiding in the forest, and telling him that when the snow melted sufficiently so his people could not be tracked, he planned to lead them north to join the Nipmuck and Pokanoket in the war against the English.

"Tell Canonchet that my wife, my son, and my daughter-in-law lie dead at the fort," Squeteague replied. "Ask him to help me find my grandson, whose name is Quannto. If he can do that, I'll join him. Otherwise, I'll continue to take vengeance on the English by myself."

A day later, the messenger returned with word that Quannto was not with the Narragansett but might have been taken prisoner by the English, who were sending Indian captives to Plymouth and selling some of them into slavery in the West Indies.

That night, Squeteague took a sentry prisoner, led him into the forest, and tied him to a tree. Then he built a pile of pine boughs around the man's feet and sharpened Epenow's knife on a rock. The Englishman, fearing torture, began to beg for his life.

"Please don't hurt me," he whined. "I have a wife and child."

"So did I," Squeteague replied. "They were slashed and burned at the fort."

"Not by me," the soldier protested. "I'm with a company that was held in reserve."

Squeteague traced the tip of the knife across his throat. "Do you want to live?"

"Yes," the soldier whimpered. "Oh, please, yes."

"Then tell me the truth when you answer my questions. Did the English take any prisoners?"

"I know of two boys who were brought to General Winslow's headquarters here at Wickford."

"Are they being held there now?"

The soldier shook his head "They were sent to Providence this morning."

"Do you know their names?"

"No," the soldier said, eyes widening in terror as Squeteague fingered the blade of the knife.

Squeteague cut the sinew that bound the sentry to the tree. The man fell to his knees and started begging for his life again.

"Please believe me. I've told you everything I know."

"I believe you," Squeteague said. "Do you know how to find your way back to the garrison?"

The soldier looked about him in the dark forest and gave a look of panic.

"Follow the footprints that brought you here," Squeteague told him, scornfully.

Squeteague knew from the moment he had set foot in the blackened ruins of the fort in the Great Swamp that the war against the English could not be won. All that remained for him was to find and save his grandson from the retribution that would surely follow defeat, and to meet his own end with honor. Later that night, he set out for Providence and arrived early the next morning at the stone house of Roger Williams, which sat in the middle of the plantation he had established there.

"Dear fellow!" Williams exclaimed. "You look exhausted. Come sit by the fire and tell me what brings you here while I have my servant fetch you something to eat."

When Squeteague had finished recounting the story of what had happened in the Great Swamp, Williams looked at him aghast. "Only yesterday did I have some word of it," he said. "How terrible a tragedy! And your family—how heavy my heart is to hear of their fate! But at least you have survived."

"I survived because I wasn't with them at the fort," Squeteague said. "I failed them when they needed me most."

"Don't blame yourself unfairly," Williams counseled. "The Lord God who loves us works in mysterious ways."

How touching that the English have faith in a loving God who allows them to burn women and children, Squeteague told himself. "My grandson is missing," he said. "His name is Quannto. I've learned that Winslow's men have taken two boys prisoner, who have been sent here to Providence. I'm hoping you can find out whether Quannto's among them."

"A contingent of soldiers from Plymouth Colony is billeted

nearby. They're waiting for the Narragansett to move north into Nipmuck country. I'll make inquries of their commander."

"I'll be greatly in your debt," Squeteague said. "The English have been selling captives into slavery."

"I'm opposed to that. Still, it's a pity the Narragansett failed to heed my warning that the United Colonies would wreak terrible punishment upon them if they should take the side of Philip."

"I'd say they've have done that and more," Squeteague observed.

"God's retribution takes many forms."

"In this case, the blackened corpses of women and children."

"I beg you not to harden your heart against Him,"

"He's not my God but yours," Squeteague replied.

Williams fell silent. Then he asked Squeteague what he intended to do?

"I'm going to find my grandson if he's still alive and take him to safety. Afterward, I'll join the war against the English and cut off as many of them as I can before I die."

Williams fell on his knees, clasped his hands together, and lifted his face toward the ceiling. "Merciful Lord," he prayed, "grant Thy servant Squeteague—he who has suffered the greatest loss a man may endure—the strength to renew his soul and obey Thy commandment not to kill."

Squeteague suppressed a grimace at the ridiculous posture Williams had assumed and the trembling plea that issued from his lips. "Don't trouble yourself about the condition of my soul," he said. "Be assured that if I had one it was left behind in the swamp with the people I loved the most—my wife, son, and daughter, whose charred bodies now lie beneath a pile of rocks."

Grasping the arm of his chair, the elderly reverend, who suffered from rheumatism, raised himself to his feet. "I'll leave now to make inquiries about your grandson. Please stay in the house until I return. Many people have fled from Providence to take refuge in the garrison at Warwick. Those who remain fear for their lives, as I do for yours, should anyone find you abroad."

Williams was gone for more than an hour. When he returned, he entered the vestibule of his house and took off his great coat with difficulty, craning his neck this way and that as he withdrew one arm and then the other. In the living room, he sat down by the fire and warmed himself before telling Squeteague through chattering teeth what he had learned. "Two boys were taken prisoner during the fight at the fort. They were brought here to General Winslow, who has sent one of them to be a servant to a friend in Boston, and the other to Plymouth to be sold into slavery."

"Do you know their names?"

"The officer I spoke with knew only that one was about seventeen years old and the other younger."

"And which of them was to be sold into slavery?"

"I should think the older, for the reason that he would be stronger and better able to perform labor."

Squeteague hoped this would turn out to be the case. "I don't suppose the commandant knew to whom the younger boy was sent in Boston."

Williams shook his head. "Governor Winslow would, of course, have many friends there."

"Yes, I would expect as much," Squeteague said, grimly. And may your wonderfully merciful God have mercy on any of them who have mistreated Quannto, he told himself.

Chapter Seventeen

Squeteague left Roger Williams's house early the next morning and set out on the trail to Boston. Traveling swiftly by snowshoe, he arrived at the Praying Town of Natick after dark. He did not know that most of the inhabitants had by now been interned on islands in Boston Harbor and was puzzled to see that smoke was issuing from only a single wetu. Weary from his journey, he selected an abandoned dwelling in which to spend the night, and the next morning he asked a squaw who had ventured outside to gather firewood whether she had seen soldiers come by with a prisoner.

Frightened, the squaw retreated into her wetu. A moment later, her husband appeared in the entranceway, hatchet in hand, and looked Squeteague up and down.

"I come in peace," Squeteague told him. "I'm looking for my grandson, whom the English soldiers took prisoner at the Great Swamp fight."

The expression on the man's face indicated that he had no idea what Squeteague was talking about. When Squeteague informed him about the attack on the Narragansett fort, he shrugged and said that the inhabitants of the village had been taken to Deer Island, where they were dying of famine and disease. "My squaw and I have been left behind to take care of the wetu," he said. "We're not of one side or the other in this war. We desire only to be left alone."

"I understand," Squeteague replied. "I'll be leaving now. Don't tell anyone you saw me."

Heading to Boston along the cart road dressed as he was in the deerskin leggings and shirt of a Narragansett warrior would be tantamount to inviting mayhem, so Squeteague kept to the woods, skirting farm settlements and following the coils of the Quinobequin River until darkness fell and he arrived at the outskirts of Cambridge. What a difference since he had last been there! A cluster of new timbered buildings housed the classrooms of Harvard College. Large dwellings surrounded a square called Market Place and lined the dirt streets that radiated outward from it. An unlit farmhouse lay between Dunster Street and the river.

Using Epenow's knife to lever open a door, Squeteague entered the dwelling and searched until he found the master bedroom and a chest full of men's clothing from which he helped himself to a heavy buff coat, a pair of broadcloth breeches, a linen shirt, a pair of buckle shoes, and a knitted wool hat. A small pile of silver shillings lay beneath the clothes. He awoke refreshed after a night's sleep in the master's bed and ate biscuits and cheese he found in the kitchen. Upon searching further, he came across a letter indicating that the house belonged to one Thomas Gibson, who had sent his wife and children for safekeeping to his brother in Boston while he went off to serve as an officer in Winslow's army. At this point, Squeteague dressed himself in Gibson's clothes, filled his pockets with Gibson's shillings, and set out along the Quinobequin to Boston in search of Quannto.

Boston had been a city of about 2,000 when he had last journeyed there during the Cuttaquin affair. Since then the population had more than doubled as merchants and sailors arrived to take advantage of the triangular trade in which ships carried rum made in New England to Africa to trade for slaves, who were then transported to Caribbean sugar plantations where they were sold for molasses that was brought to New England to make rum. But where in this bustling town should he start looking for his grandson? Squeteague decided to start at the wharves of the waterfront where matters of commerce were a constant topic of conversation.

Knocking at the door of the rum-exporting firm of Hubbard & Son, he indentified himself as a ship captain just arrived from Narragansett Bay with some young Indian captives to sell as dock workers or household servants. The clerk at Hubbard could not help him, but the price he asked was so cheap that word soon spread along the waterfront about a swarthy mariner who was selling Indians at bargain rates. Squeteague set up informal headquarters at the nearby Blue Heron Tavern, where he described his imaginary human wares to merchants who needed stevedores to unload casks of molasses arriving from the West Indies. During these sessions, he made sure to tell his would-be customers about the origin of his cargo, and in this way inform them of the victory won by General Winslow's army in the Great Swamp.

On the second day, his gamble paid off when a ship owner named Stubble offered one pound each for the Narragansett captives.

Squeteague smiled and shook his head. "Strong young Indian boys should fetch more than that—thirty shillings apiece at the very least."

Stubble frowned. "A neighbor of mine has just received such a boy as a gift from General Winslow. Perhaps I'll make inquiries of him in order that I might be favored in like manner."

Squeteague took a long sip from his glass of rum and regarded the merchant in silence. Then, with a shrug, he told Stubble that he believed him to be mistaken. "The Great Swamp fight took place a mere four days ago—hardly time for the general to send a young captive all the way to Boston."

Stubble glared at Squeteague in irritation. "I'll have you know I've seen him with my own eyes—yesterday at the house of

Master Ralston, which is hard by mine!"

Squeteague held up the palm of his hand in appeasement. "Why, then, I owe you an apology, good sir. Let me demonstrate my regret for doubting you by buying you a drink, and offering you the sturdy Narragansett lads in my custody at the price you offered to pay—twenty shillings each."

"Done," the merchant said, who also accepted Squeteague's offer of a second and third glass of rum. Before taking his leave, he arranged to conclude the bargain on the next day, but failed to notice that he was being followed as he left the inn and made his unsteady way home via the backside of Beacon Hill.

Squeteague thought of how ridiculous he might look to a fellow Wampanoag as, wearing the clothes of a colonial gentleman, he trailed the weaving figure of Stubble and tipped his hat to passers-by in the courteous manner he had observed during previous visits to Boston. The peninsula of Shawmut was surrounded by the harbor and the Charles River, and Governor Winthrop had founded a settlement there called Trimontaine (later shortened to Tremont) after the three hills that dominated the area. On the highest of these—Beacon Hill—a sixty-five-foot-tall pole had been erected and topped with a flame pot to be lit in the event of enemy attack, and a cluster of small, timber-framed houses had been built around the summit. Following in the wake of Stubble's wobbly gait, Squeteague could smell the smoke of wood fires spilling from stone chimneys into the cold December night.

At last, Stubble paused before the doorway of a house with a steeply pitched gable roof and, fumbling in his coat pocket, withdrew a set of keys from which he selected one with difficulty and tried inserting it in a lock several times before succeeding. When he disappeared into the house, Squeteague looked about and saw that there was only one other dwelling immediately adjacent. This one had a similarly steep roof above an overhanging half-story with a tiny window. The ground floor had a small center door flanked by a pair of casement windows with leaded, diamond-shaped sections.

Squeteague peered through one of the windows but could see little in the interior because the glass was glazed rather than clear. A moment later, he rapped on the door, which was opened by a gray-bearded man. Squeteague removed his hat. "Master Ralston?" he inquired. "Beg pardon for disturbing you at this hour, but the merchant Mr. Stubble has informed me that you have recently been sent a Narragansett boy to be your household servant, and I'm here to request your indulgence that I might obtain some information from you regarding him."

"Why, he only arrived yesterday!" Ralston exclaimed. "And, might I venture to say, bears no little resemblance to you?"

"I'm a ship captain whose dark and weathered countenance has witnessed the rise and fall of many suns at sea," Squeteague explained. "The worthy Master Stubble told me about you because I have some Narragansett lads to sell as slaves or servants."

Ralston stepped back and opened the door wide. "Come inside," he said. "'It's a cold night to be abroad."

"That it is," replied Squeteague, who was soon sitting before a blaze in an open hearth and sipping from a glass of rum provided by his host.

"You say you're a trader of Indians as slaves or servants," Ralston told him. " I should tell you to begin with that I have no use for slavery. Service is another matter. Ten years of good service and I'll release the lad General Winslow has sent me."

"You're a kind man, Master Ralston," Squeteague murmured. "A man of principle."

"I'm a religious man, Captain...?"

"Teague," Squeteague supplied. "I would ask that, if you should know anyone who wishes to purchase Narragansett boys as servants, they should contact me at the Blue Heron Tavern."

"Have you and your captives also come from Narragansett country?"

"Thanks to a fair wind that blew me here with news of General

Winslow's magnificent victory over the heathen."

"I've heard nothing about it from the lad. He seems frightened dumb by what happened there."

"Hasn't he told you about the terrible fire that consumed the fort?"

"He's unable to talk," Ralston said. "I've decided not to attempt any training of him until his spirit mends and his tongue returns."

"A commendable course," Squeteague replied. "Someday the boy will come to realize how fortunate he has been to end up in service to you."

"I'll endeavor to treat him in a manner that will lead him to such a conclusion."

"In my travels, I've dealt with fur traders of the Algonquin tribes," Squeteague continued. "Thus I'm able to speak their language, including some of its many dialects. Perhaps I might be of service to you by translating your gentle intentions to this afflicted lad."

"I'd be much in your debt," Ralston replied. "My wife also, who says that such is his fright she can't get anything across to him. I'll have her fetch him."

A few minutes later, Squeteague beheld his trembling grandson, who was disheveled from his long journey through the snow from Providence, and seemed paralyzed with fear.

Squeteague spoke to him in the Narragansett dialect they used when they had lived in adjacent wetu at Pettaquamscutt, but Quannto did not recognize him in his English clothes.

"Quannto, dear boy," Squeteague said, gently. "Don't you know your grandfather?"

The boy's eyes widened and, for a moment, Squeteague feared he was about to jump into his arms.

"Don't let on who I am," he cautioned. "Just know that I've come to take you away from here this very night."

"I suppose the boy sleeps under the eaves," he said to Ralston.

The man nodded his head. "It can be bit cold up there at night, but I'll provide him with sufficient blankets."

"What a fortunate boy," Squeteague murmured, with a smile.

"Of course, I take the precaution of locking him in."

"As would any sensible master," Squeteague replied. "But might he not escape through the window?"

"It's not easily opened and in any case gives off to a roof that's too steep to afford purchase."

Squeteague nodded gravely and turned to his grandson. "Now listen carefully to me, Quannto. When everyone's asleep you'll open the window in your room by cutting away the sash with the knife I'm going to pass to you. Then you'll squeeze through the opening and slide down the roof into the arms of your grandfather, who will be waiting below. Do you understand?"

"Yes, grandpa, I'll do exactly as you tell me."

"Thanks to you, he seems to have found his tongue!" Ralston exclaimed. "What says he?"

"He says he feels confident that he'll be safe here."

"How glad I am to hear it! My wife and I have wondered that he might run away."

The pair of night watchmen who patrolled the byways of Shawmut with muskets on their shoulders had passed Ralston's house by the time Quannto climbed through the window and onto the gable roof. Hesitating, he looked down at his grandfather standing below, who told him to jump and broke his fall by catching him in his arms. At the waterfront, Squeteague freed a rowboat that had been tied to a dock and rowed them up the Quinobequin until they reached a landing near Thomas Gibson's house, where Squeteague had left his deerskin leggings, shirt, and moccasins. They hid in the house that night and the next day, before resuming their journey upriver under the cover of darkness to the Praying Town at Natick, where Squeteague found a canoe that had been left behind by one of its interned residents. The following night, they paddled north across Lake Cochituate and then along a stream that flowed out of the lake and into a river leading past Concord, which had been turned into a garrison town with armed militiamen patrolling the streets.

As they were gliding through the darkness, Quannto remembered what had happened at the fort in the Great Swamp. "When Papa was wounded and lying on the ground, he told me to run away," he whispered over his shoulder. "A warrior helped me pass through a hole in the wall, but he was shot by an English soldier, who made me march with him all night through the snow. The next day, a Narragansett boy and I were taken to a house with other prisoners, and from there I was sent to the place you found me."

Squeteague laid his paddle across the gunwales of the canoe and bowed his head. To think that, with his last breath, Epenow had commanded Quannto to run and save himself, just as his own father had shouted for him to run as he was being taken prisoner by Hunt's seamen! The symmetry was overwhelming, as was his self-blame for having left his family behind at Pettaquamscutt.

"Grandpa, I know my father must be dead, but can you tell me what happened to mama and grandma?"

Blinded by sudden tears, Squeteague remained silent until he was able to compose himself.

"We'll talk of it when we're no longer in danger of being discovered," he replied.

At Concord, a river known as the Musketaquid (place where water flows through the grasses) was formed by the confluence of the stream they had been following with another of similar width. After a second day of paddling through waters that were beginning to freeze over, he and Quannto arrived at the Praying Town of Wamesit, where the Musketaquid emptied into the Merruasquamack, to find it burned to the ground and inhabited only by the charred bodies of people too old and frail to leave when its younger residents fled north to take refuge with the Pennacook. A sign nailed to a tree declared, "We are sorry for the English who have driven us from our praying to God and from our teacher."

That night, after a dinner of perch speared through a hole in the ice, Squeteague told Quannto that his mother and grandmother had been killed by English soldiers at the fort in the Great Swamp. Then he told Quannto to keep the knife he had taken from his father's hand and which the boy had used to escape from Ralston's house. "It was your father's since the day he became a warrior. Now it is yours. Keep it close to you for as long as you live."

The Merruasquamack was a great river flowing powerfully toward the sea. Squeteague had sailed into it soon after he had acquired the *Nauset*, trading for furs with the Agawam who lived near its mouth and with the Pennacook who lived on a bluff overlooking rapids at Namoskeag, which was famous as a place for netting and spearing shad and salmon. At the time, the Pennacook were a powerful confederacy led by a revered sachem named Papassaconnaway, who, like Massasoit, had warned his people not to make war against the English. Squeteague now hoped to find refuge for Quannto with Wonalancet, Papassaconnaway's son and successor, but when he and Quannto reached Namoskeag, they found the village abandoned and learned from a weir fisherman that Wonalancet had led his people north to Lake Winnepiseogee (Winnepesukee) in order to stay out of the conflict between the English and Philip.

Leaving their canoe at Namoskeag, Squeteague and Quannto traveled north by snowshoe over the frozen Merruasquamack until they came to its confluence with a river flowing south from Lake Winnepiseogee. There, they met a party of Pennacook who conducted them to the village of Winnisquam, where Wonalancet was spending the winter. Squeteague informed the Pennacook sachem about the burning of the Narragansett fort in the Great Swamp and the loss of his wife, son, and daughter-in-law. "The boy I have brought with me is my grandson, who survived the fire," he explained. "Will you grant him safekeeping until I can return to fetch him?"

"Your grandson is welcome among us" Wonalancet replied. "We've given sanctuary to many people who have fled from the war. The English have warned us not to accept refugees, but they don't understand that it is our sacred obligation to do so. Meanwhile, they're taking our lands as well as those of the Abenaki, who have gone to war with them. Last summer, they sent a captain named Mosely, who burned our wetu and cut down our corn."

"Mosely kills Native People whenever and wherever he can," Squeteague said. "Those few he takes prisoner he sends to the West Indies to be sold as slaves."

"I'm determined to keep peace with the English, as my father wished, but if this Mosely comes among us he won't find captives to sell as slaves. He will find warriors who will cut him off."

That night, Squeteague told Quannto he had made arrangements for him to stay with the Pennacook.

"But I want to stay with you, grandpa."

"I'd like that, too, but it isn't safe for you to be with me because of the war."

"Why can't I fight alongside you"

Squeteague placed a hand on the boy's shoulder. He was thinking that in two years Quannto would be as old as his father had been when he killed his would-be Mohegan assassins, and, in four years, as old as he himself when he had shot arrows at Standish and his soldiers. "I'll return for you as soon as the war has ended," he said. "Meanwhile, you'll be safe here, as your mother and father would have wished."

For some moments Quannto looked at his grandfather with eyes that had filled with tears. Then he shook his head, as if to clear them away. "By the time you return, I'll have become a warrior," he declared.

Squeteague took him in his arms. "In that case, your grandfather, who is proud of you already, will be prouder than before."

Chapter Eighteen

After bidding farewell to Quannto, Squeteague left the winter camp of the Pennacook and traveled south until he reached the deserted Praying Town of Natick. There, he learned from the caretaker he had encountered earlier that Philip and the Pokanoket had made their way west to Schahgticoke in the Hudson River Valley, where Philip was trying to enlist the support of the Mohawk in the war against the English. As for the Nipmuck and other Native People, they remained in winter camps near Wachusett Mountain, where they were surviving by hunting game and foraging for food left behind in cabins and farmhouses abandoned by English settlers.

A sudden January thaw persuaded Squeteague that it was time to return to the Great Swamp to give a proper burial to Alawa, Chepi, and Epenow. He had not encountered any English since the night he had freed Quannto from Ralston's house in Shawmut, but as he was passing near Rehoboth he came upon some settlers who were butchering a moose they had tracked and killed in the snow-covered forest. Squeteague debated whether to stalk and kill the hunters, who, immersed in their bloody work, presented easy prey. In the end, he decided against it, reasoning that such an act might bring pursuit and delay him from carrying out the grim task that lay ahead.

Skirting Providence and staying well to the west of the English settlement at Warwick, he entered the Great Swamp several days later to find Ninigret and a party of Niantic burying the bodies of Narragansett women, children, and warriors, as well as those of English soldiers and their Mohegan allies who had perished in the fight at the fort. When Ninigret asked him why he had returned, he told the Niantic sachem that he had come to bury his wife, his son, and his son's wife.

Ninigret winced in sympathy. "I am saddened for you," he said. "I have come to bury the bodies of the Narragansett because they are kinfolk and their deaths weigh heavily on our hearts. I am also burying the bodies of English soldiers and their Mohegan allies in order to show the magistrates at Plymouth and the Bay Colony that I intend to keep my people out of a war that can have no good ending for them."

"What of Pessacus and Canonchet?"

"They and their warriors, women, and children are still in hiding, together with the people of the squaw sachem Weetamoo. Now that warmer weather has come, I expect they'll trek north along the Kittacuck River into Nipmuck territory to continue the fight with the English."

Squeteague was gazing at the stone cairn that rose above melting snow on the hummock beyond the scorched palisades of the fort. As if anticipating his thoughts, Ninigret offered to provide him with the help of some Niantic warriors and their tools.

Squeteague accepted the offer of a spade but declined the assistance. "What I do here I must do myself," he said.

The hard work of digging through the packed earth and tangled roots of the swamp soon had him laboring for breath. Pausing to wipe his brow, he tried to gauge how deep and wide the grave must be, but the limits of his energy and the latticed web of cedar and other roots dictated that it would have to be deep and narrow, and that his loved ones must huddle together in death as they had so often in life when sleeping in the open. When he had finished digging, he began to dismantle the cairn, pulling away one stone at a time and laying each beside the grave so they could be reassembled on top of it.

The sight that greeted his eyes when the last stones were removed was a tableau of horror—twisted limbs, blackened faces, and eyes frozen shut in unseeing silence—which he would carry with him to the end of his life. Squeteague knew that the spirits of these precious dead had long since fled their discolored faces and contorted bodies, but also that the faces and bodies were all that remained to him. Tenderly, he gathered each one in his arms and lowered them into the grave—Epenow first, Chepi on top of him, and last of all Alawa, whose cold and shriveled face he touched with the tips of his fingers. Then he covered over the grave, stomped the earth firm beneath his moccasins, and rebuilt the cairn to mark the place. When he had finished, he fell on his knees, placed his forehead against the cold stones, and, spreading his arms, embraced them.

Ninigret, who had been watching, approached and offered him sanctuary with the Niantic. "You have served my kinsmen Miantonomo and Pessacus when you supplied them with weapons and spoke for them to the English, and you have served me in the same way. Now we're both old men who deserve to live our remaining days in peace. You're welcome to stay among us."

Squeteague thanked the Niantic sachem but declined the offer. "My heart is too heavy and full of rage to live anywhere in peace," he replied. "I will now hunt down the English and cut off as many of them as I can."

"You have much reason to avenge yourself, so I will not try to persuade you otherwise," Ninigret told him. "But I must warn you that the English have become too numerous and powerful to resist no matter how many you and others may cut off."

"What else is there for me to do?"

"I have agonized over the same question," Ninigret said. "In the end, I have decided to place the safety of my people foremost by keeping them out of war. They are all I have left."

"Except for my grandson, I have no one left," Squeteague replied.

In January, Josiah Winslow's army pursued four thousand Narragansett, Pocasset, and Sakonnet—nearly half of them warriors—northwest along the Kittacuck River into Nipmuck territory. The gnawed carcasses of stolen horses and cattle left by the trail gave testament to how famished the trekkers had become, but the English soldiers found themselves in similar straits as supplies ran out, temperatures dropped below freezing, and flu swept through their ranks. Soon the army was no longer following the enemy as much as it was engaged in what its soldiers called the "Hunger March." By the time they reached the frontier between the Massachusetts Bay Colony and Nipmuck country, disease, desertion, cold, and near starvation forced Winslow to disband his forces and allow his troops to return home. Thus did the colonists lose an army while the ranks of the Native insurgents were strengthened by some two thousand vengeful warriors. Meanwhile, Philip's attempt to enlist the support of the Mohawk failed when the Mohawk fell upon his forces at Schaghticoke and forced the Pokanoket sachem to beat a hasty retreat back to the Connecticut River Valley.

As for Squeteague, he shadowed Winslow's army as it made its agonizing way home, waylaying stragglers whose bodies he left face down in a familiar circle of snowshoe tracks, with their heads pointing northwest in the opposite direction from the abode of the great god Kiehtan, with whom in Wampanoag legend the souls of the dead were believed to find sanctuary. The English soldiers soon took to calling him "the snowshoe killer."

One evening, near Mendon, he came upon a boy who had fallen behind because his frostbitten feet wouldn't allow him to keep up. The boy sat huddled against a tree and looked at Squeteague with the same terror in his eyes that Squeteague imagined Alawa must have looked at the Englishman who had killed her.

"Are you a soldier?" Squeteague asked.

Too afraid to speak, the boy merely nodded.

"I'm not going to hurt you," Squeteague said. "You're only a boy. My grandson would be about your age."

"I'm fifteen," the boy replied in a whisper. "I'm a bugler."

"A bugler," Squeteague repeated. "You sound the alarm for battle and retreat?"

The boy nodded.

"Were you at the Great Swamp fight?"

The boy nodded again.

"Did you sound your bugle there?"

The boy gave another nod.

"And what did you see there?"

"Smoke," the boy replied, "and fire."

Squeteague squatted on his haunches before the boy and thought of the flames that had scorched the faces of Alawa and Chepi. Then he unlaced and removed the boy's boots and began rubbing his feet in his hands. The feet were ice cold and had turned blue. "What's your name?" he asked.

"Daniel," the boy replied, wincing in pain as the circulation began returning to his toes.

"And where do you come from?"

"Duxbury."

"Captain Standish lived there," Squeteague told him. "On land given to him by Massasoit."

"Captain Standish was a great soldier," the boy declared.

Squeteague smiled without reply. *I tried to kill him when I was your age,* he was thinking.

The boy's face registered renewed fear even as his feet grew warm because of Squeteague's brisk ministrations.

"Did you fight at the fort, Daniel?"

The boy shook his head. "I was told to stay outside."

"And you saw nothing of what was happening inside?"

"I could hear yelling and screaming," the boy said.

"Of women and children who were being killed by the soldiers."

The boy nodded. Tears began streaming over his cheeks.

"What kind of soldiers hack women and children to death with their swords and burn them with fire?"

Weeping, the boy made no reply.

"When you return to your home in Duxbury, who'll be there?" Squeteague asked.

The boy choked out a reply. "My mother and father, my two sisters, and my brother."

"Is your father a soldier?"

"He's a member of the militia that guards the town."

"What will you tell your family when you see them again?"

"I'll tell them about the fight in the Great Swamp and what happened there. And how I fell behind when I couldn't walk any farther. And of meeting you."

Squeteague wrapped the boy's feet in a rabbit fur hat he was wearing and built a fire to warm his boots and socks. Then he shared some cornmeal cake with him and built a shelter of pine boughs to ward off a chill wind that swept across the snow. Afterward, he and the boy lay down on a deerskin and, huddling together for warmth, slept through the night, except when Squeteague got up to refresh the fire. At first light, they drank snowmelt and set out for the outskirts of the settlement at Marlborough, where the remnants of Winslow's army had encamped. On the way, they encountered a Praying Nipmuck scout who had been sent out to guard the army's flank. Squeteague gestured toward the boy and told the Nipmuck who he was. The conversation was brief and ended when the man nodded and waved them on.

When they arrived on the outskirts of Marlborough, they could see smoke issuing from dozens of fires the soldiers had built to keep warm. "Here's where you go back to your people," Squeteague told Daniel. "Look how foolishly they huddle together in the open. Instead of posting post sentries at the edge of the forest, they rely on Praying Indians to protect them from attack, but Praying

Indians don't always turn against their own people, as you saw this morning."

The boy was looking at Squeteague with gratitude. "You saved me from freezing to death" he said. "How shall I explain it to the soldiers when I return among them?"

"Tell them you met a warrior who doesn't kill women and children. Tell them you've been saved by the man who circles their dead with snowshoe tracks."

The boy nodded and started away.

"Tell them to send you home to your family," Squeteague called after him.

Following his encounter with the bugler boy, Squeteague snowshoed north to Lake Chaubunagungamaug (fishing place at the boundaries) where some of the Narragansett who had escaped from Winslow's army had camped for the winter. The lake lay close to the Connecticut Path leading from Boston to Agawam (Springfield) and Hartford and the surrounding forests and swamps had been blanketed with knee-deep snow. Thanks to this impediment, deer could not move easily and tended to yard up in cedar swamps, where Squeteague and other skilled hunters killed them with their bows and arrows, thus providing badly needed food while saving precious supplies of powder and gunshot that were needed to continue the war. In addition to shooting deer, Squeateague served as a gunsmith for Narragansett warriors to keep their flintlocks in good repair.

Hunting deer and repairing flintlocks kept him busy and helped combat a deep depression that lay upon his spirit like the snow that covered the land.

In February, several hundred Nashaway, Nipmuck and Narragansett Warriors led by the Nipmuck sachems Monoco (also known as One-Eyed John) and Sagamore Sam raided and burned the English settlement at Lancaster, and made prisoners of Mary Rowlandson and her three children, one of whom died of a gunshot wound, as well more than twenty other residents.

Later that month, they burned the town of Medfield, twenty miles southwest of Boston, killing twenty-three of its inhabitants and wounding many others. In early March, a Puritan army of six hundred mounted soldiers commanded by Major Thomas Savage was ordered to Menemesit to attack a large group of Nipmuck led by Mattaump. Thanks to a skillful rearguard action carried out by a handful of warriors, the Nipmuck sachem devised a daring escape, ferrying some two thousand warriors, women, children, elderly people, and captives (among them Mary Rowlandson and her two surviving children) on makeshift rafts across the swollen Poquaig (Millers) River without the loss of a single life. Finding the river too turbulent to cross, Savage gave up the chase, while Mattaump took his people to the Connecticut River Valley to join Philip, who had returned from Schaghticoke after being routed by the Mohawk.

Mattaump, Canonchet, Pessacus, and Philip now met to map out a three-pronged strategy for continuing the war. According to the plan, the Pocumtuck and River People would drive English settlers from the Connecticut valley so that in the spring its fertile soil could be planted with the corn, beans and squash that would be necessary for survival; the Nipmuck and Pokanoket based in camps around Mount Wachusett would begin a series of raids on the colonial towns west of Boston; and the Narragansett would return to their homeland to attack settlements that the colonists had built in southeastern Massachusetts and Rhode Island. The Native forces would thus be in a position to threaten colonists living in a wide area stretching from the Merrimack River on the north to Narragansett Bay on the south, and from the Connecticut River on the west to the Atlantic Ocean on the east.

By this time, Squeteague had made his way north to the Wampanoag encampments around Mount Wachusett that would serve as bases for the planned assault on the English frontier towns. There, he found himself struck by the lack of provisions available to feed the large number of women, children, and elderly who had crowded into the camps, and realized that a desperate need for grain and livestock must lie behind the decision to attack the English settlements. Squeteague also noted a profound change in Philip, whom he encountered for the first time since he had interpreted for John Easton during his unsuccessful attempt to persuade the Poanoket sachem to submit to arbitration.

Philip wore the haggard look that might be expected of someone who had dodged his English pursuers from swamp to swamp since the start of the war, and had then made his way through snow and cold to the Hudson River Valley, where he had hoped to make a pact with the Mohawk, only to have them turn on him and inflict a heavy defeat. Upon his return to New England, he found that the Nipmuck and Narragansett, who had carried the brunt of the war against the English in his absence, had lost much of their prior respect for him. Pessacus, Canonchet, and other Narragansett sachems believed that, instead of fleeing his homeland, he and his Pokanoket should have stayed to fight against Winslow's army, while Mattaump and Monoco were disappointed by his failure to join the Nipmuck in their attacks on the English settlements west of Boston. Though fatigued, the Philip whom Squeteague encountered as the snow cover was beginning to melt remained as defiant as ever, and determined that the springtime offensive he had helped to plan would succeed. "We'll need you to supply us with more flintlocks, powder, and shot as we drive the English toward the sea," he declared.

"Unfortunately, my ship was captured by the English after the Great Swamp fight," replied Squeteague, who, aware that the single-minded Philip would consider acknowledgment of personal tragedy to be a sign of weakness, chose not to reveal that he had lost three members of his family during the battle.

"Then we'll have to supply ourselves with weapons taken from the dead bodies of our enemies. Now that our Narragansett brothers have joined us, there'll be more than enough of those."

Squeteague wondered if Philip believed in this grandiose prediction, or whether he realized only too well the overwhelming odds he faced and was trying to maintain a good face in spite of them.

"Once the colonists are forced to abandon the settlements along the frontier, they'll lose heart for more fighting," the Pokanoket sachem continued. "When that happens, the English will either agree to respect our territory or return to the land from which they came."

"After seeing the outcome of the fight in the Great Swamp, I don't believe this war can be won," Squeteague said. "I believe that your great father was right when he urged the Wampanoag to keep peace with the English."

Philip's face darkened. "My father would have come to see the English as his enemy had he lived to witness the full measure of their untrustworthiness!"

"I doubt it."

"Do you dare doubt what what I tell you about my own father?"

"What I don't doubt is that your father remained a friend of the English all his days."

"You've become become weak, old man," Philip sneered. "If you hadn't done me service in the past I'd smash your head!"

"I don't fear anything you might do to my head," Squeteague replied. "What troubles me is the calamity I've helped bring upon our people."

Nipmuck warriors had already mounted a daring raid on Weymouth, a town on the coast a few miles south of Boston. A few days later, they attacked Hingham and Scituate, two other towns on the coast, killing a resident in each. On March 13, Monoco attacked the village of Groton, burning the meetinghouse and more than sixty dwellings. On the day Squeteague met with Philip, the sachem Totoson overran William Clark's garrison on the Eel River, south of Plymouth, killing eleven settlers who had taken refuge there, including a number of women and children.

Squeteague was revolted when he learned of the massacre. After coming upon the charred remains of Alawa and Chepi in the Great Swamp, he had no stomach for the murder of women and children, and after saving the young bugler boy from freezing, he had lost the desire to indulge in further killing.

That same week, he left Wachusett and made his way south along the Kittacuck River toward Narragansett Bay with the idea of locating the *Nauset* and liberating her from English custody.

He had decided to leave the war.

Chapter Nineteen

Fury against Native People had grown among the inhabitants of Boston to such a degree that authorities of the Bay Colony found themselves forced to guard the Praying Indians against attack by angry colonists who wanted row out to Deer Island and slaughter them. English clergymen inveighed against what they considered to be deep-rooted traits of treachery lodged in the Native character. Some commanders in the militia refused to use Natives as scouts, even though they had proved to be invaluable, because of a conviction that they could not be trusted. Such was not the case on Sunday, March 26, when Captain Michael Pierce and a company of sixty-five Plymouth Colony soldiers, together with twenty Native auxiliaries from Cape Cod, set out from the town of Rehoboth along the Pawtucket River and stumbled into an ambush laid by a large force of Narragansett led by Canonchet. Rushing after some warriors who pretended to be limping, Pierce's men suddenly found themselves surrounded and trapped against the riverbank. The soldiers fought desperately against the onslaught until forty-nine of them, including Pierce, had been killed. Nearly a dozen Native auxiliaries also died. Nine men were captured and led to a nearby swamp called "Nine Men's Misery," where they were tortured and killed. Two days later, Canonchet and his warriors fell upon Rehoboth, burning houses, driving off cattle and horses, and carrying away stores of food.

The Narragansett sachem's next target was Providence, from which most of the inhabitants had fled, leaving the elderly Roger Williams and forty men, who had barricaded themselves in a fortified garrison house, to defend the settlement. Upon learning that Squeteague had been seen traveling south along the Kittacuck, Canonchet sent a messenger requesting that he come to Providence to assure Williams that he would be safe whatever happened.

On the morning of March 29, Squeteague found himself standing with several warriors on the heights above Providence Harbor, watching the bent figure of Williams who was leaning on a staff as he labored uphill to meet them. As always, he harbored ambivalent feelings toward the venerable minister who had often proved to be a friend of the Native People, but just as often appeared to consider them inferior. When Williams reached the top of the bluff, he paused to gain his breath before turning to Squeteague. "I trust you haven't thrown in with these cutthroats," he said, gruffly.

Squeteague smiled with appreciation for the old man's outspokenness. "I trust you'll be glad to learn that, thanks to you, I was able to rescue my grandson from servitude in Boston."

Williams turned to the Narragansett. "You'll never win this war! The Bay Colony can raise thousands of men against you, and as fast as you may kill them the King of England will send more!

"Well, let them come," one of the Narragansett replied. "We'll be ready for them. But as for you, Brother Williams, you're a good man. You have been kind to us these many years. Not a hair on your head shall be touched."

Hearing shouts from below, Williams looked down on the plantation and saw his house go up in flames. "How can you do this to someone you acknowledge has been kind to you?" he cried.

"My house burning before my eyes has lodged hundreds of you over the years. Yet you run about the country like wolves killing innocent people!"

"We're in a strange way," another warrior admitted, "but you English have made us so."

"What can he be talking about?" Williams asked Squeteague.

"Perhaps he's talking about the massacre of women and children in the Great Swamp," Squeteague replied.

Williams, who didn't like to be reminded of atrocities committed by the colonists, gave him an angry look. "It will soon be time for you and us to plant corn and beans," he told the warriors. "How can that happen if it's not safe for anyone to go into the fields?"

"We have little need of planting," came the reply. "We can live off the corn and food the English have stored away, once we kill them and take their cattle and sheep."

"God will punish you for such a barbarous strategy!"

"God is not with you but with us. Come to the river and see for yourself where Captain Pierce and his men lie unburied."

Williams's face flushed with fury. "Fight in the open and not by ambush and you'll be the ones who will lie unburied!"

The meeting ended with the Narragansett advising Squeteague to accompany the minister back to the garrison house in case some of their younger and angrier colleagues might seek to do him harm. By this time, thirty of the fifty dwellings in Providence Plantation were engulfed in flames. Although virtually all of the inhabitants had taken refuge in the garrison, a religious eccentric named Wright, who had convinced himself that, while he held a Bible in his hands, he would be safe, had his belly ripped open and the Bible stuffed inside.

Roger Williams, who would later refer to the raid as taking place on the "burning day of God's wrath," paused at the door of the garrison and offered Squeteague the opportunity to take sanctuary inside.

"There's no sanctuary for me," Squeteague told him. "Either

inside or out."

Canonchet had returned to southeastern New England to carry the fight to the colonists and to retrieve badly needed seed corn buried at Seekonk so it could be planted in the rich soil of the Connecticut River Valley. The mission would prove to be his undoing. On April 9, he and his warriors were surprised by forty Connecticut soldiers led by Captain George Denison, of Stonington, who, together with some Native auxiliaries, had been ordered into the area following the massacre of Pierce and his troops. As Canonchet raced through the forest to escape his pursuers, he tossed aside his silver-laced coat and wampum belt but slipped on a rock as he tried to ford a stream and was seized by a fast-running Pequot in a manner that was eerily similar to the way his father, Miantonomo, had been seized by the swift Mohegan Tantaquideon more than thirty years earlier.

When a young English lieutenant named Robert Stanton came upon the scene and presumed to question Canonchet, the Narragansett sachem regarded him with disdain. "You're just a child!" he declared. "You aren't old enough to understand matters of war! Take me to your chief. I'll answer to him."

Canonchet was then brought before Major Palmer, commander of the Connecticut force, who told him that his life would be spared if he would agree to submit the Narragansett Nation to the United Colonies. The sachem refused, telling Palmer that killing him would not end the war.

One of Palmer's senior officers reminded Canonchet that he had threatened to burn English settlers in their houses and had broken his promise to turn over Wampanoag refugees who had fought against the colonists.

"Haven't you English burned my people in their houses?" Canonchet replied. "Have you ever delivered up a single Englishman who had killed a Narragansett?"

A day later, forty-three Narragansett warriors who had been taken prisoner at Seekonk by the Connecticut soldiers were executed, and Canonchet was transported to Stonington, where he was informed that he would be put to death.

"I like it well," he replied. "I shall die before I have said anything unworthy of myself."

In order that their Native allies might share in the glory of killing such a prominent enemy, Connecticut authorities allowed the Pequot to shoot Canonchet, the Mohegan to sever his head and quarter his body, and the Niantic to burn the quarters. Canonchet's head was then taken to Hartford and presented as a trophy to the Connecticut Council of War.

Squeteague, who had remained in the vicinity after the burning of Providence, heard about the capture and execution of Canonchet from Narragansett warriors who had escaped captivity. He knew at once that the uprising of the Native People had been dealt a mortal blow, because the Narragansett led by Canonchet were its most capable fighting force. Aware that English soldiers were scouring the area for any remaining warriors, he headed south along Sakonnet Bay, hoping to escape detection. To his surprise, he encountered the squaw sachem Awashonks, who had returned with her people to their homeland on Sakonnet Point.

Squeteague had met Awashonks at Pettaquamscutt when she and the Sakonnet had sought protection with the Narragansett at the start of the war. Following the Great Swamp fight, she and her people had trekked north to spend the winter near Mount Wachusett, but by late March she realized that the fortunes of war had turned against Philip and decided to abandon the conflict. Upon meeting her again, Squeteague inquired whether she feared reprisal at the hands of the colonists.

"Not at all," she replied. "I have a friend and protector in Captain Benjamin Church, who tried to persuade me to join the English before the war and with whom I've made amends. He was wounded in the Great Swamp fight, but is now recuperated and living at Aquidneck."

Squeteague began to wonder about the nature of the relationship between Church and Ashawaonks when she revealed that the captain had dined with her in her wetu on many occasions and had shown her scars on his hip and thigh. Upon questioning her further, he found her more than willing to discuss her friendship with Church.

"The captain has promised immunity to the Sakonnet if we submit ourselves to the rule of Plymouth Colony. He has great influence there because his grandfather was a passenger on the ship that brought the first English to our shores."

Which means that his grandfather was probably among the English soldiers I tried to kill as a boy, Squeteague told himself. "What else has the captain told you?" he inquired.

"That he killed the warrior who wounded him during the Great Swamp fight. That he begged General Winslow not to allow his soldiers to set fire to the Narragansett fort but use it as a shelter for the wounded. That Winslow's surgeon said the wounded would freeze to death if they weren't evacuated to Wickford, and threatened not to treat the injuries to his hip and thigh but let him bleed to death if he did not agree to this. That he had no choice but to accept the decision to put the fort to the torch and join in the retreat. And that he's a true friend of the Sakonnet and other Native People."

"And you believe him?" asked Squeteague, who had learned from a Sakonnet elder that Church had recently concluded an agreement with the magistrates at Plymouth under which he and his men would receive half of any profits gained by selling Native captives into slavery.

"Yes, I believe him," said Awashonks, with a smile. "He has become my dearest friend."

And perhaps more, Squeteague decided. Whatever the case, he regarded the squaw sachem's defection from Philip as another indication that the war against the English would soon come to an end. Locating the *Nauset* now became a priority. With that in mind, he crossed over to nearby Aquidneck Island by canoe and made his way at night to Newport Harbor, where he broke into a shop and stole a pair of sailor's slops and shirt. Thus disguised, he prowled the waterfront until he spied the rakish hull of his sloop riding at anchor among many other vessels.

At dusk, he commandeered a dinghy, rowed out to the *Nauset*, and hailed a pair of armed guards who were patrolling its deck. One of them took his musket off his shoulder, rested its barrel on a gunwale, and took aim at Squeteague's head.

Squeteague lifted his hands to show he had no weapon. "I'm looking for a berth," he said. "Might this be a vessel to ship out on?"

"Ye'll find no berth here," the guard replied, "but in any case ye should be applying at the shipping office on shore."

At this point, Squeteague heard the rattling of chains coming from within the hull. "Passengers on board?" he inquired.

"Heathen passengers," said the other guard, who had crossed the deck to join his colleague. "Bound for Barbados to be sold."

When Squeteague had rowed out of earshot, he shipped the oars, slipped over the side of the dinghy, and swam to the bow of the *Nauset*. There, grasping the anchor chain between his knees and fists, he climbed hand over hand to the hawsehole, where he paused to catch his breath before swinging himself over the rail and onto the deck. Crouching behind a keg of coiled rope, he surveyed the length of the ship and saw that one of the guards was walking toward his hiding place in the bow as the other marched toward the stern. When the first guard had reached the keg and started back, he rose to his feet, clamped a hand across the man's mouth, and, yanking his head back, slashed his throat to the neckbone with his knife. Then he picked up the man's musket, which had fallen with a clatter on the deck, shouldered it, and started walking toward the stern on the starboard side. As he passed the second guard on the port side amidships, he heard a soft taunt.

"Drop ye're gun did ye, Eben? Some soldier ye'll be goin' to make."

When the man had passed by, Squeteague crept across the deck, came up behind him, and brought the butt of the musket down on his skull. The guard sagged to his knees and fell across the gunwale. Squeteague bent over, lifted the man by his legs, and pitched him overboard. Then he went to the main hatch, which had been fastened with an iron bar, and wrenched it open to be greeted by the stench of urine and feces rising from the hold. Lighting his way with a torch saturated with whale oil, he descended a gangway to find himself amid a score of Narragansett warriors, who rattled their chains and greeted him with joy, telling him that they had surrendered to Connecticut troops but would have fought to the death if they had known they were going to be sold as slaves.

"Our brothers whom the English executed were more fortunate than we," one of them cried.

Squeteague examined the chains and leg irons that fastened the Narragansett and saw that they had been joined together in fours, right legs to left legs, and were secured with large iron padlocks. For the next hour, he tried to force the padlocks by jamming knives and other instruments into their keyholes. Then he attempted to hammer them apart. Finally, he resorted to placing links of chain against the ship's anvil and striking them over and over with the iron bar that had been used to lock the hatch of the hold. Nothing worked. Meanwhile, the hour had slipped well past midnight. Day would soon be breaking.

Squeteague apologized to the Narragansett captives for his inability to free them, but they would have none of it. "Brother Squeteague, that you have come amongst us is a miracle," one of them said. "You have done your best. We're in your hands."

"I'm going to slip anchor and set sail. Perhaps we'll be able to reach Niantic country in time to find help."

At that point, he went on deck and let the anchor chain fall over the side. Then he set the jib and mainsail and slid away to the south between the other ships anchored in the harbor. Before long, however, he realized that an alarm had been raised and that several vessels were not only in pursuit but also gaining on him as a result of having set greater sail. Squeteague lashed the helm, went below, and told the captives that the sloop would soon be overtaken.

"Don't let it happen," one of them told him. "We'd rather die than live as slaves,"

"Kill us!" another implored. "Put us to the knife! Don't let them take us captive again.

"There are too many of you for that," Squeteague said.

"Then sink the ship!"

On the one hand, Squeteague was appalled at the prospect of killing the Narragansett captives and of losing the precious sloop he had just regained. On the other hand, he knew he couldn't abandon these men to the fate that awaited them in the West Indies.

"I'll do my best," he told them.

"Do what you must!" they begged.

Squeteague went back up on deck and saw that a pair of brigantines under full sail were closing fast upon him. Tacking off to the windward, he gained time on his pursuers and brought the *Nauset* closer to shore south of Conanicut Island. Then he went below again, bade the trapped Narragansett a solemn farewell, and opened bilge-cocks that allowed geysers of water to begin filling the hull. Returning to the deck, he waited until he felt the ship start to settle into the sea. When the water had reached the gunwales, he re-lit the whale-oil torch and set fire to the sails and whatever else he could find that was combustible. Then he jumped over the side and swam to the shore at Pettaquamscutt, where he and his family had found sanctuary for so many years. Behind him, the ship he loved second only to them was sinking beneath the surface of the sea, sails blazing at daybreak.

Not a murmur came from the hold where the Narragansett were meeting their end.

Exhausted by the time he reached land, Squeteague spent the night in the open near the site of his old wetu, and then sought refuge in the Great Swamp with some Narragansett warriors who had gone there after avoiding capture by the Connecticut soldiers at Seekonk. The silence of the chained and drowning men in the hold of the *Nauset* tormented him, as did the cries of women and children meeting their fiery end at Fort Missituck so many years before, and what he imagined to have been the terrifying final moments of Alawa, Chepi, and Epenow, who lay beneath a cairn he could not bear to visit. Weary of his seventy-plus years, he wrapped himself in a blanket and sat in silence by a fire tended by his hosts, who understood without asking that a great sadness had befallen him.

The following week, he learned from newly arrived refugees that a thousand Nipmuck, Pokanoket, and Native warriors had descended from their strongholds near Mount Wachusett and attacked the English settlement at Sudbury, whose inhabitants quickly sent a request for help to Concord and other nearby towns. A dozen men from Concord rushed to the rescue, but were surprised and cut down to the last man by warriors concealed in tall grass beside the Musketaquid River. A larger group of soldiers led by Captain Samuel Wadsworth, of Milton, and Captain Samuel Brocklebank, of Rowley—both of whom had taken part in the Great Swamp Fight—hastened to the scene from the garrison town of Marlborough. When they drew near Sudbury, they encountered several Indians who pretended to be surprised and fled as they approached.

What took place next had happened many times before. Unaware that they were rushing into an ambush, the two officers and their troops pursued their quarry over a hilltop only to run headlong into an overwhelming force of Nipmuck and Pokanoket, who were hiding out of sight on the other side. Realizing that they were about to be surrounded, Wadsworth and Brocklebank ordered their men to retreat to the top of the hill, where they succeeded in holding off their attackers for several hours. However,

the warriors set fire to dry grass and brush surrounding the hilltop, and flame and smoke soon engulfed the soldiers at the summit, who broke ranks and fled for their lives only to be chased
down and tomahawked to death by the enemy. A handful survived by taking cover in an abandoned mill, but seventy-three
Englishmen lay dead, including fifty soldiers, among them
Captains Wadsworth and Brocklebank.

The attack on Sudbury turned out to be the last major action undertaken by the Nipmuck and their allies against the
English. After prolonged negotiation, it was agreed that Mary
Rowlandson would be released for the sum of twenty pounds
and a pint of liquor. Philip opposed the ransom on the grounds
that he could strike a better bargain, but Rowlandson was considered to be the property of Weetamoo and her fifth husband,
Quinnapin, so the final decision was theirs. Following the release of Rowlandson, the Nipmuck sachems proposed an immediate cessation of hostilities with Massachusetts, and during
the rest of May they negotiated for a peace treaty with the colonists. Finding the treaty unacceptable and fearing betrayal,
Philip gathered his remaining forces—among them Weetamoo
and those Pocasset who remained loyal to her—and returned
to his homeland to continue the war.

The Nipmuck decision to seek a separate peace was influ-
enced in great measure by a catastrophe that took place on the
western frontier. Famished River People, as well as many hungry Nashaway, Poctumtuck, and Quabaug, had established a
fishing camp at Peskeomscutt, which was situated where rapids on the Connecticut River made conditions ideal for setting
weirs. Realizing that the Natives at Peskeompskut presented
easy prey, Captain William Turner, commander of English
troops garrisoned in Hatfield, gathered a mounted force of
one hundred and sixty men and charged into the midst of the
fishing camp at dawn on May 19. The men, women, and children who did not die in the initial fusillade directed at the
wetu were shot as they tried to escape by swimming across

the river, or drowned as they were carried away by the turbulent rapids. Upon discovering half a dozen elderly people and children hiding beneath the riverbank, Captain Samuel Holyoke, grandson of William Pynchon, the founder of Springfield, set about slashing them to death with his sword. Nearly two hundred Native People—most of them women and children—were killed. Turner lost one man, who was shot accidentally by a fellow soldier.

The tide of battle turned quickly, however, as a large group of Pocumtuck and Nipmuck closed in on Turner's men, whose retreat from Peskeompskut soon became a rout as pursuing warriors harassed their flanks. Turner was shot through the back and thigh and left to die as he tried to cross the Green River, and by the time the weary expedition straggled into Deerfield almost a quarter of its men had been killed. Nevertheless, the fight at Peskeompskut turned out to be a major victory for the colonists, because it spoiled the plan of the desperately hungry Native People to carry on the war by replenishing their food stocks with dried fish and newly planted corn. Nipmuck morale suffered an additional blow a few days later when English soldiers captured the wife of Mattaump, a chief of the Quabaug, as well as the wife and children of Sagamore Sam, a sachem of the Nashaway, who were taken prisoner while fishing in a pond near Lancaster.

Meanwhile, a morose Squeteague, mourning the loss of his beloved family and treasured sloop, remained in hiding in the Great Swamp until a day in early May when buds were opening on the shad bushes, fiddlehead fern were poking through the ground, and a Narragansett warrior who had taken part in the Great Swamp fight came to him with news that would shake him out of his depression.

"I saw your son die," he said.

Squeteague got to his feet without a word.

"He had been wounded already when he shot an English captain who was running toward him through the fire and smoke.

The Englishman fell to the ground, but then got to his knees and fired at your son and hit him full in the chest."

"And the women who were with him—his mother and his wife?"

"There was too much smoke for me to know more than I have told you. Except for the name by which I heard the soldiers call the wounded captain as they carried him away. They called him 'Church.'"

Part Five

AFTERMATH

Chapter Twenty

Squeteague stood beside the stone cairn marking the grave in which his family lay, his spirit echoing with the sights and sounds of horror—the swath of Hunt's cutlass as it slashed through his father's torso, the thud of the ball from Church's musket piercing Epenow's breast, and the swords of the colonial militiamen hacking away at the helpless Alawa and Chepi. Now he realized that he could not leave the war—a war he had spent a lifetime helping to bring about—until Church was dead. He also realized that his best chance to kill the English captain lay in the possibility that Church might pay another visit to Awash-onks, who appeared to be enamoured of him. With that in mind, he crossed Narragansett Bay by canoe from Pettaquamscutt to her homeland at Sakonnet Point, and waited for the Englishman to show up.

Meanwhile, Church had recovered from his wounds and, missing the excitement and glory of battle, had decided to return to a war he had come to relish. For reasons of pride, he was unwilling to serve under Major William Bradford, son of the former governor of Plymouth Colony, who had been placed in command of an army of several hundred men. He would raise his own force from settlers living at Aquidneck and go after Philip on his own. In an effort to recruit Sakonnet scouts for this mission, he arranged to meet with Awashonks on the shore of Sakonnet Bay, and was followed there by Squeteague, who concealed himself in a thicket of beach plum bushes. To Squeteague's chagrin, the encounter turned out not to be an assignation but a feast of eels, flounder, and clams attended by several hundred Sakonnet to celebrate a forthcoming peace treaty between them and Plymouth Colony. Under its terms, the Sakonnet would submit themselves to the authorities at Plymouth, who would guarantee to spare the life of every Sakonnet man, woman, and child, and not to transport any of them from their homeland or sell them into slavery.

At the conclusion of the feast, Ashawonks lit a ceremonial bonfire and performed a frenzied dance like the one she had performed for Church just before the war began. Her warriors then circled the blaze—each with a spear in one hand and a tomahawk in the other, before striking his spear into the ground and swearing allegiance to the English in the presence of the squaw sachem and her guest. Fearing discovery, Squeteague stole away and disappeared into the surrounding forest long before the festivities ended.

Bradford had moved his army north by boat with the intention of intercepting Philip at Montaup Bay, while Major John Talcott, who commanded a force of Connecticut soldiers and Mohegan scouts, attacked the Narragansett, killing and capturing nearly two hundred men, women, and children in the swamp at Nipsachuk from which Philip and Weetamoo had escaped a year earlier. Farther north, the war was winding down. The magistrates of Massachusetts Bay Colony had issued an offer of mercy to all Nipmuck warriors who would surrender, except those judged guilty of starting the war and committing atrocities. The Nipmuck sachems Mattaump and Sagamore Sam wrote a letter asking to be included in the amnesty and begging the English to care for their wives and children, who had been taken prisoner a few weeks earlier. However, the colonists were not inclined to grant mercy to Sam, whom they considered a war criminal for having led the attack on Lancaster that resulted in the kidnapping of Mary Rowlandson, or to Mattaump, whose warriors had killed sixty-four soldiers at Bloody Brook. As a result, Sam and Mattaump sought the protection of Wonalancet and the Pennacook, and the English sold their wives and children into slavery in the West Indies.

During the next few weeks, hungry and exhausted Nipmuck combatants gave themselves up in large numbers to colonial authorities, creating a situation that produced acts of betrayal on both sides. The English offered amnesty to a Nipmuck chief named Sagamore John if he would surrender and hand over Matoonas, a fellow sachem who had attacked Mendon at the start of the war. John and one hundred and eighty of his followers not only brought in Matoonas when they gave themselves up, but also shot him to death on Boston Common, beheaded him, and affixed his head to the top of a pole. By executing Matoonas, John hoped to ingratiate himself with the English, but he soon found out they had no intention of honoring their promise of amnesty and were preparing to hang him. At that point, he fled to the Pennacook, where he asked Wonalancet to grant him the refuge he had already afforded the Nipmuck sachems, Mattaump, Sam, and Monoco. The English proceeded to execute eight of his followers, sell thirty others into slavery, and exile the rest to Deer Island, where they died of exposure, starvation, and disease.

Meanwhile, Church had gathered a force of some thirty men, including a number of Sakonnet scouts, and set out to close the trap on Philip and a mixed group of Pokanoket and Narragansett, who were dodging from one hiding place to another in the vast wetlands north of the Titicut known as the Hockomock Swamp. On the run but still dangerous, Philip attempted to raid Bridgewater at the end of July, but was beaten off by determined resistance on the part of the town's militiamen, who killed ten of his warriors—among them his aging uncle, Akkompoin. A day later, Church and his men arrived on the scene and captured Philip's wife, Wootonekansuke, and their nine-year-old son, which prompted the Reverend Cotton Mather to observe, "It must be as bitter as death to him to lose his wife and only son, for the Indians are marvelously fond and affectionate toward their children."

Squeteague had been shadowing Church through forest and swamp for several weeks, waiting for a chance to come upon him alone and off guard. Days passed without his even catching sight of Church, and he began to wonder if he had grown too old to keep up with the English captain. Then, just as his resolve had reached its nadir, he was blessed by a stroke of luck. He had risen at daybreak on a misty morning, after spending the night near the ford on the Titicut, where Mohegan assassins had tried to kill him more than twenty-five years earlier, and had crawled on hands and knees to a grassy bank above a slow-flowing stretch of the river. He was preparing to slide down the bank and douse his face with water when he heard a sound so faint it might have been made by an eddy in the current. A moment later, he heard a tiny splash that could not have been made by an eddy, but might have been that of a trout rising to the surface to eat a caddis fly or a kingfisher sprearing a minnow. Whatever it was, it caused Squeteague to freeze into the stillness of a rock. Not a muscle moved, his breathing subsided to a whisper, and only his eyes betrayed life as they flicked from side to side in an effort to determine where the sound had come from and what had made it. For a full minute, he lay motionless at the top of the riverbank; then, like a mirage, a shaggy head and bare torso rose out of the mist before him as Captain Church, who had gone to the river for the same reason, got to his feet from where he had been kneeling at the water's edge, and, with an expression of astonishment, found himself at eye level with an equally astonished Squeteague.

In an instant, Squeteague cupped his hand behind the nape of Church's neck and pulled him off balance by yanking him forward. Then he grabbed a fistful of Church's hair and, using it for leverage, twisted him hard about so that he faced in the opposite direction, with his back leaning against the riverbank, his head lying flat on the ground, and his face turned to the sky. Squeteague held him fast by locking a forearm under his chin, and planted the tip of his knife in the soft spot below his ear in a way that drew a trickle of blood.

"A single sound or the slightest move and I'll drive this dagger into your brain," he said, quietly.

At this point, Squeteague found himself wondering what more he should say to Church before killing him. He would tell him that he was the father of the young man he, Church, had shot and killed during the Great Swamp fight, and that soldiers under his command had hacked his wife and daughter-in-law to death. He would inform him that he was now going to pay for this atrocity by forfeiting his life to someone who had sworn vengeance against him, followed him night and day for a month, and finally made him his prisoner.

"My name is Squeteague," he began. "When I was ten years old my father was kidnapped by English sailors and later killed and thrown into the sea by their captain who was taking him across the ocean to be sold into slavery."

As Squeteague continued to pronounce the sentence of death on his prisoner, he kept looking around him, expecting that Church's comrades might come searching for him, and that he would have to kill him sooner than he wished. However, nothing moved in the forest except for the tranquil flow of the river beneath the mist. Squeteague was describing how he had witnessed the fiery massacre of the Pequot at Fort Missituck, when Church gasped that he had not even been alive when it occurred.

Squeteague tightened his grip on Church's neck. "Were you alive when the Pocasset surrendered to Plymouth on the promise of amnesty but were sold as slaves in Spain?"

"I had nothing to do with that."

"What about the transaction that pays you and your men half of the money from the further sale of captives into slavery?"

When Church remained silent, Squeteague told him it was time for him to die. "Not only because you have killed those dearest to me, but also because your people have come among mine with evil hearts. You have stolen our land, burned our villages with our women and children inside, and sold the men and boys you took prisoner into slavery."

"I am not afraid to die," the captain replied. "A soldier must be prepared to die."

Church had no sooner spoken these words than Squeteague witnessed the appearance of something that seemed to be even more of a mirage than the head and torso of the Englishman that had materialized from the mist a few minutes earlier. What passed before his eyes was a great white owl—a raptor rarely encountered in that region and never in summer—that glided by on motionless wings, as if buoyed by the curtain of fog that hung above the river. Its very color conjured up ill fortune, because Wampanoag legend considered white creatures to be omens of dread and owls to be harbingers of death. As denizens of the night, they were associated with the supernatural and were said to carry messages from beyond the grave. Thus the sudden appearance of a white owl, especially during the day, could only be construed as ominous.

Squeteague crouched above his prisoner and watched the ghostly bird as it remained within sight for a remarkable length of time, before disappearing around a distant bend in the arch of foliage that enclosed the mist-shrouded river. As a young man he had scorned the foreigners' God, who was said to have brought disease and death upon the Wampanoag and other Native People as punishment for their reluctance to accept English religion and rule. Nor had he accepted the power of Native powwaws, who claimed to be intermediaries between mortals and the inhabitants of the spiritual world, as well as possessors of the power to heal sickness. Indeed, except for his dream about Wianna's husband, Webcoit, he had rarely considered the realm of spirits, let alone believed that they might take the form of apparitions warning of future happenings. But could the sudden appearance of a white owl just as he was about the plunge his knife into Church's neck be accidental?

Squeteague hesitated, and suddenly, the will to kill Church left him as swiftly as the bird of omen had slipped from sight. Squeteage got to his feet and stood over his prisoner with a foot pressed against his neck, where blood drawn by the tip of his knife had begun to trickle. Then he picked up Church's flintlock, which was lying in the grass nearby, threw it end over end into the middle of the river, and, with a disdainful toss of his head, told Church he was free to rise and leave.

"Go, Englishman, but look carefully upon my face so you won't forget it."

Following his confrontation with Church, Squeteague made his way south through swampland, which was being combed by English soldiers vying with each other for the honor of tracking down and killing the beleaguered Philip. The question of where to go was decided when he learned a few days later that authorities of the Bay Colony had set bounties on the heads of Mattaump and Monoco, who had taken refuge with the Pennacook, and were threatening to retaliate against Wonalancet if he refused to hand them over. So he must turn around and head north at once to rescue Quannto whom he had left in Wonalancet's care and could now be in danger. Toward evening, he came upon a pair of squaws lamenting over the naked and headless body of a woman that had washed ashore near the mouth of the Titicut River. The squaws told him the corpse was that of Weetamoo, daughter of Corbitant and widow of Massasoit's son Alexander, who, while fleeing the English had drowned trying to cross the river on a makeshift raft. English soldiers had found her body, cut off its head, and sent it to the Town of Taunton, where it had been placed upon a pole to taunt some Pocasset prisoners who were being held there. Remembering how the once-lovely Weetamoo had tried to charm him at Mattaposiett, Squeteague turned away from her ghastly remains, waded out into the river, and swam across to the opposite shore.

That night, after making camp, he recalled Weetamoo's father, Corbitant, accusing Massasoit of having made an evil bargain by allying himself with the Pilgrims, and warning that the Native People must arm themselves with muskets before trying to drive the invaders from their homeland. As the war had demonstrated, however, by the time they had acquired enough muskets to rise up, the English had become too numerous and powerful to overcome. So when had it not been too late? During the winter that followed the arrival of the starving settlers at Plimoth, when Massassoit could have had them slaughtered, only to decide that he needed their weapons to counter the threat posed by Corbitant and the Narragansett? After the massacre of the Pequot, when the people of the region—the Narragansett, Nipmuck, Nashaway, Massachusett, Mohegan, Pequot, Pokanoket, Pocasset, Pennacook, and Sakonnet—had good reason to set aside their differences and make common cause against the newcomers? But if they had risen up that early, could their bows and arrows have prevailed against the muskets of the foreigners any more than had those of the Pequot? The questions Squeteague posed became secondary to the conjecture that had followed him all of his adult life: What if some Nauset warriors—among them a young scout of sixteen—had been willing to charge into the fire and noise of weapons they had never encountered before and driven Captain Standish and his handful of soldiers into the sea?

Before daybreak, he pressed on through the lush late-summer forest that resounded with the singing of cicadas.

During the next two weeks, he retraced the route he and Quannto had taken a few months earlier. Traveling at night to avoid detection, he made his way to Concord, paddled downstream on the Musketaquid River to Namesit, and then up the Merruasquamack to the great falls at Namoskeag, where the Pennacook had their ancestral home, only to find the place empty. Upon making inquiry, he learned that Wonalancet and two hundred Pennacook, together with the Nipmuck sachems to whom he had given refuge, and an equal number of their followers, had gone to Quochecho, an English garrison on the Piscataqua River, to accept an offer of amnesty from the colonial authorities. When he arrived at Quocheco two days later, he approached Wonalancet, whose Pennacook, together with the Nipmuck, were arraigned in a line opposite a large number of English soldiers.

"Is my grandson Quannto with you?" he asked.

Wonnalancet shook his head. "I sent him and other children for safekeeping to Odanak, an Abenaki settlement on the St. Lawrence River, in Quebec. It was the only way I could ensure they wouldn't be harmed."

Squeteague was alarmed to see the Pennacook and Nipmuck warriors raise their muskets in preparation to fire. "What in the name of the spirits are they doing?" he demanded.

Wonalancet's voice exuded calm. "We're conducting a joint training exercise with soldiers under Major Richard Waldron, the English commander here. He's promised that the Nipmuck under my protection will be given amnesty by the Bay authorities in Boston."

"A joint training exercise," Squeteague wondered aloud. "What does that mean?"

"A sham fight in which the Pennacook and Nipmuck will fire their muskets in the air, followed by Waldron's soldiers firing theirs."

"Don't allow it," Squeteague warned. "You're being tricked."

But Wonalancet had already given the order to fire, and as soon as the smoke cleared from the muzzles of the muskets carried by his warriors, English soldiers with loaded weapons separated the Nipmuck from the Pennacook, and marched them under guard to ships anchored in the Piscataqua, which promptly sailed for Boston. Fortunately for Squeteague, Wonalancet was able to prevent the soldiers from doing the same to him by claiming that he was his personal prisoner and servant.

Because of a peace treaty Wonalancet had signed with the

colonists, he and his Pennacook followers were allowed to return to Namoskeag, where they discovered that English settlers had taken advantage of their absence to occupy some of their choicest land. Meanwhile, word came that several weeks earlier Captain Church and his men had tracked Philip down in a swamp near his home at Montaup and that he had been shot through the heart by a Pocasset named Alderman and had fallen face down in the mud. Church described him as looking like a "great, naked, dirty beast" and ordered that none of his bones be buried, "because he has allowed the bodies of many Englishmen to lie above ground to rot."

Philip's body was dragged to a knoll, where it was drawn, quartered, and beheaded by a Sakonnet executioner, who declared, "You have made many men afraid, but now I'm going to chop your arse for you." The quarters were hung on the limbs of trees to putrefy. One hand was sent to Boston as a trophy; the other, mutilated by an old gun accident, was given to Alderman, who pickled it in a jar of rum and went about the country exhibiting it for a fee. The head was taken to Plymouth, where it remained fixed to the top of a pole for some thirty years and became a skull in which wrens nested in sockets that once held eyes.

An exultant Cotton Mather declared, "God has sent us the head of Leviathan for a feast!"

Chapter Twenty-one

The Wonalancet who returned to his ancestral home was a disillusioned man. Not only had English settlers seized valuable tracts of land during his absence at Quochecho, but also word came that Mattaump, Monoco, and the other Nipmuck sachems, to whom he had given sanctuary had been hanged at Boston. The rest of their followers—two hundred men, women, and children—had been sold as slaves in the West Indies, with Waldron profiting from the transaction.

"I should never have trusted Waldron to honor the amnesty he promised," Wonalancet told Squeteague, as they shared a meal of dried salmon and corn cakes before a fire. "He was an evil man as a fur trader and equally as a soldier. It's said that he used to tip the balancing scales in his favor so he could claim that beaver pelts being sold to him weighed less than they did, and that he failed to cross off debts in his account book even when they had been paid in full. How painful to me that I allowed my Nipmuck friends to be betrayed by such a man!"

Squeteague, who had no words of comfort to offer, offered none. He had begun to doubt the wisdom of his decision not to kill

Church when he had him at his mercy at the riverbank, especially now that the English captain had succeeded in hunting down and killing Philip. Only the realization that, if he had carried out the execution as planned, he would surely have experienced a similar fate at the hands of Church's soldiers and thus been prevented forever from being reunited with Quannto, allowed him to regard the decision as warranted.

A disconsolate Wonalancet talked into the night. "When I was a young man, English soldiers led me away with a rope around my neck and held me captive for more than a year. When they sent an emissary to my father, he refused to receive him. 'Tell the English that when they restore my son to me, I'll talk with them,' he said. My captors released me but only after forcing my father to sign a treaty of submission. He never trusted them again. Nevertheless, he kept the peace with them and even sold them land."

"Selling land to the English was the great mistake of Massasoit," Squeteague declared, "It only whetted their appetite for more."

Wonalancet threw a log on the fire before continuing. "In his later years, my father spoke to a great springtime gathering of his people who had come to Namoskeag to harvest salmon and shad. He told them that he had become like an old oak that would soon fall. He reminded them that he and they had fought many battles with the Mohawk and other warlike people, but that the Pennacook could not prevail against the English. 'Peace with the white man is the only path for us to follow.'" he said. "But soon the Court of Massachusetts gave settlers the right to make farms on the island of Natticoke, where we had planted our corn for generations to keep it safe from deer. My father had to petition for us to use a tiny portion of what had been our former territory. He died a short while later. By then we had become beggars in our own country."

"Weren't you ever tempted to resist the encroachments of the English?" Squeteague inquired.

Wonalancet gave a rueful smile. "More of late than before.

When Philip went to war we decided not to join him. Nevertheless, even when the English burned our wetu at Wamesit, with our old and infirm brothers and sisters inside, we didn't retaliate but left them a sign telling them we never did harm to them and were leaving."

Wonalancet fell silent and peered into the embers of the fire. "The English capacity for cruelty is strong, even toward women and children. A sachem of the Saco named Squandro was a friend of the English until sailors from a ship anchored in the Saco River overturned a canoe carrying his wife and infant son to test their belief that our young ones have the ability of wild animals to swim even if thrown into water. Squandro's squaw dived into the river and recovered the child, but it died of chill shortly afterward. Do you wonder that Squandro refused to come to Quochecho to accept the false amnesty offered by Major Waldron? Or that he has begun raiding English settlements along the coast?"

Pokanoket and Nipmuck refugees were now making their way north from their former homelands, bringing news of what had happened in southeastern New England following Philip's death. Late in August, the Narragansett sachem Quinnapin, husband of Weetamoo, had been executed by firing squad after being promised amnesty if he surrendered. At the end of the month, Benjamin Church captured the wife and children of Tuspaquin, sachem of the Nemasket and one of Philip's staunchest allies. Early in September, he captured Annawon, Philip's oldest and most trusted captain, in a swamp near Rehoboth.

Annawon was taken to Plymouth and put on trial. Church then tricked Tuspaquin into surrendering by leaving word that his life and the lives of his wife and children would be spared if he agreed to fight the Native People in the region north of Massachusetts who had risen up against the English. However, both men were put to death soon after their arrival in Plymouth and their severed heads exhibited on poles beside that of Philip. Tuspaquin's wife and children were sold into slavery in Bermuda, as were Philip's wife, Wootonekanuske, and their nine-year-old son. Church, who profited from the sales, claimed that he had interceded with the authorities for the lives of Annawon and Tuspaquin but had been overruled.

The dispersion of the Native population of the region began in earnest as remnant bands of Wampanoag, Narragansett, Nipmuck, and other Algonquian people fled north and west to escape being hunted down and sold into slavery by the English victors, or killed by bounty hunters operating under the aegis of the Massachusetts Bay and Plymouth Colonies. Some groups joined Abenaki communities in territory south of Canada, or went to Odanak, the Abenaki settlement in Quebec, where Wonalancet had sent Quannto. Other groups moved west to live with the Mahican and Schaghticoke, who inhabited the region around the Hoosic River, near Albany. In spite of their long alliance with the colonists, the Mohegan fared little better as English settlers found legal and quasi-legal ways to divest them of large parcels of land. The General Court of Massachusetts "dissolved" the Praying Towns and partitioned empty Nipmuck territory for English settlement. Elsewhere, individual Natives drifted into hiding in the wilderness or hired themselves out as farmhands and servants to English masters.

Fear of execution and enslavement was the major impetus for the Diaspora. For more than a year, the authorities of Plymouth Colony had been killing adult male captives and selling younger ones into slavery. Indeed, Plymouth had sold more than a thousand Native People as slaves in Bermuda, as well as in Barbados and elsewhere in the West Indies. In Rhode Island, male and female prisoners were distributed as servants to heads of households—thanks largely to the Reverend Roger Williams, who served as chairman of a five-member committee that decided the lengths of servitude as follows: "All who are under five years of age shall serve until they are thirty; those above five years of age and under ten shall serve until they are twenty-eight; those between ten and fifteen until they are twenty-seven; those between fifteen and twenty until twenty six; those from twenty to thirty shall serve for eight years; and all above thirty for seven."

Between wartime casualties, flight, forced removal, and slavery, the Native People of New England were reduced in drastic fashion. In 1670, they had made up nearly a quarter of the region's inhabitants. After the war, they constituted only a tenth. As a result, the General Court issued a proclamation setting aside a day of thanksgiving declaring, "Among those tribes and parties that have risen up against us there now scarcely remains a family who live in their former homes for they have either been slain, captured, or fled into the wilderness."

Upon reading the proclamation, Squeteague winced with the bitter knowledge of how much he had helped bring about the destruction of his people, and wished that he had killed Benjamin Church when he had the chance.

The only choice for him now was to lie low. Already wanted in Rhode Island for having scuttled a ship full of Narragansett captives before they could be sold into slavery, he was being sought by authorities in Massachusetts Bay Colony who had set a price on his head for running guns to the Native insurgents, for waylaying and killing stragglers and sentinels in General Winslow's retreating army, and for helping a bondage servant escape from the home of a prominent Boston merchant.

His fugitive status prevented him from accepting Wonalancet's offer of sanctuary, especially in light of what had happened to the Nipmuck refugees who had been betrayed at Quochecho by Major Waldron. The decision about what to do next came easily, however, because he knew that his grandson was living in Quebec with the Abenaki, and being taught in a school run by French Jesuits, who were known as Blackrobes.

He would travel north to find Quannto.

At the age of seventy-two, Squeteague could no longer make lenghty treks through the forest, so when he left Namoskeag he decided to travel up the Merruasquamack by canoe. However, his birch bark craft needed repair. One of its gunwales had been split when he had overturned in rapids near Namesit, which required reinforcement with pieces of maple sapling. He then replaced several lengthwise splints that had also been damaged with thin strips of ash and secured them with pine hoops to the gunwales. After applying a coat of pine pitch to the canoe's seams and cracks, he was ready to venture out on the river again.

The warmth of a false summer that accompanied the last harvest had fallen over the Merruasquamack. The foliage of trees that lined the banks had begun to turn from green to muted yellow. Tiny whirlpools created by his paddle trailed in the wake of the canoe and disappeared in the current. The easy rhythm of his strokes lulled him into an uncharacteristic state of complacency, so that a few hours after leaving Namoskeag he nearly ran headlong into a large war party of Mohawk, who were paddling downstream on their way to their homeland. A dozen warriors sat in each of several elm-bark canoes, presenting a fearsome spectacle with shaved heads surmounted by a strip of hair running from forehead over the middle of the skull to the nape of the neck. Squeteague was able to avoid them only because he heard them chanting in time to take cover behind the branches of a tree that overhung the riverbank. As they glided past, he saw the head of Pessacus mounted on a pole that had been affixed to the bow of the lead canoe. He would later learn that the Mohawk had killed the Narragansett sachem as he was fleeing from English retribution through a forest near the Piscataqua River.

Since he had no way of knowing whether he might run into more Mohawk, he dragged his canoe ashore and waited for several hours before resuming his journey. Two days later, he reached the fork where the Winnipesogue (Winnipesaukee) River led northeast to the lake of the same name, and the Pemigewasset

River led northwest into the mountains. He took the Pemigewasset, because it was the shortest route to the land of the Abenaki, but he soon became too weary to paddle against its current, so he abandoned the canoe and struck out overland on a trail that led through the mountains.

It was early October and the leaves of trees along the river valley and on the hills that rose on either side had turned colors that Squeteague had never seen before. Stands of maple had become scarlet and orange; those of birch and beech had turned various shades of yellow, and groves of oak alternated between dark red and russet brown. Scattered among this riot of color were daubs of dark green that marked the presence of spruce, and streaks of lighter green that revealed alders growing in wetlands beside the the river. In whirling eddies beneath boulders lay fat trout that could be tickled with fingers and snatched by hand. Thickets of dogwood held grouse that he shot with well-aimed arrows. An occasional rabbit or squirrel provided more substantial fare. After two days of winding along the riverside through notches between mountains, the trail climbed a summit where Squeteague found himself higher above the sea than he had ever been and looking toward a distant cliff that bore the resemblance to the profile of an old man.

He had heard of this place. There had been a legend about it when he was young and living among Wianna's Massachusett. "Follow the great river north," the legend went, "and you will come to a mountainside with a great stone face."

A day later, he arrived at the upper reaches of the Connecticut River, which he crossed on a raft fashioned from tree trunks. On the western bank, he made camp and built a fire to dry his clothes. While he warmed himself, some Abenaki warriors who were paddling downstream, stopped to see if he were friend or foe. Squeteague kept his flintlock within reach, but when the Abenaki learned that he was heading to Odanak, they gave him dried deer meat and directions to his destination. They also showed him where they had concealed a canoe and offered him the use of it so he might make the journey upriver to an east-west trail that led to Lake Memphremagog, in Quebec, and from there to the Saint-François River, which he took downstream to his destination.

Odanak was a dispiriting village of reed and sapling huts that was situated where the St. Francois emptied into the St. Lawrence River. The largest building was a wooden chapel with a bell out front that a black-robed Jesuit rang at various times of the day to summon the inhabitants to worship. Peering into the chapel, Squeteague saw a large cross from which hung the carved figure of a dead man, with arms outstretched, head lolling to one side, palms nailed to the horizontal member and feet pinned to the vertical piece in the same fashion. Beside the chapel stood a smaller building that served as a school, with rows of wooden benches upon which sat a dozen boys, who were chanting in a tongue he couldn't understand. The same Jesuit who rang the bell was leading the chant, and when it was over he clapped his hands—a signal for the boys to jump to their feet, rush through the doorway, and start a vigorous game of kick ball in the dust-filled yard outside.

One of the first to emerge was Quannto.

Turning to watch his grandson, Squeteague was unaware that the Jesuit had come up beside him until he heard himself addressed in the strange language of the chant. The Jesuit then spoke to him in an Algonquin dialect he could understand. "I am Father Phillipe Lefebre," he said. "You don't appear to come from this region."

"I'm from far to the south," Squeteague replied, and nodded in the direction of the boys playing in the yard. "I've come for my grandson."

"One of the Pennacook sent here for safekeeping?"

"Sent for safekeeping by the Pennacook but not of them."

"Which is he?"

"The tall one kicking the ball."

"Quannto!" The Jesuit exclaimed. "My Quannto!"

Squeteague took note of the pronoun. "My grandson," he told

the Jesuit, firmly.

"Yes, he looks like you," Lefebre said. "He happens to be my prize pupil. He's already learned to speak fluent French and has mastered the catechism."

"And what is the catechism?"

"A manual used to instruct those who would be converted to our religion."

"Why is it you Europeans are so desirous of converting us to your religion when we already have our own?"

"We wish to lead you in the paths of our Lord that your souls may be saved and you will enjoy His salvation."

"Don't our souls belong to us?"

"The souls of all men—even those of the *sauvages*—belong to God."

"*Sauvages*," Squeteague repeated, wondering if it meant the same as the term the English used to describe Native People.

"It's the French word for forest dwellers," explained Father Lefebre, who regarded Squeteague as he might have looked at a child in need of instruction. "Once a person has been shown the way, he can accept the existence of the Holy Trinity, which is God the Father, Jesus our saviour, who is the Son of God, and the Holy Ghost, which is the spirit of Jesus. Acceptance of the Trinity means eternal life. Rejection leads to everlasting damnation."

Sorcery even more lunatic than that of our powwaws, Squeteague decided. "Preachers of the English religion describe their beliefs in much the same fashion."

"I'm not familiar with how English preachers go about their teaching," the Jesuit replied.

"Believe me when I tell you that the differences between them and you are small. In any event, I haven't come all this way to be converted to anyone's religion. I've come to claim my grandson."

"You can't do that without permission," Lefebre said. "Such decisions are made by Capitaine Pierre de Saurel, who commands the regiment in this region."

Chapter Twenty-two

Two weeks passed before Squeteague was granted an audience with Capitaine de Saurel. Meanwhile, he became reunited with Quannto, who had been living with a Pennacook family that had been given refuge by the Abenaki. The boy seemed happy with his new life and overjoyed to see Squeteague, who realized that, after the terror of the Great Swamp fight and the turmoil of captivity, rescue, and flight, Quannto must welcome the advent of tranquility. He told Squeteague that he liked his language studies and his teacher Father Phillipe, who was going to save his soul.

Squeteague held his tongue. The time would come to deal with the Jesuit and his penchant for salvation. What mattered for the moment was that Quannto was content with his life, as a fourteen-year-old boy should be.

Captaine de Saurel was a veteran of the Carignan-Saliere Regiment that had taken part in the campaigns against the Iroquois ten years earlier. A resplendently uniformed officer, he sat in a high chair behind a large oak table in the great hall of a palisaded fort on a hill above Saint-François du lac—the French name for Odanak. He had been been informed that Squeteague was an Algonquian-speaking Wampanoag, and he treated the newcomer with courtesy.

"You are welcome among us," he said, using Lefebre to translate. "I'm given to understand that your grandson has been living here for some time."

Squeteague had determined to be respectful but not obsequious. "He has, Your Excellency, and I'm thankful for your safekeeping of him, as well as for his instruction at the hands of Father Lefebre."

"Who no doubt desires to save his soul," de Saurel observed, with a wry glance at the Jesuit.

Squeteague took note of the Commandant's teasing of his priestly interpreter. "When my grandson comes of age, he'll be able to decide for himself who shall be the custodian of his soul."

"Well said," de Saurel replied. "Now, tell me, how goes the war between the *sauvages* of *Nouvelle Angleterre* and the English?

"Poorly for the Native People. Most of their warriors have been killed in battle or captured and executed. Hundreds of other prisoners—men, women, and children—have been sold into slavery. Villages and cornfields have been burned. The power of the Narragansett, Nipmuck, and Wampanoag has been destroyed and what remains of them has been dispersed."

"I'm sorry to hear it, for we had hoped their insurrection might weaken our English enemy. This leaves them free to make alliance with the Iroquois in order to displace us from the St. Lawrence and gain access to the fur trade. It means there will be war between France and England for years to come, and also that you and your grandson will not be able to return safely to your homeland any time soon."

"That's undoubtedly the case," Squeteague replied.

"Which means you will be forced to remain under our protection."

"With gratitude, should it be granted."

"And leads me to wonder where you intend to live and how

you propose to make your way?"

Squeteague found himself at a momentary loss for words.

"Father Lefebre tells me the boy can remain in school if he continues to apply himself to his lessons," de Saurel continued. "The good Father has already taken considerable pains to ensure your grandson's education, just as the regiment I command has kept him safe from the depredations of the Iroquois."

Squeteague remained silent as he wondered what the captain might be driving at.

"Naturally, we have the right to expect something in return. In other words, what might you be prepared to offer as a contribution to the common welfare?"

"I've been a fur trader," Squeteague said. "I've also owned and sailed a ship."

De Saurel allowed himself a slight smile. "It wouldn't sit well with our *coureurs de bois* for me to set you up in competition with them for trapping beaver. Nor would it be acceptable to our river traders for you to ply the waterway, except possibly as a crew member, for which you appear somewhat too old. May I ask what other talents you possess?"

"I've been a fisherman," Squeteague replied.

"Interesting," de Saurel declared. "Have you knowledge of eel fishing?"

"I've fished for them all my life."

"Excellent!" the captain exclaimed. "The eel-fishing concession here has gone begging since the death of its last holder, who drowned in the river a year ago. Suppose I were to grant it to you in return for a quarter of the catch, salted and put down in barrels?"

"I would accept," Squeteague said.

"You won't regret it," de Saurel told him. "I'm informed that, with good weirs, one can land a thousand eels on a single tide at Batiscan and Lotbiniere."

Fortunately for Squeteague, de Saurel assumed that Native People everywhere trapped eels in weirs and nets, as they did in the St. Lawrence, whereas Squeteague's experience in catching the slippery creatures had been confined to spearing them in the muddy bottoms of tidal ponds or through holes in the ice in winter. He soon found out from an elderly Huron squaw that he had much to learn. To begin with, most of the wicker weirs at Odanak had not been removed from the river during the previous winter, with the result that they had either been destroyed or badly damaged by ice floes. Thanks to the squaw, he was able to enlist the help of other Huron women to weave new sections of weir and install them in V-shaped configuration in time to trap some of the silver eels that were still migrating downriver to the Atlantic Ocean. The women packed the eels between layers of salt in flour barrels and then removed, washed, and repacked them for shipment. In the town of Quebec, Squeteague found a Breton merchant who would buy and transport them across the ocean to France, where they were considered a delicacy.

With the money earned from his first catch, Squeteague paid the Huron women to weave enough nets so that the following spring he was able to section off a considerable stretch of shore along the river, and harvest an abundance of elvers that were returning to the headwaters from their spawning grounds at sea. Meanwhile, he acquired a vacant Huron longhouse and, after assuring Father Lefebre that Quannto would continue his studies, brought the boy to live with him. Grandfather and grandson now entered a period of domestic tranquility they had not enjoyed since they had lived at Pettaquamscutt before the massacre in the Great Swamp.

During the next several years, Squeteague and Quannto lived peaceful and productive lives in Quebec. The extensive co-habitation that had taken place there between French soldiers, settlers, hunters, and traders with Huron and other Native women, as well as the official policy of French authorities to treat the indigenous population as allies, produced a far more conciliatory atmosphere than in New England, where the Pilgrims and Puritans had considered the Native People inferior from the start.

Quannto excelled at school, especially in his knowledge of French and mathematics, and Squeteague found satisfaction in improving and expanding the eel fishing concession he had been granted by de Saurel.

Thanks to his business arrangement with the shipper at Quebec, he soon amassed a small fortune in *livres*, the local currency. However, his success engendered envy among some of the local Huron, who petitioned Captaine de Saurel for return of the eel concession. Because the officer was under strict orders not to alienate his Native allies, he informed Squeteague that it could no longer be his.

"I regret having to make this decision because you've revived the eel-fishing enterprise hereabouts. Perhaps there's something I can do to compensate you."

"Might your Excellency see fit to grant me permission to acquire a fishing boat? I've been the captain of a ship before and I'm hoping that my grandson will agree to serve as crew."

"Let me see what I can do," the captain said.

Squeteague told Quannto about the request he had made of de Saurel while they were wading ankle deep in a mass of writhing eels that had been funneled by weirs into a large wicker trap from which there was no escape. For a few minutes, the boy did not reply. Then, with a smile, he informed Squeteague that he had been misnamed.

"You told me they called you Squeteague because, like a fish, you squirmed through the arms of the English sailors who took your father captive. But they should have named you after these eels we're standing in, because you're as slippery as they are. In any case, you don't fool me, grandpa. I know what you're up to."

"And what might that be?"

"You want a boat so that we can leave this place."

Squeteague looked at his grandson with relief. "You'll join me then?"

"Of course!" Quannto replied.

"I worried you might be swayed otherwise by the teachings of Father Lefebre."

"The Father and I have had a disagreement."

"May I ask what about?"

"An Abenaki girl."

"Ah," Squeteague said, "you don't have to tell me any more."

"Father Lefebre saw us go into the woods. When I revealed at confession what we had done, he told me to say words of contrition one hundred times a day for one hundred days or I'd be consigned to burn in hell."

"And did you say them?"

Quannto shook his head. "I've decided they're a form of sorcery in which I don't believe."

"You're right to think so, but don't tell the Jesuit. Let him suppose you're penitent."

"What shall I do about the girl?"

"You're young and so is she," Squeteague told him. "Enjoy your time together."

Administrative procedure ground as slowly at Quebec as elsewhere in the New World, but several months later, thanks to the intercession of de Saurel, Squeteague was granted permission to purchase a boat and to fish in the river as far east as the Gulf of the St. Lawrence, so long as the Micmac who lived in that region did not object and he did not engage in trade. Since he had no intention of either fishing or trading, the restrictions were of no consequence. However, finding a suitable boat was another matter. For several weeks, he and Quannto searched along the St. Lawrence without success. Then, on the Ile d'Orleans, a few leagues downriver from the settlement of Quebec, they came across a bateau that had been claimed for debt by a local fur-trading merchant after its owner had abandoned it and refused to pay the cost of salvage. The boat was in need of repair and the merchant was glad to sell it, especially when he saw that Squeteague was prepared to pay in cash.

The year was 1684. Squeteague had turned eighty and Quannto was in his early twenties. They had been living in Canada eight years by the time they refitted the bateau and sailed down the great estuary that broadened until they could no longer see land on either side.

Three days later, they reached the Gulf of the St. Lawrence, where they inhaled a delicious rush of salt air from the sea, and embraced one another.

Chapter Twenty-three

Not long after after Squeteague and Quannto rounded the lands known as Acadia and sailed into the Gulf of Maine, the uneasy peace that had followed the end of King Philip's War began to fall apart. Wonalancet was succeeded by his confrontational nephew, Kancamagus, who led the Pennacook into territory to the east. There, they allied themselves with the Wabanaki Confederation whose members—the Abenaki, Maliseet, Micmac, Passamaquoddy, and Penobscot—had begun to resent the English colonists, who were building settlements along the coast and infringing on Native lands in the interior. In 1688, disputes broke out between the Abenaki and settlers who had strung nets across the Saco River to catch salmon, thus depleting a major Native food source, and had allowed their cattle to trample on Abenaki cornfields. When repeated protests met with deaf ears, ill will toward the colonists reached a boiling point. At that point, Kancamagus devised a stratagem that led to the capture of the garrison houses at Quocheco (Dover) and a terrible revenge against Major Richard Waldron for his long history of dishonesty toward Native People and his treacherous treatment of the Nipmuck and Nashaway to whom Wonalancet had offered sanctuary.

Kancamagus's plan was simple. Two squaws were sent to each garrison house to ask permission to spend the night and, when everyone was asleep, they opened the gates to Pennacook and Abenaki warriors, who rushed inside and proceeded to kill those inhabitants who resisted and take the others prisoner. Waldron, then seventy-four years old, seized his sword and tried to defend himself, but was dragged into the great hall of his house, where the invaders slashed his face and chest with knives, informing him as they did so they were "crossing out their accounts" as he had long refused to do. They then severed the joints of his fingers, asking him, "Does your fist still weigh enough to tilt the scales in your favor?" Finally, they cut off his nose and ears, forced them into his mouth, and, holding his sword on end, made him fall on it.

For his part, Squeteague entertained little sympathy for Waldron, a deserving victim of Pennacook revenge, but neither did he derive any satisfaction from the manner of Waldron's death. What it evoked was a whole series of vengeful acts that had taken place during his long life—the senseless murder of Peskuot and Wituwamit by Miles Standish; the mistaken revenge taken by Sassacus against Captain Stone; the grisly torture of the English hunter Tilly by Pequot warriors; the hideous torment inflicted upon the Pequot captive Kiwas by Uncas and his Mohegan; the immolation of hundreds of women and children at Fort Missituck by Puritan soldiers; the drowning at sea of bound Pequot prisoners by John Gallop; the heartless sale of Native women and their children into slavery by the Pilgrim descendants at Plymouth Colony; the tearing to pieces of an elderly Pocumtuck woman by Mosley's dogs; and the starvation of Praying Indians on Deer Island by vindictive Bostonians—the list unrolled in his mind as if it were endless, until Squeteague concluded that both sides in the war had soaked themselves in the blood of revenge to the everlasting shame of both. He came to understand how each act of retribution generated another and then another and still another until their sheer multiplicity defied all reason and left those seeking vengeance sinking into a morass of inconsequence and futility. In this frame of mind, he began to reconsider his vow to avenge the deaths of Aawa, Epenow, and Chepi at the hands of Benjamin Church and the soldiers under his command.

The attack on Quocheco came a year after the start of King William's War (1688-97) between England and France, which was mostly fought in Europe, but to some extent on the North American continent, where it pitted the English colonists of Massachusetts and the regions that would become Maine and New Hampshire, against the French in Canada, their allies in the Wabanaki Confederation, and other Native People who had been driven out of New England by the colonists after King Philip's War. By this time, Squeteague and Quannto had obtained a Breton schooner at Port Royal, which they named *Nauset II*, and were making their living cod fishing in the Gulf of Norumbega and selling their catch to settlers living in small towns along the coast. They also landed cod at Gloucester, Salem, and Boston, where Squeteague roamed the streets in sailor's garb—his transgressions against the Bay Colony long erased from the memory of anyone by the passage of time and the onset of old age, which had creased his weathered face beyond recognition.

It was in a tavern on the waterfront of Boston that he and Quannto learned of the outbreak of the conflict named after King William, which the colonists called the Second Indian War.

"The savages have resorted to more of their barbarity," they were informed by a sailmaker sitting at the next table. "They've destroyed the garrison at Quocheco, but they're about to meet their match in Major Church, who'll be leading an expedition to punish them."

"A major now," Squeteague mused. "Imagine that!"

"Would you deny him promotion?" the sailmaker demanded.

"Who would deny promotion to the valiant soldier who hunted down and killed King Philip?" Squeteague replied.

Quannto turned a puzzled face to his grandfather. "You have never spoken of this man to me," he said.

Squeteague waited until the sailmaker had left the tavern. "That's because I have unfinished business with him that I've become too old to undertake."

"Is it your wish to speak to me in riddles?" Quannto asked.

Squeteague gave a sigh. "I'm reluctant to say too much about the matter, because I fear you'll feel obliged to become involved in it, and I'd rather you didn't."

"If you fear I'll feel obliged to become involved, it must be something that concerns me."

"Yes," Squeteague acknowledged, with a sigh.

"Then tell me what it is."

Squeteague took a deep breath. "Benjamin Church is the man who killed your father, and soldiers under his command killed your mother and grandmother."

Not surprisingly, Quannto queried Squeteague about the details surrounding the deaths of his parents and grandmother at the hands of Benjamin Church and his soldiers, and by the time Squeteague had finished telling him the story his fists had become clenched and his mouth tight with rage. "From this day on it will be my solemn duty to avenge them," he declared.

Squeteague, who remembered vowing vengeance on learning of the murder of his father by Captain Hunt, placed a hand on his grandson's arm. "Hear me, Quannto. After I left you with Wonalancet and the Pennacook, I returned to the Great Swamp and buried our loved ones. Then I followed General Winslow's soldiers through the snow as they retreated north and took revenge on them by bludgeoning their stragglers and sentries with your father's tomahawk. I cut off so many Englishmen that I became known among them as the snowshoe killer because I left their bodies surrounded by the same circular pattern of webbed tracks. One day, I came across a boy of about your age, a bugler who'd fallen behind because his feet had become frostbitten. He was terrified I was going to kill him, even when I warmed his feet in my hands and held them near a fire. I'm sure that after my encounter with him my need for vengeance would have run its course if I hadn't learned it was Benjamin Church and his soldiers who had killed your father, Alawa, and Chepi. At that point, I followed Church for a month with the intention of ambushing and killing him, but when I finally had him in my power a strange thing happened that persuaded me to set him free. To this day, I'm not sure why. Perhaps I wanted him to know that I would stalk him for the rest of his life. Perhaps I had become sick of shedding blood. Whatever the reason, I realized it was more important for me to go to Odanak and find you than to seek revenge, and now I've grown too old to be able to seek it at all. More important, I've grown old enough to know that revenge serves no good purpose."

"Perhaps not for you, grandfather," Quannto said, grimly, "but for me it's a different matter."

"No, not for you either. Seeking vengeance will poison your heart and weaken your spirit. Promise me that you won't follow that path."

Quannto fell silent, not knowing what to say, and saw that tears were flooding Squeteague's eyes.

"Dear grandson, the truth of the matter is that, if I hadn't sailed from Pettaquamscutt to Long Island to buy guns for the Narragansett, I might have been able to save our family. Thus the burden of what happened rests with me and shouldn't be passed on to you. For this reason, I ask you to promise me you won't undertake something that will bring you neither satisfaction nor happiness."

Quannto had not known the extent to which his grandfather blamed himself for not having been at the side of his wife and family during the Great Swamp fight. Reluctantly, he granted Squeteague's wish. "Very well, grandfather, I promise not to seek revenge against this man."

Squeteague and Quannto stopped fishing in the Gulf of

Norumbega when French and English frigates began interfering with fishing vessels there and decided to ply their trade on the Georges Bank off the coast of Cape Cod. With the onset of old age, Squeteague became less and less able to help with the hard work of setting sail and handlining cod, and when he suffered a stroke that crippled his arm, Quannto put into Nantucket Harbor with the idea of hiring Native seamen to assist him. What he learned there was enlightening. He already knew that the Wampanoag had harvested whales since ancient times by waiting for them to strand themselves, and had also used canoes to corral, frighten, and drive them ashore. Soon after he arrived on Nantucket, however, an English merchant informed him that Basque fishermen had been hunting whales for more than a hundred years off the coast of Newfoundland in a much more efficient way. "They launch small boats from ships, row close to the animals, and kill them by lancing them with harpoons," he said. The merchant went on to tell Quannto that a company had recently been established on Long Island to sell the oil from extracted whale blubber as fuel for lamps. He claimed it could fetch as much as twenty shillings a barrel, and that he was planning to start a similar business on Nantucket.

Quannto realized at once that whaling could bring far greater profits than cod fishing, and that the Wampanoag of Nantucket, who had been hunting whales for generations, would provide ideal crewmen to row and steer the whaleboats and harpoon the animals. Over the next few months, he hired a number of Natives to serve in this capacity, promised them a fair share in the proceeds, and ordered several double-ended boats to be built and equipped with oars, harpoons, and hundreds of feet of heavy line.

He told Squeteague about the venture he was planning to undertake as they sailed north to Boston, loaded with cod after a final fishing trip to the southern portion of Georges Bank. The day before, they had been buffeted by a powerful northeast storm that had driven the *Nauset II* close to land, but the new day had turned sunny with strong breezes from the southwest that put them in the lee of outer Cape Cod, whose long stretch of sand cliffs could be seen off the port side. Squeteague, now in his middle eighties and somewhat deaf, was having difficulty comprehending the new business on which his grandson was embarking, and Quannto was trying to explain it to him in a way he would understand.

"During early times, our people waited for whales to beach themselves so they could strip them of their meat and blubber," he said, patiently. "Then they began looking for them from high points along the coast and driving them ashore from canoes. On Nantucket, I learned that foreigners are hunting them in a new way and making great profit by selling the oil from whale blubber as fuel for lamps They hunt whales from ships in the open seas and kill them with harpoons thrown from small boats that can be lowered over the side. They call it whaling and I'd like to give it a try. What do you think?"

Squeteague looked at his grandson with affection and amusement. "It's not necessary to treat me like a child just because I've grown old," he said. "As it happens, I engaged in this business called whaling many years before you were born."

At that point, he motioned Quannto to sit down beside him and pointed to the sand cliffs off the port side. "There's where I was born and grew up," he said. "We called it the Narrow Land because it's slender between the ocean on this side and the bay on the other. One day, our sachem, whose name was Aspinet called for me while I was stripping blubber from a whale that had beached itself on the bayside. When I reached him, he was standing at the edge of a cliff overlooking the sea and pointing in this direction toward something I had never seen before—a ship with sails that I took for clouds, which was heading in the same direction we are now. He made me his scout and told me to run along the beach and keep the ship in sight. So I followed it one whole day and part of the next until it anchored in the deep water off Meeshawn. There, I watched the first Englishmen come from it and walk upon our land. A few days later, we tried to drive them away, but they had a new kind of weapon that gave off noise and fire so we ran from them in fear."

Quannto had heard Squeteague tell this story many times before, but he did not let on. Instead, placing his hand on his grandfather's crippled arm, he recited the ending.

"If you had known to seize advantage of how long it took the Englishmen to reload their muskets, you could have charged into them, driven them into the sea, and slaughtered them with your tomahawks," he said.

"Yes, it fills me with comfort and sadness to think so," Squeteague replied, and closed his eyes.

When Quannto saw that his grandfather wanted to rest, he left his side to tell the helmsman to take the ship farther offshore in order to avoid shoals that lay ahead. An hour later, he went to his grandfather again, saw that his eyes remained closed, and, reaching down to touch his face, realized that he was dead.

At sunset that afternoon, Quannto and one of his crew members rowed ashore in the ship's dinghy and carried Squeteague's body, which had been sewn into a sailcloth shroud, up a steep cliff to a plateau that marked the end of Cape Cod when the first Wampanoag had arrived ten thousand years before. There, as a falling sun illuminated the dunes behind which a young scout had lain in hiding as the *Mayflower* made landfall, they dug a grave in sandy soil and lowered Squeteague into it, together with the knife he had taken from the hand of his dead son, Epenow, and a cod jig he had carved from a seal bone. Following Wampanoag custom, they had excavated the grave so that Squeteague's head pointed in a southwesterly direction, toward the home of Kiehtan, the Wampanoag god of life, which also happened to be the direction of the Great Swamp, where he had buried his wife Alawa, his son, Epenow, who was Quannto's father, and Epenow's wife, Chepi, who was Quannto's mother. After refilling the grave, Quannto sent the crewman back to the beach to stay with the dinghy, while he spent the rest of the night kneeling beside the rectangle of freshly smoothed earth and striking sticks together to let his grandfather know he was keeping vigil.

When the sun rose above the sea behind him, he returned to his ship, weighed anchor, and sailed away.

Epilogue

When the Second Indian War began, Benjamin Church was commissioned by authorities of the United Colonies to command a force of two hundred and fifty volunteers, including Native auxiliaries, and engage French forces and their Wabanaki Confederacy allies, who were raiding English settlements along the coast of Maine. In 1689, he led an expedition against Pennacook and Abenaki forts on the Androscoggin River, where he captured the wife and children of Kancamagus, killed Kancamagus's sister, and took a large number of prisoners. Some of these prisoners, including women and children, were murdered in cold blood by soldiers under his command. It was an atrocity Church must have known about, because he ordered two elderly squaws to be spared so they could deliver a message to Kancamagus and other sachems that he, the vanquisher of King Philip, had come among them, and that if they wished see those of their wives and children still alive they would surrender without delay. Kancamagus, whose wife and child were among Church's hostages, bowed to the ultimatum and signed a peace agreement at Casco Bay, near present-day Portland.

In 1692, Church undertook an expedition against the Penobscot, who lived on an island in the river of the same name, but failed to come to grips with the enemy, who escaped by canoe. Four years later, following the capture of Fort Pemaquid (now Bristol) by French soldiers and Wabanaki warriors, he carried out a retaliatory raid against people living on the Isthmus of Chignecto—the land bridge that connects Nova Scotia and the mainland of Canada. Although Church (by now a colonel) weighed two hundred and fifty pounds, he personally led his troops in destroying villages on Chignecto and killing dozens of their inhabitants, including many women and children.

The Treaty of Ryswick ended King William's War in 1697, but hostilities soon broke out again with the start of Queen Anne's War (1702-1713), which was known in Europe as the War of the Spanish Successsion, and in America as the Third Indian War. In February, 1704, French soldiers and Pocumtuck warriors, who had been driven from their homes in the Connecticut River Valley following King Philips War, avenged Captain Turner's massacre of two hundred women and children twenty-eight years earlier at Peskeomskut (now called Turners Falls) by attacking Deerfield, killing fifty-six settlers, and taking one hundred and nine captives. A few months later, Church led a retaliatory night raid on a village of the Passamaquoddy, who lived in northeastern Maine. During the attack, he ordered the settlement to be destroyed and the heads of people hiding in its wetu, including women and children, to be bashed in, claiming not to care whether they were French or Indian "because they're enemies alike to me." Defending himself against subsequent accusations of cruelty, he acknowledged that he had been in a "great passion," and that in the heat of battle, "I shouldn't be held to account for every word I've spoken."

By this time, Quannto had become a successful whaler and the owner of a tryworks on Popponessett Bay in Massipee, where whale blubber was boiled and oil extracted from it. He had married a beautiful young Massipee woman, as his father Epenow had done, and become the loving father of two boys—one of whom he named Epenow and the other Squeteague. He owned several whaling ships—all of them manned by Native crews from Massipee and Nantucket—which ranged far out to sea in search of spermaceti whales, and he lived with his family in a large house he had built, which his children inherited when he died.

Quannto had followed the admonition of his grandfather not to seek vengeance against the man who had killed his parents and his grandmother, but he had made it his business over the years to keep himself informed of Benjamin Church's military activities, as well as his whereabouts. As a result, he not only learned about the atrocities Church had committed in war, but also that he had built homes in Bristol, Fall River, and Sogkonate—the latter place being the site of his meetings with the squaw sachem Awashonks. Quannto kept track of Church with the vague idea that he might someday confront him, if only to take his measure, but he did not get around to it until January 17, 1718, which happened to be the day Church died at the age of seventy-eight.

Church's activities on that day have been chronicled by Samuel G. Drake, a renowned historian whose works are cited by many authors who have written about the English colonists in New England. In a seven-hundred-page compendium entitled, *History of The Early Discovery Of America And Landing Of The Pilgrims: With A Biography Of The North American Indians*, which was published in 1854, he writes about Church as follows:

> *In his latter years he had become very corpulent, and a burden to himself. The morning before his death he visited his sister, Mrs. Irish, who lived about two miles from his residence. While returning home, his horse stumbled and threw him upon the ground with such force that a blood vessel ruptured in his neck, which caused him to die about 12 hours later.*

As it happens, this description of the death of Benjamin Church omits something that could not have been known to Drake by any dint of research or stretch of the imagination. Which is to say that his account of the misfortune that befell the veteran of the Great Swamp fight on that fateful day is accurate in every respect, except that just before his horse stumbled and threw him to the ground, he had been sufficiently startled to shift his great bulk in the saddle (and send his equally startled horse off balance) as he caught sight of a man standing beside the sun-dappled bridle path whose countenance triggered a flash of recognition in his memory for a younger man he had shot to death during the battle of the Great Swamp many years before, who turned out to be the look-alike son of the man who had taken him by surprise at the Titicut River with the intent of killing him, but, for some reason he would never fathom, had released him with the adjuration not to forget his face.

After being carried home by servants who had been sent to look for him, Church lingered for a day, spitting up blood and babbling incoherently about a strangely familiar Indian he had encountered, which, because of his renown as an Indian fighter, family and friends at his bedside took to be the last words of an old soldier reliving his glory days as he was about to expire.

The End

Native People In Alphabetical Order

ALAWA, a Pequot refugee who became Squeteague's wife and the mother of their son Epenow. She was killed by English soldiers during the Great Swamp fight in 1675.

ALEXANDER (originally Wamsutta) who became sachem of the Pokanoket upon his father Massasoit's death in 1661. He died in 1662 after developing a mysterious fever while in English custody.

ANNAWON, a chief counselor of Massasoit and Philip, who was taken prisoner by Church in September 1676 and beheaded at Plymouth.

ASPINET, sachem of the Nauset who ordered Squeteague to follow the Mayflower, and led his warriors in the confrontation with Miles Standish and his Pilgrim soldiers at First Encounter Beach. He died of plague in 1623.

AWASHONKS, squaw sachem of the Sakonnet, who lived on a peninsula east of Narragansett Bay. She fought against the English to begin with, but ultimately threw in with the colonists.

CANACUM, sachem of the Manomet, who lived a few miles south of Plymouth Plantation, and died of plague in 1623.

CANONCHET, a son of Miantonomo, who became a leader of the Narragansett. He and his warriors killed Captain Pierce and forty-nine of his men at the Pawtucket River in March 1676. Shortly afterward, he was captured by Connecticut Colony soldiers and executed at Stonington.

CANONICUS, sachem of the powerful Narragansett, who was an avowed enemy of Massasoit and the Pilgrims.

CHEPI, a girl who lived in the Christianized village of Massipee (now Mashpee) on Cape Cod, where Squeteague, Alawa, and Epenow went after an attempt on their lives by Uncas's warriors. Chepi and Epenow met there, fell in love, and married. She died at the hands of English soldiers during the Great Swamp fight.

CORBITANT, sachem of the Pocasset who occupied territory at the northern end of Buzzards Bay. He bitterly opposed Massasoit's treaty of friendship with the Pilgrims.

EPENOW, a sachem who lived on the island of Noepe, which the English explorer Bartholomew Gosnold named Martha's Vineyard. He had been kidnapped by English seamen, taken to London as a captive, and later escaped. Like Corbitant, he opposed the peace treaty Massasoit had made with the settlers at Plimoth.

EPENOW, the son of Alawa and Squeteague, who was born in 1644 in Narragansett territory, where Squeteague and Alawa had gone to live. He was named after the sachem Epenow, whom Squeteague had met and admired after leaving his Nauset home. He was killed by Captain Benjamin Church while defending his family during the Great Swamp fight in 1675.

IYANOUGH, sachem of the Cummaquid, who lived in territory near the Cape Cod town of Hyannis, and died of plague in 1623.

KANCAMAGUS, nephew of Wonalancet and sachem of the Pennacook. He captured English garrison houses at Quocheco on the Piscataqua River in New Hampshire in 1689 and executed Richard Waldron, an English fur trader and soldier, who had abused and betrayed Native People over a period of many years.

MASSASOIT, sachem of the Pokanoket and supreme leader of the Wampanoag Confederation. He lived in Sowams at the head of Narragansett Bay and signed a treaty of peace with the Pilgrim settlers at Plimoth (later Plymouth) in 1621. He died in 1661 after keeping peace with the English colonists for forty years.

MATOONAS, a Nipmuck warrior who attacked the English settlement at Mendon in July 1675. He was betrayed the following year by a Nipmuck sachem named Sagamore John, who brought Matoonas to Boston, tied him to a tree, and shot him to death.

MATTAUMP, sachem of the Quabaug, a Nipmuck tributary. In September, 1675, he ambushed Captain Thomas Hutchinson and twenty-five troopers who had been sent to apprehend Matoonas, killing eight English soldiers and wounding Hutchinson who later died. Mattaump was executed at Boston in 1676.

MONOCO (also known as One-eyed John), a Nipmuck sachem, who helped plan and carry out the ambush of Captain Hutchinson. Later, he attacked the English settlements at Groton, Lancaster, and Medfield. He was executed at Boston in 1676

NANUSKOOKE, daughter of the Pocasset sachem CORBITANT and wife of KING PHILIP, leader of the Pokanoket during the war named after him. She was captured by Benjamin Church in August 1676 and sold into slavery in Bermuda with her nine-year-old son.

NINIGRET, a sachem of the Eastern Niantic, who was influential in Narragansett affairs. He opposed English encroachment but managed to keep his people out of King Philip's War.

OBTAKIEST, a Massachusett sachem whom Massasoit suspected of plotting to attack the Pilgrim settlers at Plymouth.

PASSACONNAWAY, revered sachem of the Pennacook, who lived in southern New Hampshire by the Merrimack River. He advised his people not to go to war with the English.

PESSACUS, younger brother of Miantonomo, who became sachem of the Narragansett after Miantonomo's death. He waged war against the English after they attacked and burned his fort in the Great Swamp, killing hundreds of Narragansett women and children. He was slain by a Mohawk war party in 1676 while fleeing execution by the colonists.

PHILIP (originally Metacom) youngest son of Massasoit, who became sachem of the Pokanoket after the death of his older brother Alexander (originally Wamsutta) in 1661. He led the Pokanoket during the Native insurrection that has become known as King Philip's War, and was killed in August 1676 by a member of the force led by Captain Benjamin Church.

QUANNTO, the son of Epenow and Chepi, who was born in Narragansett territory in 1664. He was taken prisoner by the English during the Great Swamp fight, but was rescued by his grandfather Squeteague. He became a pioneering whaler and lived into the 18th Century in Mashpee on Cape Cod.

QUINNAPIN, a Narragansett sachem, who became the fifth husband of Weetamoo. He was executed by firing squad at Newport, Rhode Island in 1676.

SASSACUS, sachem of the Pequot, who raided English settlements after English soldiers destroyed his villages. Soldiers from the Massachusetts Bay Colony and Connecticut Colony burned his fort at the Missituck River in 1636 and massacred hundreds of its inhabitants, mostly women and children. Sassacus was killed by the Mohawk while seeking refuge in New York a few weeks later.

SQUANDRO, chief of the Saco, who lived by the river of that name in what is now southeastern Maine, and became a bitter enemy of the colonists after English sailors threw his infant son into the Pisquataqua River to test the theory that Native children could swim at birth.

SQUETEAGUE, a Nauset boy living on Outer Cape Cod when the Mayflower arrived in 1620. His father Pocassonnet had been kidnapped and murdered by the English Captain Thomas Hunt, in 1614, and his mother had died of plague. Squeteague was the father of Epenow and the grandfather of Quannto. He devoted his life to arming the Native People with muskets and encouraging them to rise up against the English invaders.

TISQUANTUM (also known as Squanto), who befriended the Pilgrims after they settled at Plimoth. He died at Monomoyick (now Chatham) in 1622.

TOTOSON, leader of a band living near Buzzards Bay, who attacked English settlers at Dartmouth at the beginning of the war. In the spring of 1676 he destroyed Clark's garrison on the Eel River near Plymouth, killing eleven settlers, including a number of women and children.

TUSPAQUIN, (also known as The Black Sachem), leader of the Assawompsett band and ally of Philip. In July 1675 he attacked and destroyed the English settlement at Middleborough. The following year, he surrendered and was executed by the Pilgrims at Plymouth.

UNCAS, sachem of the Mohegan, who lived east of the Connecticut River. He was a staunch ally of the English colonists and a bitter enemy of Sassacus, leader of the Pequoit, and of Miantonomo, leader of the Narragansett. He assassinated Miantonomo with English permission and tried unsuccessfully to assassinate Squeteague and his family

WAMSUTTA (also known as Alexander), eldest son of Massasoit. He became sachem of the Wampanoag following his father's death in 1661 and died under mysterious circumstances after being arrested and detained by Plymouth Colony authorities in 1662.

WASSAUMON (known to the English as John Sassamon), a Massachusett who served as an interpreter for Alexander and later became secretary and interpreter for King Philip. He was a spy for the English at Plymouth Colony and was found dead under the ice of Assawompsett Pond in 1675.

WEETAMOO, daughter of Corbitant and squaw sachem of the Pocasset, who inherited her father's mistrust of the English colonists. She married Massasoit's son Wamsutta and blamed the English for causing his death. She joined Philip at the start of King Philip's War and drowned in the Titicut River while fleeing English soldiers in 1676.

WIANNA, squaw sachem of the Massachusett, who became Squeteague's lover and benefactress during the early 1620s.

WITUWAMAT and PECKSUOT, Massachusett warriors murdered in 1623 at Wessagussett by Captain Miles Standish, who suspected they were plotting to attack the Pilgrims at Plimoth Plantation.

WONALANCET, son of Passaconnaway, who became sachem of the Pennacook upon his father's death. After English settlers seized his lands, he sought refuge in Canada.

WYANDANCH, sachem of the Montaukett, who lived at the eastern end of Long Island. He resisted the efforts of Miantonomo to enlist the Montaukett in the fight against English expansion and sold most of his land to English settlers.

www.ingramcontent.com/pod-product-compliance
Lightning Source LLC
Chambersburg PA
CBHW031217020726
47499CB00002B/615